HUNTER

A Reed Security Romance

GIULIA LAGOMARSINO

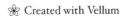 Created with Vellum

To my book reviewers. Your constant support and encouragement mean the world to me.

CAST OF CHARACTERS

Sebastian "Cap" Reed- owner
    Maggie "Freckles" Reed
    Caitlin Reed
    Clara Reed
    Gunner Reed
    Tucker Reed
    Lily Reed
    Carter Reed
    Julia Reed

Team 1:

Derek "Irish" Cortell- team leader and part owner
    Claire Cortell
    Janie Cortell

Hunter "Pappy" Papacosta
    Lucy Papacosta
    Rylee Papacosta
    Colt Papacosta

Rocco Turner
 Brooke
 Evelyn Rose Turner

Team 2:

Sam "Cazzo" Galmacci- team leader and part owner
 Vanessa Galmacci
 Sofia Galmacci
 Leo Galmacci
 Max Galmacci

Mark "Sinner" Sinn
 Cara Sinn
 Violet Sinn
 Asher Sinn

Blake "Burg" Reasenburg
 Emma Reasenburg
 Ryker Reasenburg
 Beatrix (Bea)

Team 3:

John "Ice" Peters- team leader and part owner
 Lindsey Peters
 Zoe Peters
 Cade Peters
 Willow Peters

Julian "Jules" Siegrist
 Ivy Siegrist
 John Christopher Hudson Siegrist
 Katie Siegrist

Chris "Jack" McKay

Alison (Ali) McKay
Axel McKay
Elizabeth (Lizzie) McKay

Team 4:

Chance "Sniper" Hendrix
Morgan James (Shyla)
Payton James

Jackson Lewis
Raegan Cartwright
Annie Lewis
Parents: Susan and Robert Cartwright

Gabe Moore
Isabella (Isa) Moore
Vittoria
Lorenzo (Enzo)
Grayson Moore

Team 5:

Alec Wesley
Florrie Younge
Reid

Craig Devereux
Reese Pearson
Grant Devereux

Training:

Hudson Knight- formerly known as Garrick Knight
Kate Knight
Raven Knight

Griffin Knight
Cade Knight

Lola "Brave" Pruitt
    Ryan Jackson
    James Jackson (Cassandra Jackson- mother)
    Piper Jackson
    Ryder Jackson
    Paige Jackson

Team 6:

Storm Hart
    Jessica Finley

Daniel "Coop" Cooper
    Becky Harding
    Kayla Cooper (daughter)

Tony "Tacos" Russo
    Molly Erickson
    Marcello Russo

IT Department:

Robert "Rob" Markum

Chapter One

LUCY

"*Y*ou're going home with me," Hunter snapped at me from the foot of my hospital bed.

"I am not," I insisted.

"You don't have anywhere else to go."

"I'd rather sleep in the gutter," I sneered.

"Why can't you just accept my help?"

"Because you're not offering, you're demanding."

"Who fucking cares? You need a place to stay and I have it."

"That's besides the point," I said, coughing harshly as my chest burned from the smoke that was still affecting me. Hunter had pulled me from a burning building, which I was extremely grateful for, but now he seemed to think he could boss me around. He stormed over to my bed and forced the oxygen mask over my mouth. I breathed in the air and relaxed into the bed. I just wanted some fucking sleep, but that wouldn't be possible with him standing over me and staring at me with fury in his eyes.

When the coughing subsided and I could breathe easy again, Hunter sank down into the chair next to me and ran a hand over his bald head. Sighing heavily, he looked up at me and for a moment, I thought he was going to go soft, but then his brown eyes turned harsh and he stood up, pacing around the room.

"This is ridiculous. You don't have a place to stay and I have plenty of room. Besides, I already fucking told you that things were going to change between us. You might as well accept that now." He leaned his large frame back against the wall, crossing his arms over his chest. His muscles in his arms bulged and stretched his shirt tight across his massive chest. I almost started fanning myself at the sexy sight of him, but that would just prove to him that I wanted him.

"No," I said firmly.

I stared at the sexy hunk of a man across from my hospital bed and refused to give in. He was the most gorgeous specimen God had ever put on this planet and by far the best I had ever had in bed. I wanted him so badly, but I absolutely refused to give in to his demands to go home with him today. If I did that, I knew it would be that much harder to hold onto my heart.

Hunter thought that I was the same as him, out for a good time and nothing else. To some extent, that was true. While I was working my way through my masters degree, I had no intention of dating anyone that might cause a distraction. I had been working too hard and too long to deal with complications when I was so close to my dream. I was starting to teach at a college outside of Pittsburgh in the fall and there was no way I was messing it up. Since it was my first year, I needed to be doing my job just as well as all the other teachers if I wanted to stick around.

In reality, I was like every other woman. I wanted to find someone that made me happy and settle down with a family. Hunter was not the man to do that with. He had always been a good lay, but I saw his wandering eyes at the bar and I took it for what it was. Hunter was a man with a voracious sexual appetite that one woman could never fulfill. So, as much as he stood in front of me and insisted that I would be going home with him to be taken care of, I couldn't let my heart believe that he was serious. Hunter was the one man I wanted and the one man I knew would destroy my heart.

But then something happened. Suddenly, everyone was in my room, trying to make demands on where I go. Hunter was fussing over me in an angry, brooding kind of way and when he insisted I go home with him, I couldn't refuse again. The look in his eyes as he caressed my cheek had me melting right then and there.

"Humor me."

I wanted to argue. I wanted to tell him that if I humored him, I would end up a gushy puddle at his feet on the floor. But I couldn't deny him, so I nodded and let him take me home. He carried me down to his truck, which I thought was way over the top, but gave me such happy feels that I let him do it without argument. When he walked around to the other side and got in, he seemed slightly less angry, but I noticed that his knuckles were still clenched on the steering wheel. It was almost as if he was angry with me.

"Did I do something to make you mad?" I asked.

His hands tightened on the wheel some more and he didn't say anything. I shrugged and stared out the window. There was nothing I could do about his brooding mood. My head slipped against the window as the scenery went by. I hadn't gotten a wink of sleep last night with Hunter pacing my room and hovering over me like I was about to die. I had been in a fire and had some smoke inhalation, but I had been cleared and was fine. All that excitement had worn me out though and I was asleep before we reached the edge of town where his house was located.

When we got to his house, I jerked upright, wide awake in two seconds. I quickly got out of the truck before he could come around and get me out. I had to keep my distance from him.

"Lucy, stop!"

I turned and looked at Hunter, who was running to catch up to me. "What?"

"You shouldn't be-"

"Walking? I'm fine, Hunter. I had smoke inhalation, not a broken leg."

"You're so damn stubborn. Why won't you let me help you?"

"Because I don't need it. I'm fine and I don't need someone hovering over me." I sighed and looked longingly toward the door where a bed waited for me. "Look, I'm tired. Can we just go inside so I can go to sleep?"

His eyes softened and he nodded. "Yeah. You can have the guest room."

I nodded, not wanting to show the hurt on my face. The guest room. This was why I had to guard my heart from Hunter. He had demanded all night that I was his and he would take care of me, but then he took me to his house and put me in the guest room. Hunter definitely wasn't ready to let a woman into his life.

He led me up to the guest room, which I knew all too well. Whenever Hunter and I had sex, we came to this room. He never let women into his room. It was his sanctuary and he didn't want it tainted. I ripped off my clothes, not wanting to sleep in sweatpants and a t-shirt and crawled under the covers.

"What are you doing?"

"Going to sleep," I said with a yawn.

"I see that, but why did you take off your clothes? We're not having sex, you know."

I glared at him, "I know we're not having sex, but I want to be comfortable. What do you care anyway? It's not like you sleep in here."

I rolled over before he could say anything and closed my eyes. I heard him walk around the bed and go over to the other side. Sinking down on the bed, my eyes flew open when I felt him making himself comfortable.

"Why are you here?"

"I'm just making sure you're okay."

"I'm sleeping, Hunter. There's not much that can happen to me in here."

"Look, you don't have anyone else to look after you. Why do you have to bust my balls over this?"

I sat up and leaned back against the wall. "If you really felt it was that important to watch over me, why did you put me in here where you don't sleep?"

His brows furrowed and he shook his head slightly. "Because this is the guest room."

"I know that. But why did you put me in here instead of in your bedroom?"

"Because that's my bedroom."

"Exactly. You can leave now."

"I'm not–"

"Yes, you are or I'll go stay in a hotel. I don't need you to watch me sleep or sit here and make sure I'm breathing. I just want to be left alone and since we only have sex, there's no need for you to do anything more than give me a place to stay."

A growl rumbled through him and he shifted on the bed into my space. "How many fucking times do I have to tell you that you're mine?"

"If I was really yours, I wouldn't be in the guest room where you fuck all your random hookups."

"It's the guest room," he exploded. "You are a guest, the last time I checked. Guest. Room. Understand?"

"Perfectly." I flipped off the covers and picked up my clothes. There was no way I was staying here. He just didn't get it and I didn't have the energy to keep explaining it. How hard was it for him to understand that I didn't want him in my space?

"What are you doing?" he asked incredulously.

"I'm going to a hotel."

He ripped the sweats from my hands and held them away from me. "You're not fucking going anywhere."

I smirked at him and walked downstairs in just my t-shirt. I had no problem going to a hotel in just my t-shirt. Sure, it would be awkward, but right now, I would do just about anything to get away from Hunter.

"Lucy! Fucking stop!" He raced after me and spun me around, hauling me up over his shoulder. "I told you that you weren't going anywhere."

"And I told you that I wasn't staying here!"

"Stop being so damned difficult. I'll stay out of your fucking room."

"Now wasn't that simple?"

I let him carry me upstairs and put me back in the room, glad when he plopped me on the bed and walked out of the room, slamming the door behind him. I was finally able to drift off and get some sleep, knowing that at least for the moment, I had successfully kept Hunter at bay.

*W*hen I woke up, it was after dark and I was starving. I got dressed and went downstairs to find some food in the kitchen. Hunter was in there, brooding at the table with a beer. His eyes raked over my body as I walked in and I could see the hunger there. It couldn't happen though. Now that I knew exactly what Hunter wanted from me for the moment, I knew I had to stay away from his bed.

"You hungry?" he asked.

"Starved."

"Sit down. I'll heat up some dinner for you."

"Thanks."

"So, I was thinking that I could take you shopping in the morning for whatever you need. Maggie dropped off some stuff for you earlier, but I'm sure it's not enough."

"I'll need to swing by the bank tomorrow and get out some money."

"That's not necessary. I can get you whatever you need."

"Hunter, we're not together. You need to get that through your head. I appreciate the place to stay, but I'm not going to let you buy me new things."

"Why can't you let me fucking help you?" he said, slamming his hand down on the counter. "You're so damn stubborn. I'm trying to show you that I want to be there for you and you just can't fucking let me in."

"Am I really supposed to just believe that all the sudden you want me for more than a quick fuck? That's all we've ever been, Hunter. I was in a fire and now you want me?" I shook my head at him. "I don't think so. It doesn't work that way."

He walked over to me and sat down in front of me, pulling my hands into his large ones. He stared at them for a minute and I saw a flash of a vulnerable side to Hunter. "My best friend was in a fire and I thought he was dead. When I saw your house on fire...you can't imagine how fucking terrified I was. And then I saw you passed out on the floor and I could have sworn my heart was going to pound out of my fucking chest. It was like seeing Knight dying in that building all over again. Only this time it was worse because it was you and I didn't even have a chance at something real with you. That's all I want is a fucking chance."

I was speechless. I didn't think Hunter would ever say something like that to me. We had never had any deep, meaningful conversations or anything that was remotely serious. This was a new side to Hunter and it gave me hope that just maybe we could have something more.

He leaned back in his chair and ran a hand across the stubble on his jaw. "Sorry," he said with a chuckle. "I know that's not really our thing, personal stuff, I mean. I just wanted you to know that I am fucking serious about this thing between us. I don't know the first fucking thing about how to be in a relationship, but I want to try with you."

He looked up at me and I could see it in his eyes. He was serious and I was finally ready to give him the chance he was asking for. "Okay, let's try."

A faint smile touched his lips before he stood and placed a gentle kiss on my forehead. When he turned away to get my dinner from the microwave, I couldn't help but place my fingers to the spot he had just kissed. It was so tender and so unlike Hunter and made it all the more special.

I ate quietly and then let Hunter lead me back upstairs. This time, he took me to his room, seeming to struggle with actually letting me in there as he opened his door. The room was masculine and cold, exactly what I would expect from Hunter. There were no signs of life in his room other than a few pictures on his dresser from his days in the military.

His bed was huge and looked like the only thing he truly cared about in the room. There was a fluffy comforter that looked so cozy I could wrap myself up in it and sleep for days. I walked over, running my hands along the comforter and sank down onto the mattress. A sigh escaped my lips when I was enveloped by the comfort of the soft mattress. It was heaven. My eyes slipped shut and that was the last thing I remembered.

A strong arm was wrapped around my waist, pulling me back against a hard body that I knew to be Hunter's. I smiled dreamily as I thought about what he said to me last night. He wanted to try. Things were finally looking up. I was going to be starting a job in the fall and I now had a man that truly cared about me. Someone that I found myself equally attracted to, but never thought I would have something more with.

The sun was shining brightly through the windows and putting me in the best mood I'd been in for days. I stretched my arms above my head, ready to relax back into the comfort of the bed when I felt a sharp bite over my exposed nipple. I had gone to bed last night in clothes, but this morning I was naked. When had that happened? Hunter was watching me intently as he laved my nipple and sucked it hard into his mouth. I moaned and thrust my chest up higher into his mouth.

His hand slipped down my stomach, gliding smoothly across my skin and dipped down beneath the covers. I shuddered when his fingers slipped through my folds and pinched my clit. My eyes drifted closed as he pleasured me and brought me to orgasm. Hunter knew exactly how to take my body from zero to sixty and always gave me an ending with fireworks.

His lips trailed up my breasts to my neck as he slid between my legs. His erection pushed at my entrance as he rocked against me. I moaned as I begged for him to thrust inside me, but he just kept teasing me, making me wetter with every thrust.

"Hunter, get inside me."

"I don't think so. I wouldn't want you to overdo it. You just got out of the hospital," he teased.

"If you don't get inside me now, you'll never have another chance again," I threatened. His eyes narrowed at me as he pushed inside me to the hilt. His cock moved slowly inside me, thrusting in long, hard strokes that had me splitting apart in seconds. I bit my lip as I felt my body clenching around his. He threw my legs up over his shoulders as he started pounding me harder.

My eyes rolled back in my head as pleasure washed over my body. I would never find anyone that could give it to me the way Hunter did. His primal need for me matched mine for him in every way.

"Fuck me harder, Hunter. Give me what I need."

He pulled out and pounced on me like a tiger. "I'll fuck you the way I want to and you'll take it."

"Then stop talking and do it."

He flipped me onto my stomach and gripped onto my hips, pulling me up against him. I felt his rough hands spread my ass cheeks as his dick rubbed against my ass. "If you weren't just in a fucking fire, I'd be a lot rougher with you."

"I'm fine," I insisted. "I can take it."

"Not today."

He slapped my ass and pushed hard inside me. He was pounding me so hard that he had to hold me up. Normally I could hold my own with Hunter, but I wasn't quite myself today and now I could see why he was going easy with me. He pulled my body up against his, kneading my breasts as he kissed my neck. He sank down onto the bed with me in his lap and continued to thrust up into me. It was gentler than what we normally did and so much more intimate. When his hand slipped down to my pussy, it didn't take long for me to come again for him. He followed me over the edge and then held me tight to him as we both came down.

"Hard enough for today?"

"Yeah," I said breathily. We laid back down on the bed, both of us slipping in and out of sleep throughout the day. When I was awake, I couldn't help but stare at him and wonder if this was real. It felt like it was a dream. Just yesterday, we were nothing to each other. How did this all happen so fast?

By the time late afternoon rolled around, I was tired of being in bed. I slipped out of bed and was making my way to the bathroom when he snagged me around the waist.

"So, you're staying?" he asked as he held me to his chest.

"Yeah, I'm staying." He nipped at my ear and I batted him away. "But you could at least give me a drawer so that I don't have to have my stuff in a bag on the floor," I said, pointing to the bag he had put in the corner that was full of things Maggie had brought for me. I pulled out of his grasp and made my way to the bathroom, blowing him a kiss over my shoulder. I almost stumbled as I saw him looking intently at my bag with a strange look on his face. I didn't want to think about what that meant. Everything was fine. I was just letting my mind go crazy, thinking about what ifs.

I showered, taking my time to scrub the remnants of the fire off me. I should have taken a shower when I got home yesterday, but I was just too tired. After drying off, I walked out of the bathroom to an empty room. I grabbed my new bag of clothes and pulled out a pair of shorts and a t-shirt. Maggie had packed me everything a girl could need and after finishing up, I headed downstairs to see Hunter staring out the window. I slipped my arms around his waist, but he stiffened when I kissed his shoulder.

"Something wrong?"

"No," he said shortly. "What do you want for dinner?"

His mood was different than before, darker and I couldn't help but wonder what had happened in the short time I had been upstairs cleaning up. I stepped back from him, a little uncomfortable with this new tension and shoved my hands in my shorts. "Uh, I'm fine with whatever you want."

"I have to run into the office for a little bit. I can just pick up a pizza on the way back," he said, but he wouldn't look at me.

"Sure. I can just hang out here."

He nodded and picked up his keys, leaving without saying good-bye. I tried to watch TV and I tried to read, but I just kept going over what had happened this afternoon. He had asked me if I would stay, or had he phrased it differently? Maybe he hadn't been wondering if I would stay, but wondering when I was leaving. That's not what his body language suggested, but maybe I was reading him all wrong. I dissected every word, every move since I had come here yesterday for the rest of the night. Hunter wasn't back by dinner time, so I made myself a sandwich and flipped through the channels some more.

When eleven o'clock rolled around and he still wasn't home, I decided to go to bed. I had to go check out the farm tomorrow and talk to my sister, Claire about what our next steps would be. When I woke up in the morning, Hunter still wasn't there and I was beginning to think I had made a very bad decision in letting him into my heart.

*C*laire had picked me up and we drove out to the farm together to see how bad the damage was. The house was in shambles, barely anything left standing. We walked through the burnt interior and found some picture frames that hadn't been totally destroyed, but there was nothing left of the photos that were once in them. There was no upstairs, which meant that all of our things had been destroyed. After ten minutes, there was no point in looking anymore. There was nothing to find.

We went to the chicken coop and took care of the chickens, but at this point, I just didn't have it in me to do anything with them any more. What was the point?

"Claire, I think we need to just sell the chickens and put the farm up for sale. I don't want to deal with this any more."

"I don't think I can make that decision right now. There are too many things to consider."

"Well, if you want the farm, it's all yours, but after everything that's happened and with Dad no longer here, I just don't see the point. I'm going to be starting a new job and the last thing I want is to be driving out here to do upkeep on a farm we don't even live on anymore."

"Alright. I'll take care of the farm from now on until I make a decision."

A truck pulled in the drive and Claire and I watched as Derek and Hunter got out of the truck. Hunter stalked toward me with his sexy swagger that had my insides lighting on fire, but the closer he got, the more I realized that he wasn't happy. My eyes flicked to Claire, who obviously was seeing the same thing as me.

"Why the fuck did you leave the house?" he snapped at me as he got closer.

"Excuse me?"

"You fucking heard me. I got home and didn't know where you were."

Claire scurried off to Derek and they quickly made themselves scarce. I crossed my arms over my chest and glared at Hunter. "The last I checked, I don't have to tell you when I'm doing something."

"You could have some fucking common courtesy and leave me a note or something."

"Like you did last night?"

His eyes narrowed at me. "I was working and I told you I would be."

"Right. You also said that you would be bringing dinner home, but you didn't call and you didn't come home."

"See, this is why I don't have relationships. I go to work and then have you nagging me when I don't come home on time."

"I'm not nagging you. I don't really give a shit if you don't come home because you're working, but you don't get to yell at me when you just did the same thing to me."

He ran his hand over his head and started pacing in front of me. "Look, we just need to take a step back here. This is too...fuck, I don't know. I don't know what the hell I'm doing here. One minute, just fucking, and the next, the next there's this expectation for more and I don't know how to deal with that."

"Hunter, let me ask you something. Did you stay away last night because of the whole drawer thing?"

He looked up at me and I could see it in his eyes. It had totally freaked him out. "It was just too much. I should have talked to you about it, but I'm not used to having to discuss shit with someone else."

"You know that I wasn't asking for more, right? You asked me to stay with you and I just wanted someplace to put my things."

"I didn't..." He rubbed his hand along the back of his neck and sighed. "I didn't know. I just thought it was moving really fast and it freaked me out."

I nodded and looked over to where Claire and Derek were walking around the house. I wanted what my sister had. I wanted a man that would cherish me the way he obviously did my sister and didn't have to second guess or hold back because of fear that I wanted more than a drawer. I would never get that with Hunter and that was clear as day. He was a great guy, but he just wasn't ready for a relationship.

"Can you take me back to your house and then to a hotel?"

He looked up sharply at me in confusion. "You don't have to go. I know I kind of freaked out, but that doesn't mean you have to leave."

"Yes, it does. Hunter, we're great together, as fuck buddies. I like you, but when I start dating someone, I don't want there to be all this second guessing. I don't need someone to ask me to move in and offer me everything within the first month, but I need to know that he's ready for a future together."

"I'm trying, Lucy. Shit. I told you I've never done this before."

"I know and I'm not faulting you for that, but you asked me to come stay with you and you freaked out after one night together. You didn't even want me in your bedroom."

"Fuck, Lucy. You have to give me time to adjust. This is all new to me."

"I know, but I don't want to go through an adjustment period. I don't want to always be wondering what you're thinking or if you're freaking out. You just said we need to take a step back and we haven't even been together a day. I'm sorry, but this isn't going to work with us."

I walked toward his truck without another word. I didn't want to stand there and argue about what was going to happen between us for the next hour. It was clear to me that even if Hunter wanted to try for more, he just wasn't equipped to handle a relationship yet.

I got lucky and found a small apartment over the laundromat in town. It wasn't much, just a one bedroom apartment, but it was all mine. It needed some work, but I didn't think that was going to happen, especially considering how cheap the rent was. Still, since I was starting a job in just under a month, I couldn't be picky about where I was going to be staying. The college where I was going to be teaching was about a half hour from me. I didn't want to move to Pittsburgh and the rent would have been higher there anyway, so this would suit me fine. Besides, Claire was going to be staying with Derek and my dad was in a retirement home now, so it wasn't like there were other people to get an apartment with at the moment.

The apartment had been vacant for some time, so they agreed to let me move in right away. I wanted to paint the walls and spruce it up a little, but that would have to wait. I didn't even have any furniture yet. I had a little in savings from working since I was seventeen, but it would only be enough to get me by until my first paycheck, I hoped. The only thing I really needed right this minute was a bed to sleep on. I could get a futon for the time being. It wouldn't be the most comfortable, but it would work.

I set my bag of clothes and bathroom products that Maggie had bought for me in the corner of my bedroom and sighed at how pitiful it looked. Grabbing my keys, I locked the door behind me and headed for the closest Walmart to get the cheapest futon, sheets, and pillows I could get. I didn't really need a blanket yet because it was still pretty warm outside.

By the time I got all my stuff picked out, I realized that I didn't have any towels or washcloths. I also didn't have dishes. There was just so much that I was missing that you don't really think about until you need it. I picked up the cheapest dishes I could find and the basics for the kitchen, not spending more than $200 on all of it. My total bill was much higher than I wanted, but there wasn't much I could do about it.

An employee helped me load the futon into my car and I drove slowly home since it was sticking out the trunk. When I pulled up to my apartment, I groaned at the prospect of dragging the futon up the narrow stairs by myself. I hauled the rest of the stuff inside first, knowing that as soon as I attempted to take the futon, I wouldn't want to do anything else.

I took the huge box out of the trunk and pushed it across the sidewalk to the entrance door. With a little maneuvering, I was able to get it through the door and started pushing the heavy box up the stairs. I was about halfway up when I lost my footing and started to fall backwards. I tried to grasp onto the railing, but my fingers just brushed it before they slipped away. My eyes went wide as I realized I was about to be crushed by my own futon, but then I hit a hard chest and arms wrapped around me to grab the box, preventing it from sliding down further.

"Thank you so much. I'm sorry-" I stopped when I turned around in the massive arms and saw Hunter standing behind me with a smirk. "You."

"Me. What the hell are you doing?" he asked.

"Moving in."

"To this dump?"

I squirmed to get out of his arms, but I was trapped between him and the box. "It's my dump. Can you let me go?"

He lifted one of his elbows for me to squirm out from under and then he started pushing the box up the stairs as I did my best impression of a wallflower. When he got to the top of the stairs, he looked at the two doors and then back at me in question. I snapped out of my haze and rushed up the stairs to let him into my apartment. When I opened the door, I tried not to let my embarrassment show. Yeah, it was a piece of crap.

"You can just slide it in and I'll take it from there."

"I'll help you set it up. Where do you want it?"

"The bedroom," I pointed to the only other door in the place and he started pushing it over.

"This place is a rat trap. I can't believe you're staying here."

"It's what I can afford for now."

"You could have fucking stayed with me."

"Hunter, you do remember how that went, right? You, freaking out over a drawer?"

He opened the box and started putting together the futon. "I may have fucked up, but you're still mine, and the next time you fucking need something, I expect you to ask for help."

"I'm not yours. That's not how this works. Do you even understand how to be in a relationship? You don't normally have to demand that the other person is yours."

He abandoned the futon and walked toward me with a glint in his eye that I knew all too well. "I don't have to demand that you're mine." He took a few more steps, backing me up until I had nowhere to run.

"You know as well as I do that you will always be mine. Your body knows it. Now we just have to wait for your head to catch up."

I shook my head slightly and glanced around for some way for me to escape. I couldn't resist Hunter and if he had his way with me, I would fall back into his arms. "We were never more, Hunter," I whispered. "It would never have worked."

"Then I need to remind you what you're missing."

His mouth latched onto mine, sucking my bottom lip into his mouth and biting gently. When he pushed me up against the wall, I was powerless to resist him. The truth was, I craved him and his touch. If I had any hope of not falling under his spell, I was going to have to go out and find someone else to give me what I needed.

Chapter Two

HUNTER

*D*erek's brothers were in town to meet Claire, so I thought I'd stop by and get to know all of them. I didn't get many chances to weasel information out of family because we were always so busy. This was my chance to see what Derek was like as a kid and maybe even get some leverage on him. I grinned at all the stories I was going to get and rang the doorbell, beer in hand and ready to chill.

"Hey, man," Derek said as he pulled the door open.

"I brought beer. I heard your brothers were in town and I wanted to-"

Lucy came walking through the sliding door, her hand interlocked with some other guy's. Her hair was messed up and her clothes weren't hanging properly. She had obviously been fucking this guy, who was most likely Derek's brother. Anger surged through me and I did my best to hold back my anger, but I was fucking pissed. How many times did I have to tell her that she was mine?

"What the fuck are you doing, Lucy?"

Lucy looked up at me in shock and the guy looked between the two of us, obviously wondering what the hell was going on. Lucy narrowed her eyes at me and then turned to the guy.

"Don't worry about it. We aren't together and who I fuck is none of your business," she said, turning back to me.

The guy took a step back and shook his head. "Whoa, Lucy, I'm just looking for a good time. I'm not getting in the middle of whatever the fuck you two have going on."

"We have *nothing* going on," she insisted. "Now, let's get out of here."

The guy took another step back and glanced at Derek. "Sorry, I don't poach what belongs to other men."

"I don't belong to anyone."

"Does he know that?" The guy asked. He shook his head and walked out of the room. Lucy turned to me and glared. I could feel the anger pouring off her. I didn't give a fuck.

"I hope you're happy."

"Why the fuck would I be happy that you're out screwing other guys?"

"Hunter, you need to get something through your head. We fuck occasionally. It's never been more than that and you can't just swoop in and change the rules when it's convenient for you."

"I flat out told you how it was going to be. I'm not fucking around on you and I expect the same courtesy."

"I never agreed to that and if you had it in your oversexed brain that we were going to have something different, that's not my problem."

I turned to Derek, trying my best to get control of my body. Derek wouldn't like it if I killed his brother. Or Claire's sister. "I'll meet your brothers some other time. I don't think it's a good idea for me to be around the man that Lucy just fucked right now."

I stormed away from Irish's house, pissed that I had been played by Lucy. I had already told her that we were more than just fuck buddies, but that didn't stop her from going and screwing another guy. And not just any other guy, Irish's brother. Goddamn that woman knew how to push my buttons.

I got to my truck and jumped inside, cranking the engine and ready to speed away, but then I saw the front door open and a very pissed off

Lucy storming toward her own car. I shut off the truck and got out, slamming the door behind me.

"What the fuck was that?" I shouted.

"Don't start with me, Hunter. I don't need your shit right now."

"My shit? *My shit?* You were just fucking my teammate's brother and you don't want to deal with my shit?" I yelled. "I can't fucking believe you right now."

She got in my face and pointed her finger in my face, her eyes blazing with rage. "Hey, we were only supposed to be fuck buddies, nothing more. I don't care how many times you think you've claimed me. I told you we weren't going to be more and you have to accept that."

I spun her around and pushed her up against my truck, thrusting my leg between hers. She was short and curvy, the perfect body for taking what I needed. Her large breasts heaved with every breath she took and I had to remind myself to focus on what was really going on here. "I won't accept that. You're my fucking woman whether you want to admit it or not."

She shoved her hands against my chest, but I didn't move. "We tried the whole committed relationship thing. You didn't even last one day!"

"You didn't give me a fucking chance."

"Because it was obvious that you didn't actually want a relationship. You freaked out after one night."

"How many times are you going to punish me for that? I told you to give me time to adjust."

"So, I can come over whenever I want? Eat your food? Leave my tampons in your bathroom?"

I got the hives just thinking about someone walking into my house unannounced. Food was negotiable, but there was no way I wanted fucking tampons under my sink.

"That's what I thought."

"There have to be boundaries," I said adamantly.

"Fine. I'll call first, but I want a drawer and half the closet. If we're really going to do this, then I want space at your place. I mean, it's not like I'll be staying there all the time, but when I do, I don't want my clothes piled up in the corner."

"Why is this such a big deal?" I asked in frustration. "We're just starting out and you already want space at my place?"

"I don't want space. It's not about the fucking drawer!" she yelled at me. "It's that you can't handle the drawer and I don't want to wait around and see if you can."

I ran my hand through my hair and cursed. "Why? Why do you need me to be okay with that?"

"Why is it so hard for you to give me a drawer?" she countered.

"Because you're acting like we're moving in together and buying a fucking house. Why can't you just take it one step at a time?"

"Do you even hear yourself? I'm fine with taking it one step at a time, but I don't want to constantly question whether or not you're going to freak out. That's not what a relationship is supposed to be like."

"And you know how it's supposed to be? When was the last time you had one?"

"I know that you don't just demand that someone is yours. I know that you take her out on a date first. I may not have had any relationships, but even I can see that you want me to be only yours, but you don't want the whole commitment. It freaks you out to think of me being in your space, and that's fine. We don't have to be some happy couple that just 'knows' like my sister and Derek, but I at least deserve some fucking respect."

"I do respect you," I shouted. "I'm trying to show you how much I want you, but you won't let me."

"No, Hunter. You want to own me and that's a totally different thing."

"What the fuck are you talking about? I know you're not a fucking pet."

"But you only want me on your timeline, under your conditions. You don't know the first thing about what it really means to be committed to someone and *that's* why I'm not interested in what you have to offer. We're done. I don't want to see you again and our fuck buddy status is definitely off the table. Don't call me!"

She stormed away from me and into her car, slamming the door. I felt like I had just been run over by a fucking mack truck. Was she right? Was I really walking all over her? Sighing, I got back in my truck and drove back to my place. I didn't know what the hell I was going to do about her, but I knew that I definitely didn't want to let her go yet. I just didn't know how to convince her that she should give us a shot.

---

*D*erek walked into my house with Sinner, Cazzo, Cap, and Burg a few days later. I rolled my eyes when Derek held up the two cases of beer and shoved his way inside. "We're here for an intervention."

"An intervention for what?"

"To set you straight on how you deal with a woman," Cap said.

"I don't need to be set straight. I know exactly how to deal with Lucy."

"Really?" Cazzo asked. "And how's that?"

I took a beer from Derek and threw the cap on the counter. "A woman like Lucy needs to know that her man is in charge. She doesn't want some pussy that takes shit from her."

"That's in bed, you jackass," Derek said. "You obviously don't understand Lucy very well if you think she wants to be bossed around."

"I'm not bossing her around. I'm just showing her who wears the pants in the relationship. That's me."

"Nooooo. No, no, no," Sinner said with a shake of his head. "You've got that all wrong. Men never wear the pants in the relationship and if you think you do, you're going to end up alone."

"He's right," Cazzo said. "You may think that you're in charge, but in the end, your woman gets her way or you don't get laid."

"You guys have got it all fucking wrong," I said. "That's why you had to hand over your balls to your women like a bunch of pussies."

"At least we're getting pussy," Burg said.

"She'll come around. She just needs to understand how it's going to be."

"I totally hear you, man," Cap said. "I thought the same exact thing with Freckles. You have to put her in her place and let her know who's boss."

"Right."

"Wrong. That's how you end up with your woman moving to another city and leaving you behind. I put a tracker on Maggie and didn't see her for months."

"I haven't put a tracker on Lucy. I'm not quite that neurotic."

"But she's not staying with you anymore," Derek said. "Claire said she got some shithole apartment above the laundromat."

"Shithole is right. There's no security. The door has a shitty lock and I'm not even sure the windows open. It's a fucking mess."

"And I bet you told her so," Burg said.

"Of course I did. She doesn't need to be living in a place like that."

"The problem is, you couldn't handle her living with you," Derek said. "I had to sit and listen to Claire bitch for an hour about how Lucy went on and on about you not wanting to give Lucy a drawer. Seriously, an hour over a fucking drawer."

"Look, it's not like I asked her to move in with me."

"But you did ask her to stay," Derek pointed out.

"Well, yeah, but I wasn't talking about forever."

"And you couldn't give her a drawer while she was staying with you?" Sinner asked.

"Look, it starts off as a drawer and then it's the closet. Then, pretty soon, she's shoving tampons under the sink and washing her laundry at my place."

"Does she have a washer and dryer at her place?" Burg asked.

"No."

"So, you didn't want to deal with tampons, sharing your closet, and letting her use your washer. So now she's staying in a shitty apartment that's not safe, she doesn't have any money for furniture, and she has to go to the laundromat to wash her clothes," Derek surmised.

"Well-"

"Yeah, sounds like you're doing a great job taking care of your woman," Cap snorted.

"I didn't fucking tell her to move out."

"Nope," Sinner agreed. "You told her that she was your woman, demanded that she stay with you, but then refused to actually let her use your space. She moved out and now you're fucking miserable. Are you catching on to why women wear the pants?"

"So, I just let her walk all over me?"

"She's not fucking walking all over you. If she was, she would have taken that shit without asking and then taken over the rest of your house," Burg said. "Take it from me. I've been with Meghan for almost a year and it's been rough at times, but you have to know when to give in."

"I think you guys are missing a major point here. Lucy and I barely had a chance to get started before she gave up. I'm not the one that walked away. I told her that she was my woman, but she's so fucking stubborn. She says I went about it all the wrong way."

"She's right," Burg said. "You normally ask a woman you like out on a date. You two have it all backwards. You've been fucking like rabbits and now you're trying to change the rules in the middle of the game. It doesn't work like that."

"You're supposed to have my fucking back."

"I do. She's also wrong. She can't just expect you to change overnight. Basically, your problem is that you're both too fucked up for a relationship. Neither of you know how it's supposed to work."

"And you do? Since when are you an expert?"

Burg grinned at me and took a swig of his beer. "Believe me, it's not all sunshine and roses, but it's definitely not the fucked up situation you have with Lucy."

"So, what the hell am I supposed to do? Beg her to come back to me?"

"No," they all said together as if that was the worst idea in the world.

"You never beg. No woman wants a man that falls on his knees for her. They think they do, but then they lose all respect for you," Sinner said after taking a sip of his beer.

"I wait for her to come to me then," I suggested.

"Nope," Cap said. "You have to still be a part of her life or she's going to think you don't care."

"Alright, so I ask her out on a date."

"Wrong again," Burg said. "She already told you that she doesn't want to see you again. If you start asking her out, she's going to think you don't listen."

"Well, then, I show up unannounced and don't give her the chance to tell me no."

Cazzo made a buzzing sound. "Still wrong. Showing up unannounced is basically saying that you don't give a shit about what she thinks. It's like going back to what you already had with her."

"You guys really fucking suck at this advice thing. I already went through all my options and you shot them all down."

"It's actually secret option number five. You stalk her. Discreetly," Sinner said with a grin.

"You've been hanging out with Knight too much."

"Hey, it worked for the man, but you won't take it to the same extremes that he did. He did the more forceful stalking thing and that won't work for a woman like Lucy."

This actually was sounding promising, so I pulled out a chair at my table and sat down. "Alright, how does this work exactly?"

They all pulled out chairs and sat down to strategize with me. "It's just like when you randomly meet a chick. You run into her somewhere, like the grocery store," Derek said. "It worked for me."

"Right, but you weren't stalking Claire."

"No, but that's just an example. If she goes to the diner in town, you show up there and sit down near her. You pretend to not see her until you're eating your meal and then you casually say hi, like the whole thing was a happy coincidence."

"And you can take it a step further than that," Cap said. "You have to make circumstances work for you. Make sure she gets a flat tire and then drive past when she's broken down on the side of the road. Boom. You've just come to the rescue and gotten in some time with her. You have to slowly break down her walls."

"Okay, I can do the whole tire thing. How about this? I could stage a break-in at her apartment. She'll need to call someone and that someone is me. I come in and put in a security system for her. Make her feel safe."

"You want to hire someone to break into her apartment?" Cap asked.

"No," I shook my head. "Her locks are shit. I could just break the lock and mess up her apartment a little. Make her *think* someone broke in."

"How do you know she'd call you?" Burg asked.

"Because, I'm in security," I said slowly. "Who else would she call?"

"Uh, me?" Derek raised his hand. "Her soon to be brother-in-law."

"Right, hmmm," I said in thought.

Sinner leaned forward, resting his elbows on the table. "Let me see if I've got this straight. You want to break into Lucy's apartment, mess it up, and then hope that she calls *you*, the man she broke up with, to come install security." I nodded along with him. "Then, she'll basically fall into your arms because you've saved her."

"Exactly."

Sinner rubbed his chin as he considered my plan. I thought it was pretty fucking brilliant. "It's not a bad idea. You terrorize her," I nodded. "get her to come crawling back to you," I nodded again. "then you have her at your beck and call for the rest of your life because she'll never feel safe in her apartment ever again." I stopped nodding as I considered that last part. "She'll be so terrified to go anywhere, thinking that people are always out to get her and then she'll be seeing a psychiatrist to keep anxiety attacks at bay." He leaned back in his seat and crossed his arms over his chest. "Fucking brilliant, man. You've taken her from a sane, fully functioning adult to the psych ward in just a few hours."

I looked around the table and saw they were all glaring at me. "Okay, so we'll put a pin in that grenade for now."

"Wise decision," Cap said.

———

I walked out of my house the next day, determined to get my plan in place. First thing I had to do was make sure her tire was flat and then swing by when she was getting ready to leave. I left a little early so that I would have time to let the air out of her tire, but when I got there, she was already standing next to her car chatting up some guy that was changing her tire. Her tire that was flat. Fuck.

I pulled over to the side of the road and threw my truck in park behind her car. Stepping out, a rumble ripped through my chest at the sight of her laughing with the douchebag that was changing her tire. Yeah, he looked like he knew what he was doing, but what really bugged the shit out of me was the fact that he was in shape and she seemed to like it.

Her eyes flicked up to mine and then back down, and then back up when she realized who I was. "Hunter."

"Lucy, why didn't you call me?"

"I just came out here and I was about to call Derek, but Jack stopped to help me. He owns the garage in town."

Jack stood up and held out his hand to me. I hesitantly held out my hand and shook his. "Hunter."

"Jack, yeah, I met you at Sebastian's wedding. You're on Derek's team, right?"

"Yeah. Good to see you again. I didn't recognize you out of the monkey suit."

"Alright, I gotta get into work. I'll be finished here in a minute." He bent down and finished tightening the lug nuts, then picked up the flat. "I'll take this to the garage and have it fixed. You can pick it up later today."

"Thanks, Jack."

"No problem, sweetheart."

He walked away with Lucy's tire, leaving me taking deep breaths to swallow my anger at her flirting with another man.

"Look, I can't stay. I have to get over to the school. I'm allowed into my office today and I want to start getting it set up."

"Why were you flirting with him?" I asked as she opened her car door.

"Excuse me? I wasn't flirting with him."

"I saw the way you were laughing at what he was saying. Were you hoping you could get a quick fuck in before you went to work?"

"Jealousy does not look good on you, Hunter." She flung the door open and sat in her car, leaning out as she went to pull the door shut.

"And by the way, I was laughing at a story he was telling me about his wife."

She slammed the door and cranked the engine, tearing out of there, probably trying to get as far away from me as possible. That didn't go at all as I had planned. I didn't save the day and I ended up insulting her. Operation Get Lucy Back was taking hits all around.

I waited a few days before deciding to run into her somewhere. I sat outside her apartment, parked a few spots down from her entrance, and waited for her to come out. When she got in her car, I followed her, hoping that I could run into her at the grocery store like Derek suggested. She pulled up to a building that I didn't recognize and got out. I quickly parked and followed her inside, only to stop in the doorway when I smelled the fragrance.

Lucy turned and her eyes bored into me. Shit. I had followed her into the spa. Why the fuck hadn't I been paying more attention? How the hell did I walk my way out of this one? The door chimed behind me and Maggie's laughter filled my ears. Shit. Just what I needed. She would go back to Cap and tell him that I had been at the spa. I would never live this down.

"Hunter. What are you doing here?" Maggie asked with a smile.

"Uh, just stopped by to make an appointment."

"Oh? What are you looking to have done?" Lucy asked. "Is it to get some manscaping done? Getting a little hairy down there?" she asked, pointing in the direction of my dick.

I looked down at my crotch and then back up at her. "What? No. I wasn't..." I shook my head violently. There was no way that I was letting someone else anywhere near my dick.

"If you weren't here for that, then what are you doing here?"

"Like he said," Maggie walked around me and stood next to Lucy. "He's making an appointment. For a girlfriend?"

Lucy's eyes flared with anger and Claire rushed to her side. "He doesn't have a girlfriend. He has it bad for my sister," she explained to Maggie. "And Hunter wouldn't want Lucy to get the wrong idea, right?"

I shook my head. I absolutely did not want her thinking that I was here to make an appointment for another girl. That would kill all chances of ever getting another chance with Lucy.

"You know, it's okay to admit that you're here for some manscaping," Claire said. "Men do it all the time in my romance novels."

"In your romance novels? That's not real life."

"I don't know. I talked to Derek about it and he said he would consider it. After all, it makes it more enjoyable for him. You know, when I go down on him," she said, blushing furiously.

Claire seemed to be the only innocent in this scenario. Maggie was looking at me with a satisfied smirk and Lucy was glaring daggers at me, just begging me to deny the reason I was really here. I didn't think that Lucy would be okay with me following her around, so I did what any sane man would do.

"Excuse me," I said to the receptionist. "I need an appointment."

"What service would you like?"

Lucy stepped up next to me and placed her hand on my arm, sending a lightning bolt through me. "He needs the grass cut around his tree. I would prefer a clean lawn, so give him The Hollywood."

"Is that what you would like, sir?" the lady at the counter asked.

"Uh, whatever the lady wants," I choked out. "But if you don't have time today, I can just make an appointment to come back."

"Actually, we had a cancellation and can fit you in now," she smiled.

I swallowed hard and nodded. "Perfect."

She rang me up and I reluctantly handed over my credit card. I was astounded by the price, but I would pay ten times that if it could get me away from them. I'd just slip away before anything was done.

"I'll take you back and be right out to help you ladies."

"Now? We're going now?"

"Uh-huh," she answered cheerily. I followed her back and then pulled her to the side once we were in the back.

"Look, I was just trying to get out of something back there. I don't really want this done. If you could just show me the back exit, I'll be on my way."

"Sir, you already paid for the service."

"I don't give a shit."

"Well, I can certainly give you a refund-"

"No!" That would mean going back out where the ladies were. "I don't care about the money. I'll just leave."

"Sir, I'm afraid that we can't accept your money if you're not getting our services. It's unethical. Is this about the pain? Because Anita is very good at what she does. I've never heard any complaints. It's pretty much pain free."

What the hell did I do? Go back out and face them or go through with this and face excruciating pain? "It really doesn't hurt?"

"Not the way Anita does it. She's very gentle."

"Alright," I sighed. "Let's get this over with."

We went into a room that looked very relaxing and had soft music playing. The woman pulled out a towel and handed it to me. "You can undress and lay on the table. Just lay this over you and Anita will be in shortly."

I nodded and started undressing after she left the room. I laid down on the table, being sure to cover all the pertinent parts and twiddled my thumbs as I waited for Anita to come in. This was insane. I couldn't believe I was actually going through with this.

"Hi. I'm Anita," a woman said as she entered. When my gaze swung to hers, I knew I was fucked. This woman was hot and I was just a guy after all. I could feel my arousal setting in and the towel lifting from my erection. This was not the time for this to happen.

"Hi," I said briskly.

"Have you ever done this before?"

"No. I just trim. You know, regular maintenance."

She smiled a devilish grin. "So, this is for a woman. Well, we definitely appreciate the lengths a man will go to for us. Now, the wax is hot, but it won't burn you. I'm going to-"

She stopped as she stared at my erection pushing up the towel and then cleared her throat and gave a half smile. "Don't worry about that. It happens a lot. It actually makes things easier because it keeps the skin taut. I'll keep you covered and only uncover you when I'm going to wax. Now, I'll make this as painless as possible."

I sat there as she went about gathering her supplies and cringed when I saw her bring the hot wax closer. "Alright. Let's see what we have to do." She lifted the towel and her eyes went wide, I assumed from the size of my cock. "Oh, well, that's a lot of hair."

"I'm Brazilian."

"Well, that explains the thickness. Let's get started."

The first drops of hot wax hit and it wasn't that bad. It wasn't excruciatingly hot like I imagined it would be and almost felt a little soothing. I could do this. I relaxed back and closed my eyes. And then she ripped. I could feel every tiny hair being pulled from my body, like a thousand pins poking me all at once.

"Holy fucking hell! What the fuck was that?" I grabbed onto the towel and held the irritated skin, hoping to relieve the pain, which only made it worse. I curled into a ball, feeling like I had just been kicked in the balls. I no longer had an erection. In fact, I was pretty sure my dick and my balls were trying to crawl up into my body to escape the pain. "You said pain free. You said it wouldn't fucking hurt."

"I'm sorry, sir, but you have quite a lot of hair. It's very thick and it's nearly painless for those that have it done on a regular basis. A few more times of this and you won't feel a thing."

"Are you fucking crazy?" I shouted. "I'm not letting you put that wax anywhere near me ever again."

"But, sir, you already paid."

"I'll pay you a thousand dollars to stop right now!"

"If you really don't want the service, that's fine, but you're going to be uneven down there."

"I don't give a shit if I'm uneven. I'll shave the rest of it if I have to."

She rolled her eyes and put the wax on another table. "Honestly, men are such babies. Women have this done on a regular basis and I've never heard one of them yell out in pain," she mumbled.

Challenge accepted. "Fine. Just get it over with. Be as quick as possible."

Her sweet smile reminded me of the devil pulling someone down to hell. She brought the wax back and got started again, ripping the hair from my body one strip at a time. I was pretty sure I had tears rolling down my face by the time she finished.

"Alright, we're almost done."

"Almost? There can't possibly be anything left."

"Here, you may want to bite down on this," she said, handing me a stick. I did as she said, placing it in my mouth and biting down in anticipation. My heart sped up when I felt her touch my dick. No, this wasn't happening. This was a bad nightmare. She placed the wax on the underside of my cock, pulling the skin taut and ripping the strip from my body. The lights flickered above me as a scream tore from my throat and the room went dark.

"You okay there, sport?"

My eyes fluttered open and the she-devil in front of me was smiling sweetly. What the hell happened?

"Don't worry about it," she whispered. "I won't tell anyone that you blacked out."

I shook my head to clear the fuzz and sat up. "Are we done here?"

"You don't want the rest?"

"The rest? You already took every piece of hair you could."

"You paid for the Hollywood. That gives you a leg, chest, and back waxing as well."

I flung the towel off, not caring if she saw me completely naked. "Lady, I don't have any fucking hair on my back and there's no fucking way I'm letting you wax another inch of my body."

"Okay, well, you'll want to pick up some Vitamin E cream. We have some out front and use that after every shower. Also, exfoliation is very important or you'll get ingrown hairs and bumps. No sex, condoms, pools, saunas, beaches, etcetera for at least twelve hours." I nodded and finished getting dressed. "Alright, we'll see you back here in four to six weeks."

"Not fucking likely," I muttered as I flung the door open and walked out.

I was lifting weights in the training center with Sinner, Cazzo, Burg, and Chance a few days later. I was sweating like crazy in more than one place and it was fucking uncomfortable. The moisture was making my boxers rub against my freshly waxed skin, making it itch like crazy. I set down the weights and tried to discreetly itch the irritated skin.

Sinner caught me and quirked an eyebrow. "Jock itch?"

"No." I turned away and itched at the skin again. It fucking burned. There was no way I was ever getting a wax again.

Sinner walked over and put his hand on my shoulder. "Dude, it's not really cool to itch yourself in a room full of men."

I looked at my shoulder where his hand was and raised an eyebrow. He pulled back suddenly as if he had been burned.

"Herpes?"

"No."

"Genital warts?"

"No," I almost yelled.

"Dude, if you have pubic lice, you need to get the fuck out of here."

Cazzo, Burg, and Chance turned and looked at me warily. I saw Chance's eyes drop to my crotch for just a moment.

"I don't fucking have pubic lice."

"Then why the hell are you scratching so much?" Sinner asked.

What the hell. Maybe one of them knew what to do. "I was following Lucy, trying to run into her, you know, like we talked about. I wasn't watching where she was headed and I followed her into the spa."

Sinner grinned, "First time, huh?"

"First time what?" Cazzo asked.

"Pappy, please tell me that you just did some manscaping," Burg pleaded.

"They did something called a Hollywood."

Sinner started laughing hysterically and Burg cringed. "What?" Chance asked. "What the hell is a Hollywood?"

"They fucking waxed every inch of him," Sinner laughed.

"Why would you do that?" Chance asked.

"Fucking Maggie. She was there for a spa day with Claire and Lucy. She insinuated that I was there to make an appointment for a girlfriend and I didn't want Lucy to think I was sending another woman to the spa."

"So you put hot wax on your junk instead?" Cazzo asked.

"I didn't fucking know they were going to do all that. I thought it would just be a little touch up."

"But why did it hurt so bad?" Sinner asked. "I've done it, but I've never itched like that," he said, pointing to my crotch.

"I have a lot of fucking hair. I usually just trim, but the woman said it was very thick."

"Still," Burg shook his head. "It shouldn't be that bad. Drop your pants."

"What? I'm not dropping my pants."

Sinner rolled his eyes. "We're all men. We've all seen a dick before. Do you want help or not?"

I looked at all of them and decided what the hell. What could it hurt? When I pulled my shorts down, they all cringed. Sinner let out a hissing noise and Chance covered his own dick like he would somehow catch the itching.

"That looks painful," Cazzo said, turning to Sinner. "Is that normal?"

"That most definitely is not normal. Did you use the cream?"

"What fucking cream?"

Sinner shook his head. "You have to use the fucking cream. I bet it feels like it's on fire right now."

I nodded.

"That's because you didn't use the cream. Didn't the lady tell you about it?"

I vaguely recalled her mentioning cream, but I just wanted to get the hell out of that place that I hadn't stopped in the front.

"I didn't think it was that big of a deal."

"And I bet you didn't exfoliate." Sinner crossed his arms over his chest.

"Exfoliate?"

"Yeah, when Meghan gets a wax, she always has cream and makes sure to exfoliate. I've even helped her a few times," Burg said with a grin.

Sinner bent down and took a closer look at my skin, which I found really uncomfortable. "Yep, see you're already starting to get the red bumps and what looks like the start of ingrown hairs. You should have fucking exfoliated."

"Let me see." Chance and Cazzo bent down in front of me and then Burg joined in. Four fucking dudes staring a little too closely at my cock.

"Oh yeah," Cazzo said. "I see what you're saying. That does look painful."

"Yeah, but look how much bigger his dick looks," Chance said.

"How the hell do you know how big my dick looks?" I barked.

"Dude, we all fucking shower in the locker room and you walk around without a towel on. It's not like this isn't something we've seen before."

"Yeah, it's just on display now," Burg chuckled.

The door swung open and Derek walked in, seeing Cazzo, Burg, Sinner, and Chance all bent over examining my groin. "What the fuck are you- shit, that looks bad. First wax?"

I nodded. He stepped further in the room and bent over closer. "I just had mine done. You didn't exfoliate, did you?"

"What the fuck? Have you all had this done before? Is this some new fucking trend that I didn't know about?"

Derek shrugged. "It makes it nicer for the ladies. They do it for us, so why not? I don't like to floss with her pubes, so I would assume they feel the same way. I kind of like it. Makes my dick look huge."

"Let me see," I told Derek.

"Dude..." he shook his head. "Not going to happen."

"I need something to compare it to. They were all just staring at my dick. I just need to know what it's supposed to look like."

Derek sighed and dropped his shorts, all of us leaning in close to inspect it.

"That's nice work. Very smooth," Burg nodded his approval.

"Where do you go?" Sinner jerked a nod at Derek.

"I went out of town to a place near Pittsburgh, *Fresh Start Spa* or something like that. Where did you go?" Derek asked me.

"The one in town. I had Anita."

Sinner laughed and slapped my back. "That fucking explains it.

Anita's a sadist. She hates men. They all do. You should never go to that spa. Go to any spa other than that and it won't be as bad."

"I'm not doing that ever again. Are you insane?" I asked incredulously.

"Do chicks really like this look?" Chance asked. "Doesn't it remind you a little too much of a little kid?"

"I like Meghan freshly waxed. I like being able to see her pussy on display for me."

"And it's nicer when you go down on your woman."

Just realizing that I was still standing around with my dick out, I started to pull up my pants, but I wasn't fast enough. Cap walked in and looked from me to Derek and then at all the guys in between. "I don't fucking want to know," he said as he turned and walked out of the room.

Chapter Three

LUCY

School was starting today and it was such a relief. I was finally getting my life going and things were going to be great. I would put this whole fiasco with Hunter behind me and move forward. Maybe I would even meet someone at work, not that that was the ideal situation. Mixing work and my personal life probably wasn't a very good idea. Still, the thought of meeting someone new was enticing.

I went straight to the offices to get my room key and was met by a very handsome man. He had dark, wavy hair that was thick and long, pulled back in a ponytail/bun thing. Usually that would be too long for my liking, but at least it wasn't hanging down around his shoulders. I never wanted to compete with a man over who had the best hair. He had a thick beard that had at least an inch or two of growth that made him look more like a man than a hipster. His smile was charming and he had sharp features that made his blue eyes stand out even more. He was lean and looked like he had a little bit of muscle under his clothes, but it wasn't obvious. Not like a certain man that was so massive that he looked like a pro wrestler.

"Hi. I'm Graham Kinsey." I blushed when he gave me a slight wink and placed my hand in his.

"Lucy Grant. I'm the new-"

"History professor. Yeah, I saw your file when I was in the dean's office the other day. It was sitting open on his desk and I couldn't help but get a closer look at the beautiful face in the picture."

I blushed even brighter and pulled my hand back. "Thank you. That's very nice of you to say."

"I don't lie," he smiled kindly. "I'm also a history professor."

"Oh. Wow, it's so great to meet you. I'd love to pick your brain about teaching methods that work with these students. I mean, I have a plan in place, but I'm always open to suggestions."

"Anytime. We have to help each other out."

"My thoughts exactly." I was practically swooning over the man and I had just met him. I needed to pull myself together. I hadn't even bothered to check if he was married before deciding I could throw myself in this man's arms. I tucked a strand of hair behind my ear and cleared my throat, hoping I could compose myself and not make a total idiot of myself on my first day here.

"Well, I'm going to check out my room. It was nice to meet you."

"I'll walk you. My room isn't too far away, so you'll be able to come to me with any questions."

"Thank you. That's very nice of you."

He chuckled and shot me a sexy grin. "That's the second time you've said that."

"Sorry. First day jitters."

He smiled knowingly at me and I ducked my head to keep from staring at his gorgeous eyes. I could definitely fall for this man. He was exactly the type of guy I needed. Sexy, charming, and not a total asshole. We walked down the hall to the elevator and took it up to the second floor. He pointed out the bathrooms and other teachers to stay away from if I didn't want my ear talked off.

"I'm two doors down on the left. If you need me, just swing by. My door is always open."

"Thank you so much. This has been great."

"Anytime, Ms. Grant."

I smiled as I walked into my assigned room, excited to have met someone so friendly on my first day. And not bad looking either. Screw that, he was gorgeous and if it weren't for the fact that he was my coworker and I was new here, I might consider the fact that he was exactly what I was looking for.

I spent half the day arranging my room just the way I wanted and then started going through the textbook for the course and planning my lesson plans for my first class. I was shocked at how much longer it took to plan than I thought it would. On top of that, I had lectures that I had to prepare. It was a little overwhelming and no amount of schooling could prepare me for just how much work I had ahead of me. The good thing was that I still had another month before school started, so I could spend every day here or at home preparing for school to start.

When I left for the night, it was already seven and I hadn't eaten anything since my measly lunch of a peanut butter sandwich and chips. My stomach was grumbling so loud that I was mortified when I passed another woman in the halls and she gave me a funny look. I was almost to my car when I saw Graham walking to his car also and carrying a briefcase. I looked down at the books and papers I carried in my own arms and considered that it might be a good idea to get some kind of messenger bag. Why hadn't I thought of that? I put everything in my backseat and was startled when I turned around and saw Graham standing right behind me.

"Sorry. I didn't mean to scare you," he said when I jolted back.

"It's okay."

"Hey, I was wondering if you wanted to grab a bite to eat. I could answer any questions you have."

"Sure, I'm actually starving."

"Good. There's a diner on the other side of campus that has great food. I go there a lot during the school year."

"Sounds great."

I followed him in my car and walked into the diner with him. We sat in a window booth and I smiled at how easy it all felt around him. I was attracted to him, but I didn't feel like sexual chemistry was all we had. There was an easiness that came from sharing similar interests. As we ordered and waited for our food to arrive, we discussed our different courses and what seemed to motivate the students best. After explaining that this was my first year teaching, he seemed a little shocked that I had gone right to teaching at a college level, but equally impressed.

We ate in companionable silence and then he insisted on buying dinner as a welcome to the college. When I left the diner, I felt exhilarated for the first time in a long time. When I pulled up to my apartment a half hour later, I was angry to see Hunter idling by the curb. Grabbing my stuff, I got out and slammed the door to my car.

"What are you doing here, Hunter?"

"I just came by to check out the apartment. When I was here the other day, I noticed that your locks weren't that good. I just wanted to make sure it was safe."

"Hunter, normally someone would call first."

"Well, I got off work and decided to swing by. I just got here. I swear, it's not like I've been sitting outside waiting for you."

"Well, it was nice of you to think of me, but the landlord handles all that stuff. I'm sure he wouldn't appreciate you changing the locks without his permission."

"I got his permission. I talked to him this afternoon and cleared everything with him."

I could feel the anger turning to rage with every word he said. How dare he talk to my landlord, as if it was any of his business.

"You shouldn't have done that. When are you going to learn that it's not okay to go behind my back and do things without my permission?"

"Would you relax? It's not like I changed your locks without telling you. I'm just trying to help you out."

"I understand that, but you should have talked to me first. You can't just keep barging into my life and taking control of every situation that you think you could handle better."

"Name one thing that I've done that was overstepping."

I ticked off the list on my fingers. "You demanded I stay with you after the fire. You told me I was your woman instead of asking me out on a date. You got upset when I slept with someone else even though our relationship never went further than sex. And you talked to my landlord without my permission about my apartment."

He ran his hand along his jaw and sighed. "I said name one. Look,

I'm not trying to piss you off. I see things that need to be taken care of and I want to do those things for you. I care about you."

I softened a little, even though I knew I shouldn't. Hunter was naturally a dominant person and he was just trying to help. "Fine. You can come check out the locks, but next time ask."

He gave a slight nod and followed me upstairs. He took the keys from me as I attempted to juggle all my books and papers while trying to open the door.

"Thanks," I mumbled as I walked inside and set my books down on the floor in the living room. He looked around the room and I could see the judgement in his eyes. It wasn't much to look at, but I was surprised when he didn't say anything. He got right to work on changing my locks on the door while I got changed into something more comfortable for the night. By the time I finished washing the makeup off my face and getting ready for bed, Hunter was finished with the locks and putting away his tools.

"Here are your new keys."

I took them from Hunter and tried to keep my eyes from roaming over his ripped body. It would be wrong to sleep with him, especially when I had already told him that we were over and couldn't be anything more. But the sight of him in my apartment, in his shirt that showed off all his muscles and gorgeous tattoos had my body shooting into overdrive. This was always my problem with Hunter. He was just too damn delicious to walk away from.

He stepped closer and I didn't step away. He lifted his hand to caress my face and I didn't tell him to stop. He took me in his arms and pressed his lips to mine and I thrust my tongue in his mouth, tasting every delicious morsel of his flavor. My hands took over when my brain should have shut this down. I ripped his shirt from his body and ran my fingertips over his impressive pecs, across the beautiful designs imprinted on his body. There was no denying that I craved Hunter like my next breath. I could give myself this time with him, but it could never be more.

"Hunter," I gasped as I pulled back. "I want you."

"I want you, too." He grabbed me around the waist and thrust his erection against me.

"This will never be more," I whispered before his lips crashed down on mine. He didn't respond, but the way his arms wrapped around me and held me close to him, I knew he didn't think the same. He would make me his if it was the last thing he did. I just didn't know if I was strong enough to stop it.

He carried me into the bedroom and laid me down on the uncomfortable futon. I didn't want gentle and I didn't want him in charge tonight. This was pure lust and I didn't want it confused with love or anything close to it. I stripped my clothes quickly, wanting to get him on the bed where I could take him, but he had different plans. He pulled his shirt over his head slowly, letting me see every muscle flex and move in a way that got me wet and charged. My eyes trailed down to the line of hair under his belly button that led down to my favorite part of Hunter.

His jeans hung loosely around his hips and showed just the top of his boxers. I couldn't wait anymore, stepping into his space and flicking the button of his jeans. I shoved them down over his hips and pushed him backward to fall on the futon. I tore the jeans from him and then straddled his hips, feeling his length press against my wet core. His eyes burned into me as I ground my hips against him, rubbing my juices against his shorts.

He took my nipple in his mouth, sucking the bud until it was rigid. I moved faster, needing the release that was so close. Hunter flipped me onto my back, taking away the power I held over him. He shoved his boxers down enough that I felt his cock spring free and press against my folds. He taunted me, entering me slightly and then pulling back, every time bringing me to the edge of insanity.

"Hunter, get inside me now or get out of my apartment."

"Patience, Lucy. Rome wasn't built in a day."

"I don't want you to build Rome. I want you to go on a sightseeing adventure," I gasped as he thrust inside me fully, stretching my insides with his massive girth.

"You can try to run from me, Lucy, but I'll always get you." He thrust in further over and over, slamming his balls against my ass. "You'll always be mine." He moved faster, my climax building to the point of explosion. "Mine, Lucy. Always mine."

One final thrust pushed me over as electricity coursed through my body leaving me convulsing from the pleasure. Hunter shattered on top of me, cursing as he emptied himself inside me. His muscles bulged from his arms as he remained above me, pressing kisses all over my face. They were tender kisses that were too reminiscent of love making and I couldn't deal with that. He was trying to win me over, but it wouldn't work. I already knew that Hunter wasn't capable at this point in his life of having a relationship with someone without dominating them.

I pushed against his chest and slipped out from underneath him. Grabbing my clothes off the floor, I went to the bathroom and quickly washed off in the shower. It almost felt wrong to wash away Hunter, but I couldn't stand to be sticky before bedtime. When I came out again, Hunter was sitting on my bed, fully dressed with his elbows resting on his knees.

"Thanks for stopping by," I said as I stood in my doorway, hoping he would take the hint and leave.

He looked up at me with what looked like hurt on his face, but he didn't say anything. He stood and gave a quirky smile before pulling me in for a steamy kiss. "I'll wear you down, Lucy. You're mine. You'll always be mine," he mumbled against my lips. I was sure he would if I kept giving into my desires for him. And even though I knew it was dangerous, I couldn't help but wonder what it could be like if Hunter actually was able to give me what I needed.

The next month passed quickly and before I knew it, school was starting and I was in the full swing of things. Hunter still stopped by, wearing me down more and more every time. He was trying to be nice, but there was still a commanding side to him that snuck out and tried to order me around. I did my best to ignore him and keep him at a distance. It was working, but I could feel his frustrations whenever he was with me.

At school, Graham turned out to be a great friend and resource. He was there to answer all my questions and frequently asked me to join him for lunch or dinner to discuss what we would like to accomplish with our classes this year. I found him to be very charming and the nicest person I had met at the university so far.

I was in my office after my classes were done for the day, trying to catch up on grading papers. The stack on my desk seemed to be growing by the minute and if I didn't take stuff home with me, I would never finish. I worked for another hour before deciding to call it quits and bring everything home with me where I could work from the comfort of my futon. At least I could eat while I worked.

Gathering up everything I needed, I shoved the papers into my messenger bag and turned to the door, only to jump back when a large, looming figure stood in my doorway. Seth Mackenrow. He was on the football team and one of their star players if I understood correctly. He had already missed several classes due to games, but he had always turned everything in on time. As far as I could tell, he was an exemplary student.

Still, there was something unnerving about him. He was quiet and always seemed like he had bottled his rage and it would explode any second. It was probably what made him such a great football player.

"Seth, what can I do for you?"

"I have a game coming up."

I nodded. "Yes, I've seen the schedule. I'll have your assignments for you tomorrow at the end of class."

He nodded, but stood there staring at me. I shifted from one foot to the other, unsure what I should do now. I didn't want a student to think I was afraid of him, but I also didn't want to be overly confident. I smiled at him and picked up my messenger bag.

"I was just about to head out for the day. I'll see you tomorrow."

He still stood there, so I shoved past him to the hallway. My heart pounded when I realized that no one else was around as far as I could see. I was all alone with a student that was easily twice my size and was known for his powerful tackles. And I was in heels. Seth pulled the door closed behind me and watched as I locked my office. When I headed for the elevator, he followed me. He was like my shadow, but a very scary shadow that I didn't want around.

When the elevator doors opened, I thought briefly of taking the stairs. I didn't want to be trapped in a steel cage with this guy, but I also was afraid of offending him. Strange that my senses were telling me to run, but I was afraid of him thinking I didn't like him. I took a deep breath and stepped onto the elevator and cringed when I felt the elevator bounce with his weight. I watched wide eyed as his large finger pressed the number one and the doors slid closed. I was sure I would never see what the outside of this elevator looked like after this moment.

All of the things Hunter had ever said to me about safety flashed in my head until I was on the verge of a panic attack. But just as I was sure Seth would turn around and slam me into the wall, the doors slid open and he stepped off, holding a hand out for me to walk ahead of him. I swallowed hard and focused on getting to my car. I could do this. I took out my keys and placed them between my knuckles so that I would have some form of defense. We walked through the dimming light to the parking lot. There were still a lot of cars here, teachers and students that were here for night classes, but it was the middle of the hour and nobody would be coming and going for at least another twenty minutes, too long for me to wait it out.

Seth kept a steady pace beside me, his eyes flicking around the parking lot as if he was watching for anyone that might notice him. I tried to step further away, but every time he stepped closer to me. His body crowded against me to the point of discomfort. I thought if I said something, maybe it would break the tension, but I couldn't find the words. The lump in my throat was too large and my throat was too tight.

I was almost to my car. All I had to do was get inside and lock my doors. Then I would be free of Seth and I could get home to the safety and comfort of my tiny apartment. As I unlocked my car, Seth's large hand clamped down on my shoulder.

"You shouldn't walk through the parking lot alone. It's not safe," he said in a dangerous tone that had me taking a step back. His hand tightened on my shoulder to the point of pain and I fought off the fear that was threatening to overwhelm me.

"Lucy!" My eyes flicked around Seth's large frame to see Graham walking toward me, his eyes running over us warily. "Hey, I was just going to grab a bite to eat. Would you like to come with me so we can talk about that conference?"

What conference? My brows furrowed, but when his eyes narrowed slightly, I finally got that he was trying to help me out of an uncomfortable situation.

"Uh, sure. That would be great. I have a lot of questions." I was trying to sound fine, but I could hear my voice shaking with fear.

Seth's fingers tightened on my shoulder and I looked at him again, hoping he had gotten the hint and would leave. "It's smart to hold your keys like that, but you should really think about getting some mace. You never know who'll follow you out here in the dark."

I nodded slightly, not knowing what else to do. When he finally released me and took a step back, I sagged slightly against my car, relieved that I was finally away from him. Graham walked over to me, his face pinched in concern.

"Are you okay?"

"Yeah," I said, shaking the bad feelings running through me. For some reason, I didn't want Graham to think badly of Seth. What if I was wrong about him and he really was just trying to help? I didn't want to get Seth in trouble. This was insane. I was insane. "He was just making sure I got to my car safely."

"You're sure? That looked intense."

"Positive," I gave my best smile. He looked back and watched Seth's retreating form, a strange look crossing his face. I wanted to ask what that was about, but then he turned back to me with a smile.

"Do you still want to grab a bite to eat?"

"Um, I have a lot to get done, but I could grab a quick bite."

"Great. Let's try someplace different tonight."

"There's a diner in my town that's pretty good, but it'll be out of your way."

"That's alright. I don't have anything going on tonight," he said with a shrug.

"Okay, it's called *Maggie's Diner*. Just follow me there."

"See you there."

He walked to his car and I made sure he was behind me as we pulled out. I noticed a third set of lights following behind and wondered if it was Seth and what the hell I was going to do about that. I didn't want to report him because if I was wrong, I would cause a lot of trouble for him. But if I did nothing and he really was a creep, I could end up in a very uncomfortable situation.

We pulled into the diner a half hour later and I waited for Graham to pull up next to me before I got out. The third set of headlights had followed us all the way to the diner and it was making me nervous. When Graham got out, he walked around to my door, watching the parking lot as he did so. When he opened my door, I could feel the unease coursing through him.

"You saw it too?" I asked.

"Yeah."

"Do you think it was Seth?" I asked nervously.

"I'm not sure. I couldn't see. Do you want to report him?"

"Not yet. Even if it was him, he's not really doing anything wrong."

"Lucy, he followed you out to your car and I saw him gripping your arm. He was being rough. Just do me a favor and don't go to your car alone anymore. Let me know when you need to leave and I'll walk you."

"I'm sure you're overreacting, but I'll do that."

"Alright. Let's go grab some food."

We went inside, but I couldn't help looking around the parking lot as we walked in. I had an uneasy feeling, but I didn't see anything unusual, so I shook it off and sat down with Graham.

"So, there really is a convention coming up in Philadelphia. It's supposed to be very interesting."

"What are they lecturing on?"

"There's a bunch of different things. Most of them are training seminars for teachers, but then there are a few guest lecturers that really get into how to engage students and get them interested in the subjects you're teaching. I'm pretty psyched for it."

"Can you send me the information? I'd love to go if I can."

"Sure, I can-"

"Looks like I'm interrupting something."

That voice. So dark and deep, it instantly wet my panties. I looked up into Hunter's beautiful eyes and glared at him. I had to keep up my defenses around him. He had the power to totally disarm me if I wasn't careful.

"Hunter, what are you doing here?"

"What people usually do in a diner. I'm here to eat. I didn't realize you would be here, let alone on a date," he said with disdain. I watched as his eyes flicked over Graham, judging him and by extension, me for being here with him. Graham was a great guy and didn't deserve the ridicule.

"Uh, I think I'll use the restroom," Graham said, excusing himself for me to deal with Hunter. I smiled at him gratefully, but that smile faded when Hunter took his seat opposite me.

"What are you doing here? Did you follow me?"

"No. I came to eat dinner. I'm meeting Derek here."

"Why do I not believe you?"

"I don't give a shit if you believe me. What's with that guy anyway?"

"What do you mean? He's a colleague."

"And the beard?"

"I think it looks sexy," I said defensively. Honestly, I didn't really care for the beard, but I didn't like that Hunter was being so cruel to a man he didn't even know.

"He looks like a fucking lumberjack. He's trying too hard."

"Because he has a beard?"

"All these young guys nowadays, they grow fucking beards because they think they're cool. They look fucking ridiculous."

"And I suppose only someone like yourself is allowed to grow a beard?"

"When was the last time you saw me with a beard? I may not shave every day, but I don't let my facial hair grow so long that I look like I belong in the wilderness."

"What's your problem? Why do you have to be so critical of him?"

"The man has a fucking man bun. I'm not being critical. I'm saying what the fuck is that? No self-respecting man wears a bun and grows a beard that long. It's like he can't decide if he's a man or woman."

"You're just jealous because he's here with me."

"He wants you and I already told you that you were mine."

"And I told you that we're over. Besides, we're just friends."

He snorted, shaking his head at me. "He wants inside your pants and if you think otherwise, you're blind."

"Well, maybe I want him inside my pants."

His face turned lethal, but before he could say anything, Graham was back.

"Everything okay here?"

"Fine. Hunter was just leaving."

Hunter glared at me, obviously unhappy with my dismissal, but stood and held out his hand for Graham to sit down.

"I'd suggest the lasagna, but I don't think that'd be a good idea for you," he said to Graham. "It'd probably get stuck in your beard."

He walked away, leaving me mortified and speechless.

"Nice guy," Graham smirked.

"I'm really sorry."

"Don't be. Some guys just don't know when to walk away. It's obvious he wants you, but I take it you don't want him?"

"It's complicated," I said, wishing that I didn't have to say anything about Hunter to Graham. I really liked Graham and thought there could be something between us. I just hoped that Hunter hadn't scared him off. "Should we order?"

He nodded and we went back to talking about the conference, but I couldn't help but notice Hunter sitting at a table not too far from us with Derek. At least Derek was nice enough to leave me alone while I sat here with Graham. Although, he did look at me and raise an eyebrow as he shook his head. Apparently, Derek didn't like him either.

When we left the diner, Graham walked me to my car and I noticed a man sitting in a car beneath the street light. I couldn't tell what he looked like from a distance, but the car looked familiar. I squinted to try and see better, but I couldn't make out who it was.

"Do you want me to follow you home?"

I looked over to see him staring in the same direction. "I'm sure it's nothing."

"Still, I would feel better if I made sure you got home safe."

"Thank you. I appreciate that."

He followed me home, but everything seemed normal when I

parked my car. I waved him off and headed inside for the night. At my door, there was a note that I figured was from the super. I unlocked my apartment door and threw the note on the counter, along with my purse. After taking a quick shower, I threw on some pajamas and picked up the note.

He's not good enough for you.

What the hell did that mean? Who wasn't good enough for me? Hunter. Damn him. Of course, this was his way of trying to keep my mind on him and not Graham. The difference was, Graham actually spoke to me whereas Hunter just demanded everything from me. I was so tired of these games he was playing with me. I just wanted him to let me go. Not only did I have to deal with Hunter inserting himself into my life whenever he could, I also had to deal with Seth Mackenrow following me around like a creeper.

Over the next week, I made sure to leave as soon as possible from school and took everything I could home with me so I wasn't stuck late at night. However, I still had to maintain office hours and that occasionally put me at the school later than I would have liked. I thought about asking Hunter to get me some Mace, but I didn't want him to start worrying about me. He would probably insist on having someone follow me to and from school and that wasn't going to happen, especially when I wasn't sure if there was even anything to worry about.

Chapter Four

HUNTER

"Who's the douchebag?" Derek asked as he sat across from me in the diner. I couldn't take my eyes off Lucy and Man Bun. She actually liked that asshole? His pants were tighter than most women wore. And he had on those oversized tennis shoes that didn't do anything but get in your way when you walked. He was obviously younger than me. Lucy was thirty, which was only five years younger than me, but still, I didn't take her for the type to date an asshole like that.

"A colleague."

"He's a teacher?" Derek asked incredulously. "What does he teach? Demystifying the Hipster?"

"What?"

He nodded. "You wouldn't believe that shit, but it's an actual college course."

"What do you think she sees in a guy like that?" I said, nodding over to Man Bun.

"I don't know, but I bet he waxes."

I pulled my gaze from Lucy to glare at Derek. "Don't start that shit."

"What? I'm just saying, the ladies like it. Maybe you need to find out if it's something she likes."

"I already know what she likes and I can guarantee he doesn't have one as big as mine."

"It's not all about size these days. Now women want you to share your feelings and shit."

"So, if a dude has a small dick and doesn't know how to use it, he'll still get the girl if he can be sensitive?"

Derek shrugged and waved over the waitress. "I don't know. All of the heroes in Claire's books are normal. This is a whole new generation of fucked up."

"What can I get you boys?" the waitress asked. She was maybe in her early twenties, but she referred to us as boys.

"Let me ask you something," I said, cocking my head in her direction. "What does your generation of women want in a man?"

"What, like a list?"

"Sure."

"Well, he needs to be sensitive and a gentle lover. He needs to be respectful of my body and realize that I am his equal in every way."

"Wait," I said, holding up my hand. "You think women and men are equals in every way?"

"Uh, duh. God created us equal."

"God also created man to be the protectors and women to bear children. The day a guy pushes a baby out of his dick and women take care of the men, then I'll believe we're equals."

She sneered at me and crossed her arms over her chest. "Did I mention that a man should be sensitive?"

"Okay," Derek held his hand up. "What else? What about style?"

"What do you mean?"

Derek rolled his eyes at me. "Beard? No beard? Short hair? Long hair?"

"Oh," she grinned. "I love my man to have long hair. It's so sexy to grip onto. And beards are all the rage right now."

"What about manscaping?" he asked.

She turned bright red and smiled. "If I have to keep it clean, so does he."

"Thanks for the help." She smiled and walked away without taking our orders. "Told you. That's what women want now."

"You're taking the word of waitress Barbie?"

"Hey, you heard her. And even if she does look like a fucking Barbie doll, that chick is hot. She could get any guy she wants and she just told you exactly what she's looking for."

I looked back at Lucy as she laughed at something Man Bun said and sneered. "How the hell am I supposed to compete with that? He's practically melting all over her."

"That's the point. He's playing his strengths, the same way you do. But his strengths are charming the fairer sex. Yours are getting them into bed. You need to combine the two if you're going to get her back."

"That's what I've been trying to do, but she won't listen to me. I've been telling her she's mine and she refuses to listen."

"You can't fucking tell her she's yours. You have to show her that you're hers in every way and eventually she'll come around."

"It would be easier if I could just hit her over the head and drag her back to my place."

"Yeah, that probably would be easier, but it also comes with a felony kidnapping charge."

★★★★

Three days later and my face was itching like crazy. I shaved every fucking morning, but for the last three days, I hadn't shaved once. At first, I told the guys that I hadn't had time that morning. The next day, I said I just hadn't felt like shaving that morning. This morning however, I didn't know what fucking excuse I was going to use. I was scratching so much that everyone would know that it wasn't just laziness. How did guys stand to have hair all over their faces? This was ridiculous.

I walked into Reed Security and I got a few stares, but the worst of it came when I entered the conference room for our meeting. Most of the guys were already in there and after a moment of silence, they all started laughing at me.

"What the fuck are you doing?" Cazzo asked.

"I'm trying a new look."

"Yeah, I can see that, but you don't have any hair on your head and now you're growing a fucking beard. You're going to look like a Guru or something. We could get you a turban and you'd fit right in," Cazzo laughed.

"That's real fucking hilarious." I gave him the middle finger and sat down.

Derek walked in and shook his head as he looked at my unshaven face. "I didn't say that you should grow a beard like that asshole."

"What asshole?" Burg asked.

"This guy Lucy was at the diner with the other night. He had a beard that would rival any lumberjack and a fucking man bun," Derek laughed.

"Shit," Chance shook his head. "A guy can't fucking compete anymore. All these women nowadays want sensitive men that look like fucking douchenozzles. Whatever happened to real men?"

"They're all sitting in this fucking room," Cazzo grumbled.

"You know what you need to do?" Sinner said. "You need to have a barbecue. Get all of us together and invite her over with Claire. She'll be reminded what real men look like."

"You just want me to feed you," I shot back.

He shrugged and smirked. "Two birds with one stone."

"I could bring her with Claire," Derek suggested. "We'll just say that we're going to a party. She doesn't need to know where."

"You really think it would work?" I asked the guys.

They all nodded their agreement and the more I thought about it, the more I liked the idea. "Alright. We'll do it this Friday night."

"Ooh, Friday's no good for me," Cazzo said. "I'm taking Vanessa to an art exhibit in Pittsburgh."

I rolled my eyes at him. "Fine, Saturday."

"I've got a date Saturday," Chance shook his head.

"So, bring her over."

"Sorry, I've got tickets to the Opera. This girl's a classy lady."

"Sunday?" I looked around the table. "Or do you have plans to get your hair done?"

"Hey," Sinner scoffed. "Don't look at me. I may have handed over my balls to Cara, but there's no fucking way I'd be caught dead doing that shit."

Chance smirked at Sinner. "Hey, laugh all you want, but I got box seats. While you assholes are sitting around with your thumb up your ass, I'm gonna be getting a blowjob to Pavarotti."

"Pavarotti's dead," Cazzo pointed out.

"Seriously?" Chance quirked an eyebrow. "She said she just saw Classical Eros Featuring Pavarotti."

Sinner barked out a laugh and held out his phone to Chance. "She talking about fucking porn." Chance grabbed the phone from him and clicked the link on the phone. Moans filled the air to the singing of *The Three Tenors*. "Oh, fuck. I already bought the tickets. Those things cost a fortune."

"Maybe she'll perform some of those acts on you during the show," Sinner smirked.

"Fuck. I can't believe I wasted my money on that. I could have had her on her back at my place, streaming porn."

"So, Sunday then? Nobody has any objections?"

"Just shave the rat off your face before then," Cazzo laughed.

I flipped him the bird and hoped to God that this worked.

I had everything in place on Sunday. The grill was going and I had gotten the beer that Lucy liked, thinking she would definitely be impressed that I remembered. The guys started showing up with their wives and girlfriends around three and every time someone walked in, my eyes shot up, excited to see Lucy. I was at the grill, flipping the steaks when I heard her voice.

"I still can't believe you didn't tell me the party was at Hunter's place."

"Huh," Derek said. "It must have slipped my mind. I'm pretty sure

I would have mentioned it had I known you were going to bring Man Bun."

My head whipped up as I saw Lucy walking toward me with a scowl on her face. Derek was shaking his head and Man Bun was setting something on the table with Claire. I narrowed my eyes, trying to see what he brought and rolled my eyes when I saw it was white wine spritzer. Seriously? I couldn't believe she brought this asshole. Of course, the women all flocked to him and praised him for his choice of beverage.

"Hunter," Lucy said as she approached me. "I hope you don't mind, but I brought Graham."

"Sure," I bit out. "The more the merrier."

I flipped the steaks and tried not to slam the lid shut on the grill. My day may be ruined, but I wasn't about to ruin the food. Steak was practically its own food group. I walked over to Derek with my beer and watched as Lucy and Claire laughed with Man Bun.

"Sorry. She just showed up with him."

I shrugged. "Whatever. Not much I can do about it if she wants to be with that prick."

Chance walked over and slapped me on the back. "Well, that kind of backfired."

"No shit."

"It could be worse," he said.

"How do you figure?"

"He could have brought friends with him."

He was right about that. The last thing we needed were more guys like him. A few hours later, I had successfully avoided Lucy and Man Bun for most of the party. I really just wanted them to leave so I didn't have to watch him fawning over her. She obviously liked him. I could see that they had good conversation and she didn't look the least bit uncomfortable around him. It fucking sucked to watch. Then, just about the time I was thinking they were going to leave, the douchebag came over and sat down with me and the guys.

"So, Lucy tells me that you all work for a security company. That's cool. You do security installations at homes and in offices?"

"Some of the time," Cap said.

"Cool," he nodded. "What other stuff do you do?"

"Protection services," Cazzo said stiffly.

"Like Hollywood celebs and stuff?"

"Among others," Derek replied.

"Shit. That's totally crazy. Have you ever had to kill someone?"

The guys glanced around at each other. All of us had killed someone at one time or another. We were all former military and had all seen heavy action.

"Not if we can help it," Cap finally said as he drank his beer.

"Well, they don't." Knight grinned maniacally. "I'm an assassin."

Graham chuckled and drank his white wine spritzer. "I could almost see that. You guys definitely look like you're all former military or something."

"We are," I said testily. I really hated this asshole.

"You are?" We all nodded and his face fell. "Really? Wow. I just...I can't believe that..."

A look took over his face that I knew all too well and suddenly, I really wanted to fight this fucker. "You can't believe that what?"

"That you're okay with being sent to other countries to basically commit murder."

"None of us ever committed murder. Well, except Knight. Like he said, he's an assassin," Sinner smirked.

"What would you call going over there and killing innocent women and children?"

"Casualty of war," Cap said fiercely. "Not all of them are innocent."

"So, it would be okay for countries to come over here and declare war on us? To have innocent women and children killed here?"

"In case you don't remember," Burg interjected. "That already happened. That's why we're over there defending our country and other people that are suffering at the hands of the terrorists that only live by their own twisted set of rules."

"How can you be certain that every person you shot was guilty? Those people are just trying to live their lives like you and me."

"The people we're at war with aren't trying to live life," I said angrily. "They're trying to destroy life and that's what we were sent over there to stomp out."

Graham snorted, "Sure. Tell me of a single war in history that was fought for a good reason."

"Aren't you a fucking history teacher?" I retorted. "Shouldn't you know the answer to this?"

"That doesn't mean that I agree with war. All of the wars throughout history could have been avoided," Graham shook his head. "And it's made worse by assholes like you that think you can go over and make the world a better place with your guns and bombs. Nothing you do will ever make this world a safer place because you don't know how to use your brains for anything other than-"

"Graham!" His head whipped around as Lucy stared at him angrily. "I think it's time you left."

"Sure, we can go now."

"No, call a cab. I won't be going back with you."

Graham glanced back at all of us and for a moment looked like he regretted shooting his mouth off. He turned and left the group, not looking back. Lucy stood there, staring at the ground, but when she looked up, she had tears in her eyes. "I'm sorry," she said quietly before she walked away.

Part of me wanted to go after her, but the other part of me said that she never should have brought that asshole around in the first place. He insulted not only every person that ever fought for their country, but also everything that we stood for, which was to defend those weaker than us.

"Now would be the time to make your move," Sinner said as he walked over to me.

I walked toward the house, knowing that he was right. I needed to go to her and let her know that I wasn't mad at her. She'd sent him away after all. I walked around the house, not finding her anywhere downstairs. I took a shot that she would be upstairs and was surprised when I found her sitting on my bed.

"Hey. I never thought I'd find you in my bedroom again."

She shrugged. "I just needed to get away. I'm sorry about that down there. He never should have said those things to you."

"It wasn't just to me, it was everyone, but I don't blame you for that. You don't have anything to apologize for."

She snorted and looked away. "I brought him here. Derek didn't tell me that the party was at your house, but I figured you would be around when he said it was a Reed Security party. I just wanted to piss you off."

"Well," I said as I sat down on the bed next to her. "You did that. It's still not your fault though. You can't help what other people think."

"You know, he really is a nice guy despite his idiotic opinions."

"I thought you were trying to apologize," I grinned at her. She shoved her shoulder into mine and I took it a step further. I pushed her back onto the bed and climbed on top of her. "I keep telling you that you're mine. One of these days, maybe you'll listen. Bringing some asshole like that around isn't going to make me run away. It's just going to piss me off and make me fight harder for you."

"Maybe I want you to fight harder for me."

My mouth was on hers the next second and I was pushing her shirt up and gripping her tits. She had perfect breasts that spilled over in my hands. I latched onto a nipple and sucked hard, needing to hear her scream for me.

"Hunter, I need you...I need you to fuck me hard."

"I'm going to," I said as I sucked her nipple back into my mouth. "But not until I make you come."

I pulled the vibrator out of my drawer that I bought for her the last time she was here. We had never gotten a chance to use it, but we were sure as hell going to now. I turned it on and ran it over her clit lightly, eliciting a moan from her. Her body jumped with every brush against her most sensitive areas. I brought it down to her pussy and started thrusting it inside her, a little deeper every time. She was so wet that it slid in and out easily. The little rabbit ears started pushing up against her clit and her hips lifted to meet my thrusts. I turned the vibrator for the ears on and she started writhing on the bed.

"Oh, God!"

My finger slipped down to collect some of her juices and I ran it back to her ass, slipping my finger through the tight hole. I fucked her slowly at first, but when she started bucking her hips, I fucked her harder, knowing she needed it. When she came a second time, I slid my finger out and threw the vibrator across the room.

"Tell me what you need," I said, running my cock along her wet folds.

"You know what I need."

I shook my head. "You don't get it unless you tell me."

"Hunter, please."

"Just fucking tell me. You know I'll give it to you. Whatever you want."

"Fuck me hard. Against the wall. On top of the dresser. Hell, I don't care if you throw me on the floor, just get inside me and give me that cock!"

I picked her up and walked over to the low dresser, flinging the shit on top to the floor with a crash. I knew that something broke, but I really didn't give a shit at the moment. I spread her legs and thrust hard inside her, yelling out when I sank deep inside. My hips started moving harder and faster as I chased my orgasm. Her fingers were digging into my back, scratching at my skin and probably leaving a bloody trail. I didn't give a shit.

"Wrap your legs around me, baby."

She did as I asked, pulling me closer to her in the process. The dresser started banging against the wall and the drawers were opening and slamming shut front the momentum of our bodies.

"Fuck, I'm gonna come in that sweet pussy."

"I'm almost there," she panted. "Harder. Fuck me harder."

"If I fuck you any harder, I'm gonna push the dresser through the fucking wall."

"Who gives a shit. Fuck me."

I gripped onto her ass as I slammed into her in long, hard strokes. I did my best to hold back, but when she clenched around me, I was powerless to stop what was happening. One more stroke and I was coming inside her, and pushing the dresser into the wall. I wrapped my arm tightly around her as the dresser started to tip back toward me and pushed the dresser back toward the wall with my other hand.

Lucy was panting hard in my ear and her body was trembling. It had always been like this with us. Explosive and on the verge of crazy. I should have known the very first time that I wouldn't ever let her go.

"Dude, what the fuck-oh shit."

I turned around to see Sinner walking out of the room and I chuckled against Lucy. It wasn't the first time I had been caught fucking someone, but usually the guys didn't have to see my ass.

I got dressed and gave Lucy some time to get cleaned up. The guys were outside laughing and drinking beer as if Man Bun had never been here.

"Fuck, man. You might want to warn someone when you're fucking your girl. I saw your fucking ass," Sinner shook his head.

"I don't want to even go there," Cap said, holding Maggie on his lap. "You should have seen what I walked in on at work."

I glared at him, knowing that he was about to out us. "That's not cool, Cap."

"Tell me," Maggie said excitedly from his lap.

"I fucking walked in on Pappy and Irish with their pants down and Cazzo, Chance, Burg, and Sinner checking out their dicks."

Maggie's mouth dropped open as she stared at all of us.

Knight dropped his beer bottle in the garbage and stood. "And on that note, I'm out."

"It's not like it fucking sounds," I growled.

"You already took me to the fucking store and made people think we were gay. Now a bunch of you are staring at each others dicks at work? That shit's fucked up."

"I had a fucking wax because of you," I pointed at Maggie, "and it was irritated and red. Sinner and Burg were telling me what I did wrong."

"So, why were Irish's pants down too?" Cap asked with a chuckle.

"Because he fucking gets waxed too and I needed to see how it was supposed to look."

"You did what?" Lucy said from behind me. I closed my eyes as the guys started laughing. "Did you say that you were checking out Derek's dick?"

"The wax job," I said slowly as I faced her. "I wasn't staring at his dick. I was checking out the work."

She was trying really hard not to laugh, but her nostrils were flaring and her lips were pressed tight. She nodded slowly and then her shoulders started shaking. "You know, I'd expect this from Derek-"

"Hey," he said indignantly.

Lucy gave him a look. "Really, Superman?"

Derek rolled his eyes and Lucy looked back at me. "Sorry, I just never expected that you would be looking at another man's...package."

"It wasn't fucking like that."

"I totally believe you," she said with a straight face and then promptly burst out laughing.

"Alright, you know what? Fuck all of you. I was doing it for you, and you didn't even tell me if you liked it."

"Sorry, I wasn't paying attention to that. Do you want to show me now? Maybe your friends want to take a look also. You know, to see how it's done."

The guys burst out laughing and I dragged Lucy away to the house, pulling her against me as we walked inside. "You just had to bust my balls about that in front of all the guys."

"I'm sorry, but that had to be one of the funniest things I've ever heard," she laughed.

"Yeah, well, you just remember that I did that shit for you. You won't be laughing the next time you go down on me."

She took a step back and the laughter had died on her face. "Hunter, this is just fun. I don't want you to get the wrong idea. We're not going to ever be anything more than fuck buddies."

I shoved my hands in my pockets angrily. "When are you gonna get it through your fucking head that I want you? This isn't a fucking game to me."

"It's not to me either. I keep telling you I don't want more and you keep coming back, expecting me to change my mind."

"You were willing to give me a chance before."

"That was before I saw how hard it was really going to be for you. I'm sorry, but I don't want more with you."

I pulled her hard against me and kissed her with everything I had. "That's not what your body tells me."

"I'm just not ready for more," she said as she pushed away from me. "I'm sorry, Hunter."

She walked out of the house and was gone. Again. Fuck, what did I have to do to convince her to take me back?

Chapter Five

LUCY

I left my apartment early Saturday morning to run to the grocery store. I was out of pretty much all food and I didn't think I could make a very good sandwich out of bread and ketchup. I walked to my car, feeling like something was a little off and glanced around. I didn't see anything out of the ordinary, so I got in my car and headed to the store.

I loaded up my cart with so much crap that I shouldn't be eating, but I hadn't eaten breakfast, so pretty much everything in the store looked good at the moment. I was pushing my cart down the snack aisle when I ran right into someone in front of me because I was too busy looking for the Nutty Bars to pay attention.

"Sorry, I wasn't paying attention."

A man turned around that was probably in his mid-thirties and good looking. As I studied him, I started comparing him to Hunter, which was never a good idea because Hunter was absolutely perfect to me. This guy was tall enough, but his hair was thinning a little on top. Not enough to be a turn off, though. But his face. Good lord that face could stop every female in her tracks. He had the most vibrant green eyes I had ever seen and his features were all perfectly shaped. I couldn't find a single flaw with him.

His body was lean and muscled, but I couldn't help notice that he wasn't as large as Hunter. Still, I was attracted to this man. A lot. It was then that I noticed his lips moving and realized that I was just standing there.

"Uh, sorry. What was that?"

"I said, it's alright. I was doing the same thing."

"You were?" I blew out a breath and chuckled. "That's good because I couldn't help but stare at you. I didn't mean to ignore you."

He held up a box of snacks and waved them slightly. "I meant that I wasn't paying attention either because I was looking for snacks."

"Oh," I flushed bright red.

"But I couldn't take my eyes off you either," he grinned.

I smiled that he was letting me off the hook for my blunder and tried to regain the confident Lucy that I took out to the bars with me. It was a little different in a grocery store.

"What a fucking cheesy line," I heard from behind me. I rolled my eyes in irritation as I slowly turned, glaring at Hunter, who stood directly behind me.

"What are you doing here? Are you following me?"

"Don't flatter yourself. I'm shopping," he grinned. "Good thing I'm here too, because this guy was about to break out the 'if you think I'm good looking, you should see my number' line."

"Actually, I was going to ask you out, but I don't use lines to pick up women. I just use my natural charm."

I smirked at Hunter and turned back to the man. "I'm sorry, I didn't get your name."

"It's Noah."

"It's nice to meet you. I'm Lucy."

"Maybe I could buy you a drink tonight."

"That would be great. I'd love to get together."

"Great. Why don't you put your number in my phone and I'll call you later. I'll make reservations and let you know where."

"Perfect," I said, taking his phone and entering my number.

"I'll see you later, Lucy. Take care."

"You too."

I turned and raised an eyebrow at Hunter. Obviously he didn't think I would accept a date with Noah.

"I'm sorry, was there something you needed?"

"You'd better hope Noah brings an ark because it looks like rough waters."

"You're such an asshole."

Hunter huffed out a laugh. "You're not really going out with that douchebag are you?"

"Why not? He's good looking."

"What about Man Bun?"

"I think we both know that that won't work out. Still, I'm keeping my options open."

"Or you could just admit that you really want me and stop fighting this."

"The only thing I'm fighting is the urge to punch you in the face."

He stepped toward me and I had to really hold back from plastering my body to his. He was right. I was fighting this thing between us, but it was only because I knew how he was and what he could offer.

"One of these days, Lucy. I'll wear you down," he whispered against my ear. I leaned back into the shelf, knocking over a few boxes as I tried to grab onto something to keep from swooning. My eyes drifted shut when I heard him inhale sharply, knowing that he was smelling my hair. I felt him pull back and I felt like I was drugged. I was in a Hunter-induced haze that I had to pull myself out of. His thumb brushed against my lip and then he was gone, leaving me a mess in the snack aisle.

✯✯✯✯

J texted Noah my address later that day. He was taking me to a fancy new restaurant in town. I was still thinking about Hunter while I was getting ready and that didn't bode well for the night. I left my hair down, putting some waves in it and put on a red dress that had a tight bodice, but a flared skirt. It was fun and dressy, but not too sexual. As good looking as Noah was, I wasn't sure that I really wanted things to go anywhere with him tonight. I was mostly going because Hunter had pissed me off.

I met him downstairs and smiled when he got out and opened my door for me. Such a gentleman. "Thank you," I said as I slid inside.

He got in and grinned at me, revving his engine. Okay, a little childish and not really appealing, but I went with it. He sped all the way to the restaurant, blowing through lights and taking corners way too fast, but I found him interesting enough to distract myself from the terrifying ride. He must have thought it would turn me on to see how fast he could drive his car.

We pulled up to a restaurant that had valet service and he led me inside. It was a little too ostentatious for my tastes. I didn't mind a nice restaurant, but this screamed wealth. It made me feel itchy. Hunter would never take me to a place like this. It just wasn't his style.

We were seated and he immediately ordered champagne, which I hated, and oysters, which sounded disgusting. I sipped at the champagne, but didn't really drink much. I preferred the water. I was actually a little surprised that he was drinking since he was driving, but maybe he wasn't planning on drinking much. By his third drink, I had already decided that I would be calling for a ride. There was no way I would be getting into a car with this guy.

The conversation flowed, but as the night went on, I felt more and more like he was just trying to impress me. He didn't really ask a lot about me and the food he ordered was all stuff that I didn't like. I stuck with the breadsticks that they had placed on the table. By the time he was ready for dessert, I was ready to leave. He was well on his way to drunk and I'd had enough. I placed my napkin on the table and scooted the chair back.

"Thank you for dinner, but I'm afraid I have to be leaving."

"We haven't even gotten dessert."

"I'm not in the mood for dessert." I picked up my purse, doing my best to make a graceful exit. I was just outside when I felt him grasp me by the arm and spin me around.

"Why are you being such a bitch? I just bought you dinner."

"A dinner that you picked out. You didn't even ask if I liked any of that food, which I didn't. And then you drank more than was necessary on a date. Pardon me for not wanting to stick around for dessert."

"You're all the same. All women come on strong and then act offended when the man tries to impress them."

"I'm not offended that you tried to impress me. I'm offended that you didn't give a shit about anything I wanted the whole night. Maybe we wouldn't all be such bitches if you thought of someone other than yourself."

His grip tightened on my arm and I tried to yank it away, but he held on tighter.

"Let her go." Hunter's large frame appeared to the side of me and Noah took a step back, still holding onto my arm.

"What the hell do you want? Didn't you get the hint in the store when she gave me her number?"

"Didn't you hear her when she said she didn't want to stick around? Remove your hands from her or I'll remove you from this earth," he growled.

Something about the way Hunter said it must have gotten through to Noah because he shoved me away, releasing me suddenly. I tripped over my feet and fell to the ground, scraping my hands on the sidewalk. Hunter moved in a flash, throwing Noah up against the wall and hissing something in his ear. He slammed his fist into Noah's stomach and then stepped back, watching him drop to the ground as he coughed.

Hunter bent down next to me and examined my hands. They were a little scraped, but nothing that I couldn't handle. I stood and brushed my dress off as Noah shuffled away to his car. Hunter's stern gaze narrowed in on me.

"You shouldn't have gone on a fucking date with someone you met in the grocery store."

"Why not? Claire did. How was I supposed to know he would drink like a fish and turn into an asshole?"

"You should have trusted me."

"Hunter, I'm not dealing with you tonight. I'm going home and forgetting this whole thing ever happened."

"At least let me drive you."

"Thanks, but I think I'll walk."

I turned and headed home. Luckily, the night was decent and the streets were well lit. Still, I felt Hunter follow me the whole way home in his pickup truck. Men. How the hell was I supposed to be mad at him when he was being such a pigheaded sweetheart?

*W*hen I got to my office Monday, there was a beautiful vase of flowers waiting for me. I smiled when I pulled out the card.

Congratulations on surviving your first few weeks of school.

*T*here was only one person I knew that was sweet enough to send me flowers, and that was Graham. He really was a very sweet and thoughtful man, even if our views were very different. I didn't agree with the things he said to the guys at the barbecue, but everyone had differing opinions. That didn't make him a bad person, just maybe a little misguided. Still, it was nice of him to think of me.

I placed the vase on the corner of my desk where I could admire it and got myself ready for the day. The morning went by fast, but the last half of the day was uncomfortable. Seth was in my next class and lately I felt like he was staring at me all the time. I was really thinking about going to the dean and having a talk with him, but I was still reluctant. He hadn't technically done anything other than creep me out. I caught him waiting around for me several times after school was out to make sure I got to my car okay. Luckily, Graham always met me at my room at the end of the day and took me to my car. He knew how uncomfortable I was and he was urging me to take action, but I would feel foolish if I was wrong about him.

"Ms. Grant?"

I was brought out of my thoughts by a male voice I recognized all too much. Seth was standing in front of my desk with his backpack slung over his shoulder. I felt small in my chair, so I stood, keeping the desk between us.

"What can I do for you, Seth?"

"You got flowers."

I glanced at them and gave a tight smile. "What did you need?" His eyebrows furrowed and I wasn't sure if it was confusion or anger. Either way, I didn't like his reaction.

"I have another game coming up," he reminded me.

"Yes, I know. Like always, I'll have your assignments to you before you leave."

"There are things that go on at this campus that aren't safe for a woman like you," he said, taking a step closer to me. His large frame filled the space that was between us until I felt like I would suffocate.

"What do you mean?"

"It's not safe to walk around the campus at dark."

I was so confused. It sounded like he was warning me against others, but he was the one that made me feel like I was in danger. "I'll be fine, Seth." I tried not to let my voice shake. I didn't want him to know that he scared me. "Mr. Kinsey walks me to my car after school, so you have nothing to worry about."

His face turned dark, making me take a step back. Maybe that was the wrong thing to say to Seth.

"Ms. Grant, there are things you don't-"

"Lucy, I-" Graham stood in the doorway with a wary look on his face. "Oh, I'm sorry. I didn't mean to interrupt."

"It's fine, Mr. Kinsey. Seth was just stopping by for his assignments."

Seth took a step back and looked between the two of us. "I'll stop by tomorrow for them."

Seth turned a glare on Graham before turning and walking out of the room. I breathed a sigh of relief, sagging against my desk.

"Are you okay?" Graham asked in concern.

"Yes, but I think you're right. I think it's time to report him. I don't want to get him in trouble, but I get this really bad feeling from him."

Graham nodded, "I think that would be wise. I'll walk you to your car, but I may not always be there and I don't trust that kid. Do me a favor, if I ever can't walk with you, call campus security to escort you."

"I will. At least when he's not traveling with the team."

He shifted uncomfortably, shoving his hands in his pockets. "Uh, Lucy. About the barbecue, I just wanted to apologize for my behavior. I get pretty worked up sometimes, but I should have kept my mouth shut considering where we were. I hope that you can forgive me and we can forget about all that."

It was so nice to hear an apology from a man because they so rarely happened. "I appreciate the apology, but I wouldn't expect any invitations to any more barbecues any time soon," I said with a smile.

He smiled and then glanced at the flowers. "Secret admirer?"

"I thought maybe they were from you," I said uncertainly.

He shook his head slowly and then looked back at the door where Seth had exited. "I think maybe we should go see the Dean now. This has gone too far."

I nodded and followed him out the door. Except, Seth had seemed angry about the flowers also. It didn't make sense if he was the one that sent them. Either way, it was time to file a complaint.

The dean was able to see me right away and despite Graham's protests, I went in alone. The dean, Mr. Miller, was a man in his sixties, with salt and pepper hair and a kind smile. He waved for me to take a seat and then sat in his own chair.

"Ms. Grant, my secretary said that this was somewhat urgent. What can I assist you with today?"

"I need to file a complaint against a student."

"I see. Which student is this?" he asked as he picked up his pen to write.

"Seth Mackenrow."

Mr. Miller put his pen down and leaned back in his chair. "Seth Mackenrow. What has he been doing?"

"He's been following me to my car at night, saying things to me about being careful and it's not safe. It sounds innocent enough, but it's more his tone of voice and his boundaries. It makes me very uncomfortable."

"I see." He nodded and studied his desk for a minute. "Has anything else happened?"

"I also got flowers today."

"Was there a signature?"

"No. It said congratulations on surviving my first few weeks of school."

He nodded and leaned forward in his chair. "Seth Mackenrow used to be a very outgoing, friendly student. That all changed last year. His sister went missing from the campus. No one's seen her since."

"Oh. I had no idea."

"That would certainly explain the warnings. I've had several female students complain that he does the same thing with them. He doesn't mean any harm by it."

"Was his sister ever found?"

"No, she disappeared when she was leaving the campus after a meeting with a teacher. The teacher was cleared, but he was the last known person to have seen her alive."

"Who was the teacher?" I asked quietly.

"Graham Kinsey. As I said, he was cleared by the police and campus security. As for the flowers, it doesn't sound like anything Seth would do, but I would suggest that you take precautions when leaving the building at night just to be on the safe side."

"I will."

"As for the flowers, maybe a family member sent them? It doesn't sound like something Seth would do, but I'll have a talk with his coach. He's been keeping a close eye on Seth this year."

"Thank you. I would appreciate it," I said, standing and heading for the door.

"Oh, and Ms. Grant?"

"Yes?" I turned back to the dean.

"I trust that everything that was said here stays private. I really don't like rumors being spread around the school."

I nodded and gave a small smile before leaving. When I got back to my office after talking with the dean, there was a note waiting for me.

. . .

*D*on't forget that you're mine.

*H*unter. This wasn't the first time that he staked his claim on me. Why would he even drive out here? I didn't give a shit if he saw that someone sent me flowers, even if they were unwanted. He had to learn that he couldn't control me and leaving me little notes to remind me that he thought I was his wasn't the way to win me over. I grabbed my flowers and tossed them in the dumpster on the way out of school. I didn't need the reminder that Seth had some kind of weird crush on me. I was going to settle things with Hunter once and for all.

I drove up to the gates of the Reed Security building and waited to be let in. When I drove up, Hunter was waiting outside with a grin on his face. I got out and slammed the car door, marching up to him and slapping him on the face.

"Stop with your damn notes. I am not yours and I never will be. Get it through your head. We're over!"

He looked completely shocked as he stared at me. "What are you talking about? What notes?"

"Don't mess with me, Hunter. All those notes you've been leaving me about me being yours. You're the only man I know that stakes your claim on a woman like a piece of cattle."

"Lucy, I haven't sent you any notes."

I rolled my eyes at him. "Stop lying to me. I don't know what possessed you to drive out to the campus today to see me, but the flowers were just a congratulations present. Not some declaration of love from another guy. You didn't have to go all medieval on me."

"Lucy, I sent the flowers, but I didn't leave you a note. I haven't left you any notes."

"But–" I thought back to the notes I received and shook my head. "But they all sounded just like you."

His face went hard. "What did they say?"

"Stuff like 'you're mine and don't forget it'. I just assumed that it was you. You've said it enough to me."

"Lucy, when I tell you that you're mine, I say it to your fucking face. I would never leave notes for you. That's fucking creepy. Do you still have them?"

I shook my head. "No, I threw them out. I just figured that..." I swallowed hard and felt a little light headed. Hunter placed a hand around my arm to steady me. "Why don't you come inside and tell me what the fuck is going on?"

I nodded and followed him inside. That feeling I got whenever Seth was around was back full force and I couldn't help but look back at the gates and wonder if he had followed me here.

"Don't worry. No one's getting in."

I followed Hunter into the building in a daze and didn't even blink when he shoved me into a chair and put a water bottle in my hand. I stared at it for a moment in confusion, but Hunter took off the cap and shoved it toward my mouth. "Drink."

I did as he said robotically and finally felt my brain coming back online. "So, if you didn't send the notes, who did?"

"I don't know. Is there anyone that you've noticed hanging around?"

"There's one student. I actually reported him today. He's been showing up at my office and he followed me out to my car a few times. He really creeps me out. He says weird things to me, like warnings."

"What kind of warnings?"

He took the seat across from me and took my hands in his. It felt so right and even I had to admit, it made me feel safe.

"Um, he said that it wasn't safe to walk around the campus at night. It's always something referring to it not being safe."

"That's it?"

"Well, it's more the way he says it. He hovers around me and he grabs onto me like what he has to say is urgent. But when I talked to the dean today, he said that Seth has done that with a few females. His sister disappeared from campus last year and I guess he just wants to make sure that other women are taking precautions. I just wish he wouldn't hover so much. It's just very strange. Graham has been there a few times and he intervened."

"Man Bun?"

"Seriously? You want to go there now?"

"Sorry. But doesn't it seem odd to you that Graham is always around?"

"No. He's been walking me to my car every night because he was there the first night Seth followed me out. He knew that it creeped me out, so he told me he would walk me out or to call campus security."

"Well, at least he doesn't sound like a total idiot. Why didn't you tell me about this kid sooner?"

"I really thought I was making it up in my head. I mean, he's just a college student and he hasn't said or done anything threatening."

"Following you to your car isn't threatening?"

"Well, if I came to you and said *a student followed me to my car and then told me not to walk alone at night,* what would you say?"

He seemed to consider this and then ran a hand over his face. "Alright, yeah, I probably would have thought you were imagining things, but you still should have told me. I can teach you self defense and I can give you mace to put in your purse. Especially if you're going to be walking alone through the parking lot."

I nodded, not sure what else to say. I was tired and now all I wanted was for this day to be over. I stood and Hunter gripped onto my arm.

"I think you should stay with me for now. At least until I have a chance to check this kid out."

"That's not necessary."

"Lucy, why do you have to be so stubborn? I just want to help you."

"What you don't seem to get is that your form of helping is more like tying a noose around my neck. You just don't know how to back off and I can't stand that."

He took a step back from me and shoved his hands in his pockets. "Fine. I was just trying to look out for you."

"And I appreciate that, but I've reported the student and if you give me the mace, I'm sure I'll feel much better about the whole thing."

He nodded and turned to leave. "If that's what you want. Follow me."

He walked down a hall to the elevator and I followed him on. We took it down to another level and then he led me to a room filled with all kinds of weapons. He pulled two cans from the shelf and handed them to me. "Keep this in your purse. This isn't the cheap shit they sell online. This shit is powerful, so be sure who you're aiming it at before you spray it."

He took my hand and led me down another aisle, pulling a gun from the shelf. I shook my head instantly. "Don't shake your head at me. I know you know how to use one of these. Claire tells us stories of how you and your dad used to go out hunting. This has a safety and it should be easy for you to handle."

"I can't carry that onto school grounds, Hunter."

"Then keep it in your car or at home in the night stand. I just want to know that if you need it, it's there."

"But it's not registered to me."

"We'll get that sorted out. For now, take it with you. I'd rather deal with the consequences of you carrying without a permit than you being dead."

I took the gun hesitantly and checked the magazine, seeing that it was fully loaded. I wasn't really comfortable with having a gun in my apartment, but that was mainly because I was scared I would get jumpy and shoot anyone that scared me.

"Thank you."

"You're welcome, Lucy. I just want to make sure you're safe. I know that I've fucked up a lot, but if you ever feel like you're in danger, please don't hesitate to call me. I'll always be there to help you."

I almost melted at his words. As much as I wanted to stay mad at him, he really was a sweet guy, he just had a very backwards way of showing it. I went home that night and put the gun in my nightstand, not wanting to have it with me on the campus. I wasn't even sure if it was allowed in my car in the parking lot. But at least at night I felt safer.

A few weeks passed and every week, I received some kind of note. It was always something about belonging to him. Whoever him was. I held onto the notes I received and after the third one, I decided it was time to bring them to Hunter. It creeped me out to know that this person knew where I lived and worked and was bold enough to walk right up to my apartment.

I stopped by Hunter's house after school the night I received the third note. It was already eight o'clock at night and I figured he would be at home. When he answered in just his jeans, I couldn't help but let my eyes trail down his beautiful body to his bare feet.

"Lucy, what do you need?"

"Uh," I cleared my throat and looked up into his gorgeous eyes. He was smirking at me. He knew that I wanted him. "I got a few more notes. I saved them for you." I handed over the plastic bag with the notes inside. The look on Hunter's face sent chills down my spine.

"When did you receive these?"

"One every week for the past few weeks."

"And you're just saying something now? Lucy, this guy could have attacked you at any time." He grabbed my hand and jerked me inside, looking past me into the darkness before he shut the door. "I should have just made you come home with me when I had the chance."

"Hunter, nothing's happened. It's just a bunch of notes. I just brought them over because you had asked about them last time."

"I'm going to give these to Sean at the police department. He needs to see what he can find out and you need to have some protection."

"I really don't think that's necessary. I mean, it's really creepy and everything, but they're just notes."

"They're just notes now. What happens when it escalates? How bad does it have to get before you'll see reason?"

"Look, I appreciate your help with this, but what would you have me do? Go into hiding because of some notes?"

"No, but I could hire someone to watch out for you."

"You want to hire a security detail for notes? Hunter, do you even hear yourself? That sounds so ridiculous."

"Lucy, this is what I do. I've seen shit like this get out of control way too fast and I really don't want you to be one of the ones that happens to."

"Look, I'll take extra precautions when I'm going places, but I'm not ready to have someone follow me around."

"If anything ever happened to you, I'd never forgive myself," he said quietly, stepping toward me. His hand brushed down the side of my face and my eyes drifted closed. I knew he had me. He was drawing me in more and more every time I saw him and soon, I wouldn't be able to resist him anymore. I stayed until morning and then did the walk of shame back to my apartment. When I got home, I got the strange feeling that I was being watched. I shook my head, hating that Hunter had ignored me and had someone follow me. I got ready for school and left, feeling someone's eyes on me the whole way to school. I didn't see a car following me, but then I wasn't trained at spotting a tail either. I was going to have to have a talk with Hunter about this when I got out of school today.

I was exhausted by the time I got home. My feet ached from the damn stilettos I had decided to wear and all I wanted to do was take them off and slide under my covers on my very uncomfortable futon and get some really bad sleep. I walked up the stairs to my apartment, each step more grueling than the last, and stopped dead in my tracks at the top of the stairs.

My door was ajar and I could see clearly that the doorknob was no longer attached like it should be. I took a step back, freaking out because there could still be someone in my apartment. The rational part of me said that I should just leave and call the police, but the sick and twisted side of me wanted to find out for myself if there was anyone in there. To prove to myself that I could live on my own and take care of anything that got in my way.

I took a step forward and slowly pushed the door open, peeking inside around the door. When I didn't see anyone, I shoved the door open the rest of the way and stood in complete devastation. I didn't have much, but what I did have was scattered and broken all over the floor. My dishes were broken on the counters and the floor, along with all my glassware. The few pieces of furniture I had were slashed and the stuffing pulled out all over the floor. Walking toward the bedroom I cringed when I saw feathers from my down pillow floating around the room in the breeze. My window was busted and the curtain was billowing from the air floating in. My futon was smashed and the sheets were slashed like someone had been in a violent rage.

But what really got to me was the message on my wall above my bed, with what looked like black marker.

You should have stayed away from him

The bathroom was no better. Makeup filled the sink basin and nail polish was spilled all over the floor. I wouldn't be getting my measly deposit back when they saw the newly painted linoleum floors. I called the police first to report the break in, but then I dialed Derek's number, knowing I would need someplace to stay tonight. There was no way I would call Claire. She would totally freak out over this and I didn't want her to see how bad it was. With a sigh, I dialed Derek's number and waited for the ring. I could hear men talking in the background when he answered and prayed that I could keep him and his army from showing up here, ready to tear someone limb from limb. It occurred to me that whoever broke in here was most likely upset because I had been seeing Hunter and when Hunter came to the same conclusion, there would be no escaping him.

Chapter Six

HUNTER

"Read 'em and weep, boys," Ice said as he placed his cards on the table. He had three sets of fish that were all the same.

I flung my cards down on the table, pissed that I had lost the whole night at Go Fish. Ice collected the pot that had close to $100 in it. $20 was from me. I was sure this time around I was going to win. There was nothing that killed a night like losing $150 at Go Fish.

"Whose fucking idea was it to play this stupid game anyway?" I grumbled.

"Yours," Chance pointed at me. "I believe you said that you were awesome at this game. How many times have you won now?" He asked around the cigar hanging out of his mouth.

"You know you look fucking stupid, right?" Chance was dressed like an old time poker dealer, complete with the visor, vest, and armbands. He brushed off his vest and glared at me.

"I look fucking awesome. You're just jealous because you could never pull off this look."

"Nobody can pull off that look, dickface." I leaned across the table and flicked my cards in his face. His cigar fell from his mouth when he jerked back and landed on his pants. He stood quickly, flinging his chair backwards as he picked up the cigar and brushed the ash from his pants.

"These were $100 pants, asshole."

"And now they're holy pants," I said, pointing to his crotch where the cigar had burned through.

Chance threw his cigar in the sink behind him and popped his knuckles as he swiveled his head side to side. "Let's go. I can take you any day."

"You couldn't take me out to breakfast." Chance was a sniper in his military days and he was damn fast in the ring, but he didn't have the bulk that I had. There was no way he would take me if we went toe to toe. Not unless I was completely distracted, which never happened.

"Hey, Lucy. What's up?"

I looked over to see Derek on the phone, his eyebrows drawn in concern. His eyes flicked to mine and my whole body stiffened.

"Why did you go in?...Alright, I'll be right there."

He swore and his eyes refused to meet mine. "What happened?"

"Lucy's apartment was broken into."

My jaw clenched in anger and Derek held up both hands. "Calm down, man. Let's just go check it out and see how bad it is."

I nodded, unable to say anything else right now. The drive over was fast, but I didn't remember any of it. All I could think of was the fact that this wouldn't have happened if she was staying with me. If I hadn't fucked it all up. I ran up the steps to her apartment and almost punched the fucking wall. The police were blocking off her doorway, but I could see her inside talking with an officer as he wrote down notes. Her place was completely trashed. There wasn't a single thing in her apartment that wasn't destroyed.

Derek let out a low whistle behind me and shook his head. "Damn, looks like they fucked up her whole place. That's rough after she just lost everything in the fire."

More footsteps clomped up the stairs and it took everything I had to tear my gaze away from the destruction in front of me. It looked as if every fucking member of Reed Security had shown up to see the damage. Sean Donnelly, a local detective and friend of Sebastian's, was leading them up the stairs. There had to be about fifteen of us crowded on the tiny landing outside her apartment. Sinner stood tall, trying to peer in and see what had happened.

He whipped around and glared at me. "I thought we fucking talked about this."

"What the fuck are you talking about?"

"We fucking told you that this wasn't a good idea," he said in anger.

"Whoa, I didn't do this shit. I never would have taken it this far."

Sean gave me a chin lift, obviously interested in the direction of the conversation. "What's he talking about?"

"Nothing."

"Doesn't sound like nothing. Why don't you just explain so we don't have any confusion as to what happened here?"

I ran a hand over my face as all my teammates stood there wanting an explanation. "I was trying to find a way to get Lucy back. I came up with this idea to pretend like her apartment had been broken into and then I would come to the rescue."

"That's fucked up," Ice said.

"I know. And when I ran it past Sinner, he explained why it was... fucked up. I swear, I didn't do this."

"You did what?" Lucy's feminine voice carried over the murmurs of the men. I bowed my head, not wanting to see the anger on her face as she tore into me. "Please tell me that you did not plan to break into my apartment and destroy all my things in some desperate attempt to get me back."

"I didn't. I was just spitballing with Derek and the guys-"

She spun around and glared at Derek, whose eyes and mouth were wide. "You were in on this? My sister is going to marry you and you thought this was okay?"

"No," he shook his head firmly. "We were trying to find ways to help him get you back, like running into you or letting the air out of your tire."

She spun and narrowed her eyes at me. "*You* gave me a flat tire?"

"No. I mean, I was going to, but I didn't get the chance. It went flat on its own."

"What else did you do?"

"Nothing. I ran into you on purpose at the store, the spa, and the diner, but someone else was always with you. This was my only stupid idea and I swear I didn't do it."

"What were you planning to do?" She crossed her arms over her chest and I could see that I was now dealing with Demon Lucy and I had to tread carefully.

I glanced at the guys and they were all slightly shaking their heads, telling me to keep my mouth shut. "Uh...Nothing."

"I don't believe you. Tell me now."

I swallowed hard, knowing that if I wasn't honest with her now, there would be no hope for us. "I was just going to make it look like your apartment had been broken into."

"Why would you do that?"

Another glance at the guys told me that I was fucking stupid if I answered that. "Because then you would call me to come help you."

"Why would I call you? We broke up. I could just call Derek."

"Told you, man," Derek said quietly.

Lucy spun on Derek in anger. "So, you schemed to help? Someone that you knew I didn't want a relationship with?"

Derek's mouth snapped shut and I watched as Lucy slowly turned and glared at all the men around me. I couldn't let them take the heat for me. This was on me, even if I wasn't the one that broke into her apartment.

"Lucy, I swear, they didn't have anything to do with this. This is all on me. I mean, not the apartment. I didn't do that, but trying to get you back, I was just...fuck, I didn't want to lose you."

"And you thought that manipulating me was a good way to get me back? Do you see why I didn't think a relationship would work? You just don't get it. If you have to get me back by manipulating me, why would you want me? That's not the basis of a healthy relationship."

She shook her head and turned to Derek. "Can I stay with you for a little bit?"

"Of course."

"Don't think that everything's good between us. I'm pissed that you went along with this."

She pushed through the men and stomped down the stairs and out the door. I realized in that minute how utterly fucked up it was to try and worm my way back into her life. I had gone about this all wrong and now every one of my teammates was here to witness my shame.

"What do you want to do?" Cap asked.

"I need to get this shit cleaned up and fixed for her."

He nodded and pulled out his phone, telling Maggie to get the girls together tomorrow to shop for Lucy's apartment. When the police came out, they cleared us to go in, saying they weren't able to pull fingerprints or anything. Whoever had done this was good.

I walked into her apartment and sighed at the state of it all. We'd have to work all night to make it look nice.

"Tell us what you want to do," Cazzo said from behind me.

"Alright, we're going to have to throw out all this crap. Just clear it all out. I'll buy all new stuff. Once it's all cleared out, we'll scrub the place down until it sparkles. I want the walls painted and new doors put on. I want the whole place secured so that she never has to worry about coming home to this shit again."

"You heard the man. Let's get to work," Cap barked at us. "Derek, call and get us a dumpster ASAP. Cazzo, see if Vanessa will go with you and get paint. Ice, your team can start carrying shit downstairs for the dumpster. Chance, your team can start cleaning. Use whatever supplies she has for cleaning and Pappy will get whatever else we need. Knight, Sinner, and Burg, get your asses back to Reed Security and get everything we need to make this place secure. Alec, Craig, and Florrie, I want a new door and windows installed by tomorrow. Get on the horn and find whatever you need. Bill it under Reed Security. Let's move!"

I was fucking astonished how everyone came together and got to work without so much as a grumble. I walked into her bedroom and was practically fuming when I saw the message on her wall. This shit had to stop. I walked back out into the kitchen and saw that Sean was still talking with Sebastian.

"Sean, have you gotten anything on the notes she's been receiving?"

"No, we didn't find any fingerprints on the notes. Whoever is doing this isn't giving us anything to work with."

"That message is directed at me. I'm almost positive. I'm the only one she's been hanging around."

"What about people she works with?"

"There's this one guy, Graham, but she only sees him at work. He came around a few weeks back, but she hasn't been hanging around him."

Sean raised an eyebrow at me. "How can you be sure?"

"Because I've been watching her as much as I can since she got those notes. This guy must be leaving them when I'm not around."

"Which means he knows you've been watching her."

I ran a hand along the back of my neck, irritated that I hadn't spotted this guy before. "I haven't seen anyone suspicious around. Sean, I swear to you. I didn't do this. I would never do something like this to her."

"I know that, but this means that she has a fucking stalker and we don't have any evidence who it is."

"I gave her a gun to keep here." I walked over to the nightstand where I told her to keep it and saw that it was missing. "Fuck, it's gone."

"Was it registered?"

"Not to her."

Sean shot me a look of disapproval.

"I was working on getting her a permit, but I didn't want her unarmed when she was home alone. Tell me you wouldn't have done the same for Lillian."

He snorted and shook his head. "Lillian wouldn't touch a gun if her life depended on it. And there's no fucking way she would have a gun if it wasn't properly registered to her and she was fully trained on how to use it. She would probably start foaming at the mouth if I even suggested it."

"Fuck, I don't know what to do. She's not gonna let me anywhere near her now. How the fuck am I supposed to protect her?"

"Calm down, Hunter. It hasn't escalated to violence yet."

"Yeah, and how many times have you seen something like this and it didn't escalate?"

He just shook his head.

"That's what I thought."

"I'm just saying we have some time. Obviously, this guy is pissed, but we still have time to figure out who he is. I'll have patrol cars drive past regularly to keep an eye on her place. You work for a security company. I'm sure you can figure out a way to keep an eye on her."

"Are you suggesting I install security cameras in her home without her knowing?"

"What? Did I suggest that? Not a chance. I'm a cop and that would be a violation of her privacy. I would NEVER suggest something like that. As a cop."

He turned and walked out of the apartment, nodding to Sebastian as he left.

"So, you want cameras installed?" Cap asked.

"Fuck yeah."

"She'll have your balls if she ever finds out you did it."

"She already has my balls. She just doesn't know it yet."

We worked all through the night and by morning, the place was fucking sparkling and most of the walls were painted. Maggie was going shopping with Claire while Lucy was teaching. When she got home tonight, it would be to an entirely new place.

I knew that Lucy wouldn't want me anywhere near her, so I had Derek call and let her know that her place would be ready tonight. I really wanted to see her face when she walked inside, but a man had to know when he was beaten.

Chapter Seven

LUCY

"Tell me more," Claire laughed. "This is too good."

"It's not funny."

"Yes, it is. I can just picture all of them, sitting around and plotting ways to get you back with Hunter."

"You can't really think this was okay."

"Of course not, but come on. The guy has it bad for you. I mean, he wanted to be with you and you went and slept with Derek's brother."

"Alright, that may not have been my finest moment, but I knew Hunter would be no good for me and I didn't want to fall in his trap."

Claire poured me a glass of wine and handed it over. "You know, Hunter is really a great guy. Sure, he has his issues. Obviously, he has no idea how to have a girlfriend, but he's definitely one of the good ones once you get to know him."

"I'm sure he is, but I don't want to be the girl he practices on."

"Why would you assume he's practicing?" Claire asked.

"Oh, come on. Do you really think that Hunter thought I was the one?"

She shrugged. "I don't know. The way he was looking at you was the same way Derek looked at me."

"And what way is that?"

"Like you're everything he craves."

"I don't want to be someone's craving."

"Well, there's obviously more to it than that or he wouldn't have given up his bachelor lifestyle for you."

"I really doubt he has. He couldn't go five minutes without hitting on someone new."

"I wouldn't be so sure about that. I don't think there's been anyone else since the fire."

"Well, let's give him a gold star for holding out a couple of months," I said sarcastically.

"Lucy, don't you think you're being a little hard on him? That's a long time for someone like him."

"So, because he wants to give up his ways to do a trial run with me, I should just go along with it and damn the consequences?"

"Well, yeah. It's not exactly like you could judge him. You don't have the most stellar track record either. Who was the last guy that you dated?"

"Fine, I see your point, but I'm not avoiding relationships because I don't want one. I just wanted to finish school before I tried for something like that."

"But you still haven't had one, which means that you don't have any more experience than him. Maybe you two should try something really difficult like talking and getting to know one another. Oh, my gosh! What a concept!"

"Hey, just because you got it all with the first guy you dated doesn't mean that everyone else gets the same thing."

"Well, you're never going to know if you don't try," she said as she finished off her wine. It was true, but after what I found out tonight, I didn't know if I could ever give Hunter another chance again.

★★★★★

. . .

*D*erek met me at my apartment the next night after I left the school. He said he had a surprise for me, but wouldn't say what it was. When I got there, I expected it to still be a disaster, but when I walked up the stairs and saw the new door, I knew that it would be as good as before the break-in. I was wrong.

When Derek opened the door, I almost fell to my knees in relief. Not only was everything cleaned up, but the walls were freshly painted a bright white, it smelled really clean, and there was brand new furniture in my living room that made my tiny space look like a cozy nook. The kitchen had been fixed up too. The stove didn't have any missing knobs and the cabinets all hung straight. He had also gotten me new dishes, silverware, and glasses.

"That's not all," he said. "Check out the bedroom."

I walked over and opened the door to see my room painted in a light lavender color with a new bed and matching bedspread. There were also beautiful curtains that hung from the top of the window to the floor. I also had a brand new dresser. There would be no more living out of bags and leaving clothes in my laundry basket.

The more I looked around, the more I noticed little details that were added to make it more comfortable. Little throw pillows, pictures of my family, cute lamps, a small coffee table. There was so much that had been done that I almost cried. It was perfect and so much more than I could ever hope for. The only question was how I was going to pay him back.

"Derek, I can't believe you did this."

"Well, the guys helped with it. We installed a security system for you and everything is hooked up to Reed Security. If there are any issues, we'll be notified right away. There's also an app that you can put on your phone and it'll show you what's going on at the apartment any time you want."

"Wow. I think I just gained the best brother-in-law a girl could ask for. How much do I owe you for all this?"

"Nothing. We just wanted you to feel at home. After everything that's happened, I didn't like the idea of you living in this dump the way it was. At least now you should feel safe."

"Thank you, Derek. This is amazing."

"There's one more thing to show you."

He walked back into my bedroom and opened the small closet. There was a new wardrobe of clothes that were perfect for teaching. I pulled them out and looked through all of them, knowing they were exactly what I would have chosen for myself.

"That was a present from Claire and me. A little graduation slash 'congratulations on the job' present."

"Wow. I don't know how I'll even begin to pay you back for all this. It's amazing."

"You're family," he smiled at me.

After he left, I walked around my apartment and took in every small detail of the place. They had done an excellent job with everything. It was a little weird being here, knowing that someone had broken in, but knowing that I had security installed helped ease some of the uncomfortableness. One thing was for sure, I would be saving every penny I made to pay Derek back. If there was one thing I couldn't stand, it was having someone spend so much money on me. It didn't matter if it was family.

*M*y eyes burned as I left the school for the day. It was fall now and the sun was setting earlier than when I first started, but I hadn't realized how much earlier because I had been leaving school as soon as I was able. As I started my trek to the parking lot, I glanced around the shadows, trying to see if anyone was hiding anywhere. I didn't see anything even though my gut was telling me differently. Why had I been so stupid as to leave this late at night?

Footsteps thundered behind me and I spun around, a scream leaving my throat as I saw a dark figure run up. The figure stopped suddenly and his hands were in the air.

"Sorry, Lucy. I didn't mean to scare you." Graham stepped into the light and my breath left my lungs in a whoosh. I sagged, almost falling to the ground in relief. Graham chuckled as a sexy smile curved his features. "You left without coming to get me. When I went past your room, I saw that you had already left. I told you to have someone walk with you."

"Yeah, I'm sorry. I was just so tired and I wasn't thinking straight."

"You should be more careful." I rolled my eyes at him and he held up his hands and smiled. "Alright, alright. Anyway, I saw that you signed up for the teaching seminar next weekend. I thought we could carpool."

"Oh, that's sounds good. I don't really know where it is, so it'll be nice to go with someone else."

"Perfect. I can drive. I booked a room at a hotel for two nights. Were you planning on staying for the whole weekend?"

"Um...I think I only signed up for Saturday."

"They have a great one on Sunday. The speaker is John Moorland."

"No way. You're kidding."

He smiled at me and shook his head. "I kid you not. I know the guy that set up the seminars. Do you want me to see if there's another spot available?"

"Yes," I said eagerly. "I would love to hear him speak."

"Alright. I'll make some calls and let you know by tomorrow morning, so you have time to book another night if you need to."

"I'll go ahead and book another night anyway. If we're driving together, I can't just take a taxi back from Philadelphia."

"Right," he smiled sheepishly. "That would make sense. How about I pick you up Friday around seven after classes?"

"Perfect. Thanks, Graham."

"How about I walk you to your car?"

I smiled as he walked next to me, his hand brushing mine innocently as we walked. I knew that Graham wasn't the guy for me, but I was still glad to have him as a friend. It was hard enough to start a new job, but he made it easier. He was also intelligent and I found our conversations about history to be absolutely fascinating. This was something I never had with Hunter. We didn't talk about anything other than our favorite sexual positions. And while that was great, how were we supposed to build a relationship off that?

He walked toward my car, placing his hand on my lower back as he pulled open my door for me. My breath caught when his lips brushed against my cheek. Was that an innocent kiss? Maybe he didn't mean to kiss me. Maybe it was an accident. But then he slid his hands around my waist and turned me so I faced him. His eyes gazed into mine, asking permission and when I gave a slight nod, he brushed his lips against mine. I knew it was wrong. I knew I didn't want this with him, but I still allowed it. There were no fireworks and we both knew it.

When he pulled back, a faint smile touched his lips and he ducked his head, rubbing his hand along the back of his neck. "Sorry. That was probably really unprofessional of me."

I cleared my throat not sure what to say. "Graham-"

"It's okay. I get it. Friends?"

I nodded and he took a step back and shoved his hands in his pockets. "I'll see you tomorrow. Have a good night."

I got in my car and headed home, stopping at the gas station in town to fill up. As I was pumping gas, I let my mind drift to my kiss with Graham. I didn't want to overanalyze the kiss, but I couldn't help it. It's what I did. It was firm, but gentle. There was no demand in his kiss, which was nothing like when Hunter kissed me. He didn't take charge the way Hunter did and it always felt like he was asking permission, no matter what we were doing. I was irritated when I realized that I actually liked Hunter's demanding ways. Apparently, that was what I wanted from a man. Not to run my life, but to tell me I was his and to know that he wanted only me.

I bit my lip, as I thought about the last time I had been with Hunter and all the things he had done to me. A truck pulled up on the other side of my station, breaking me from my daydream. Hunter stepped out and stopped dead in his tracks when he saw me. He stared at me for a minute and then cleared his throat.

"Hi, Lucy."

"Hi." I tried my best to hold it together. I didn't want him to see how angry I still was at him. I didn't want him to know that he still held this power over me.

"You look good."

"Thank you."

"How's school?"

I rolled my eyes and looked away. "Really? Are we going to stand here and do this?"

He went over to his pump and started filling his tank. "No, I guess not," he said quietly.

I finished pumping and grabbed my receipt, opening my car door and getting inside. I tried not to look over at him. I tried to ignore the feel of his eyes on me, but it was there and so intense. He still wanted me and if I was honest with myself, I still very much wanted him. I started my car and drove away, refusing to look in the rearview mirror to see if he was watching me.

Chapter Eight

HUNTER

I watched her drive away as I stood there pumping gas. I had fucked up so badly and there was nothing I could do to fix it. I had let her slip through my fingers because I couldn't figure out how to hold onto her without being a total asshole. Derek had told her that he paid for her apartment to be fixed up. I knew she wouldn't accept it if it had come from me. She didn't want anything from me and that included me helping get her apartment in order.

Sebastian had made sure that her apartment was monitored around the clock. No one watched the camera feed, but the sensors would go off whenever something moved in the apartment. She had a security system, so if the code wasn't entered, we would figure that someone had entered without permission and we'd go check it out. It was the best I could do under the circumstances.

I kept an eye on her from a distance over the next week, but I didn't let her know I was watching. Someone from Reed Security was always there around the time she left from work, watching her from the back of the parking lot. That had been Derek's idea. Mine had been for him to escort her every day to and from work. He didn't think she would approve of that, and insisted that this was the only way to keep an eye on her without totally pissing her off.

All I could think about most days was Lucy and the guys had been giving me a hard time about not being able to concentrate when we were training. Now I knew how Derek felt. I didn't understand it before Lucy, how a woman could captivate my every thought to the point of distraction. Which was exactly what I was right now: distracted.

I walked out of the pharmacy and straight into a woman carrying a bunch of grocery bags. The groceries were sprawled all over the ground in a mess and she was bent over shoving them back in the bags. I squatted down and started helping the woman pick up all the groceries.

"I'm sorry. I wasn't watching where I was-" I looked up into Lucy's captivating eyes, stuck in a trance that I never wanted to escape. She dropped her gaze, breaking the spell she had over me and bringing me back to my reality. The one in which she wanted nothing to do with me.

"It's fine. I shouldn't have picked up so much stuff at the store."

"Where's your car?" I asked, looking around as if it would magically appear.

"In the shop. It was making a noise, so I brought it in to be fixed."

"What kind of noise was it making?"

She laughed a little and shook her head. "You know, some clanking and then a grinding noise."

"Where was it coming from?"

"The car," she said with a smile.

How did we not know about this? Someone had dropped the ball on informing me of what was going on with Lucy. Had I known that her car was making noises, I would have made damn sure that it was checked out immediately and I would have had it checked for tampering. Now she was walking home alone and no one was with her. I looked around, seeing one of our SUV's parked down the street. I breathed a sigh of relief that she wasn't alone.

"Alright, I get it. You don't know what the noise was."

"So, anyway, I went to the store for a few things and ended up getting half the store."

"Here, I'll take some of those for you." I held out my hand for some of the bags, but she seemed reluctant to let me take them from her. "Come on. It's too far to walk with all those bags. Besides, it's the least I can do after I knocked you over."

I could see the wariness on her face and I knew she didn't want anything to do with me, so I was surprised when she nodded and handed over a few of the bags. "Thank you."

"No problem."

We walked in silence for a few minutes before I couldn't take it anymore. "Lucy, I really am very sorry for the way things went with us."

"Please, let's not do this, Hunter. I just want to move on."

I stopped her, placing my hand on her arm, turning her to face me. "Please, let me say this and then I'll never bring it up again." She bit her lip and looked away from me, but then nodded. "I never thought that I would want someone the way I want you. I don't know the first thing about being in a relationship and you're probably right that I'm not ready to let someone in as much as you need. But I wanted to try with you, and I can see how I fucked that up. I know that I can be too domineering and that pissed you off. I know you're not the kind of woman that wants to be ordered around. I just...I've lost a lot of people in my life and when you were in that fire, my instincts were to protect you no matter how I had to do it. I just couldn't stand the thought of something happening to you. And then when I fucked it all up, you didn't want anything to do with me and it fucking killed me. I'm not trying to make excuses here. I know that it was wrong to try to manipulate you. Maybe someday you can forgive me. I'd really like for you to not hate me."

She sighed and looked up at me with those eyes that seemed to look straight into my soul. "Hunter, I don't hate you. I just can't be with someone that doesn't have any boundaries."

"I know." We continued walking and even though nothing was resolved, the weight on my chest didn't feel quite so heavy anymore. "So, how's teaching going?"

"It's good. I really like it. The students are definitely challenging and it's a lot harder to teach at a college level than I thought it would be."

"What do you mean?"

"Just keeping the students interest is different. They already know a lot, so I want to be able to hold their interest and make it more exciting for them. I think most college professors think that the students are adults once they're in college and they have to put in the effort to do the work if they want to succeed, which is true. But I also want them to be excited to come to my class. I remember a professor I had in college and his world history class was what made me decide that I wanted to be a teacher. He was so engaging and made me really want to learn. I guess I want the same for my students."

"It sounds like you'll do a good job."

"I hope so."

"Have you made any friends?"

"There's Graham," she said hesitantly. "He's a history professor also. He's been helping me get my footing and we've spent a lot of time discussing strategies."

I knew I didn't have a right to be jealous. I had ruined things between us and showing my jealous side would only push her further away. Since we seemed to have a truce, I swallowed my wounded pride and smiled. "That's great. I'm glad you have someone to help you out."

She looked a little shocked, but hid it quickly. We walked for another block in silence and then we were at her apartment. I didn't want her to go, but I didn't have any reason to stop her. She hesitated and didn't walk upstairs right away.

"Hunter, can I ask you a question?"

"Of course."

"What made you not want relationships?" I studied her eyes and thought about not answering, but now wasn't the time to hold back. "Sorry. I shouldn't have asked. I just thought that there must be some reason that you have such a hard time letting people in. I'm probably wrong, but I thought I'd ask."

"There's no great reason," I said before she could walk away. "I don't have some fucked up past or a woman that left me untrusting. I guess the only reason I have is that my parents weren't the best role models. They didn't fight a lot, but they just existed together. When I think back to them, I see two people that basically tolerated each other. My parents slept in separate rooms and I don't know if that was because they didn't love each other or if my dad snored. They didn't go out on dates. Maybe because we didn't have a lot of money, but maybe they just didn't want to. I guess, I just don't know what really happened with them. They didn't give me any good example of how two people in love behaved. They divorced when I went into the military and I always assumed that they never really loved each other." I shrugged. "I just don't know any other way. I'm trying to figure this out as I go. Apparently, the first time I tried it, it didn't go so well," I said jokingly.

She smiled and laughed lightly. "Maybe you'll do better the next time around. Thanks for walking me home, Hunter."

"You're welcome."

She took the bags from me and walked upstairs. I shoved my hands in my pockets and headed for my truck. I didn't have her back, but at least she understood a little of where I was coming from. I walked along the deserted streets, looking up at the sky and wondering what it would be like if Lucy ever decided to give me a chance. I knew that if I had the chance again I wouldn't blow it.

I hit the ground, my face smacking against the pavement. My eyes blurred as something filled my vision, but I vaguely saw a figure running away from me. I tried to shake my head to try and see better, but my body wouldn't cooperate. I didn't understand what was going on. The world started slowing down in front of me. Even my eyelashes seemed to blink at a slower rate. Had I been drugged? The next time my eyes slid closed, they didn't open again.

"*D*umb fucker got shot walking down the street."

"Sebastian, are there any jobs that went wrong? Anyone that would want to take a shot at him?"

"Sure. There are always jobs that go wrong, for the other guy. I can't think of anyone off the top of my head that would go after him."

I pried my eyes open and hissed at the pain that shot through my head.

"Welcome to the land of the living." Derek was standing next to me, grinning at me like it was his birthday.

"So, what can you tell us?" Sebastian asked.

"About what?" I was confused as hell. I looked around the room and saw Sean Donnelly, Sebastian, Derek, and Knight all crowded in my small hospital room. What the hell was I doing in the hospital? "What happened?"

"Shit. We were hoping you could tell us," Cap said.

Sean stood at the foot of my bed with his notepad. "Why don't you tell us what you do remember?"

I blinked hard, trying to focus, but my head was throbbing. It took me a minute to clear the fog. "I ran into Lucy and walked her home. Then, I headed back to my truck. That's the last thing I remember."

"You were just down the block from the grocery store," Sean said as he wrote down something in his notebook.

"You still haven't said what happened."

"You got shot in the head."

"And I'm still alive? Unlucky shot."

"Or lucky," Knight said. "The bullet only scraped your skull."

"What caliber?" I asked.

".22," Sean replied. "I would say that whoever shot you wasn't trained."

There was probably a logical reason he was saying that, but my brain just wasn't functioning at the moment. "Why's that?"

"Because, a trained shooter would have made sure you were dead."

"So, this wasn't related to us," Cap said.

"I would guess this is a gang initiation or something," Sean said. "I can't say for sure, but that's what it looks like to me. Unless you've pissed off some random citizen."

"Not that I can think of," I muttered, though something was nagging at the back of my mind.

"You haven't slept with someone's wife or girlfriend?" Cap asked.

I shook my head gingerly. "You're such an asshole."

"Look, I know you have a thing for Lucy, but that doesn't mean you haven't strayed."

That was it. "The notes to Lucy. Someone was pissed that she was seeing me. At least, I'm pretty sure it was me."

"So, he gets pissed that she's still hanging around you and he tries to eliminate the competition," Sean surmised.

"Is someone still with Lucy?" I asked Derek worriedly.

"Someone's been on her twenty/four, seven. No one's approached her yet. After you left Lucy at her apartment, Chance stayed with her."

"Unfortunately, there are no cameras where you were shot and there were no witnesses. So, unless you can remember something, we've still got nothing," Sean said.

I laid my head back against the pillow and closed my eyes as the guys continued to talk around me. It got quieter or maybe I had drifted off. I wasn't sure which one, but when I opened my eyes again, the room was empty except for Knight.

"Why are you still here?" I asked, clearing my throat of what felt like sand.

Knight handed me a cup of water. "I couldn't leave. I kept thinking about all that time that you thought I was dead and now I know what that feels like."

"Except I didn't die."

"No, but when Cap called me, all he said was that you had been taken to the hospital with a gunshot wound to the head. Not many people survive those unscathed."

"Not many people survive a knife to the chest in the middle of a fire."

"Guess we're lucky bastards," he smirked.

"So, when are they letting me out of here?"

"Don't know. The doctor said he would stop by when you were awake and check you out. I would assume since you're fine, they'll let you go soon."

"Anyone else stop by while I was out?"

"You mean Lucy?"

I sighed and stared at the ceiling. Guess it was too much to hope that Lucy would make sure I was okay. Of course, since she wasn't my girlfriend, there would be no reason for her to come.

"Do you want me to call her?" he asked. I shook my head. Just because I walked her home didn't mean that everything was fixed between us. If anything, I had proven to her that I would never be ready for all she needed.

The doctor checked me out an hour later and said that I was good to be released. He suggested I take some time off work until the symptoms of the concussion I received were gone.

Knight drove me home and shut off the truck when we pulled in the drive.

"I'm fine. You don't need to stay."

"You're always supposed to have someone stay with you after a head injury."

"I've had a severe head injury before. Believe me, this is nothing."

"I'll help you inside and make sure-"

"Knight, I'm fine. I don't need a babysitter."

"You're so fucking stubborn."

"No, I'm just fucking tired and I don't need someone watching over me."

"Fine, but I'm checking up on you in the morning and if you don't answer, I'll tear the fucking door down to get inside."

"No need. There's a spare key hidden in the loose board in the porch on the right side of the door."

I slammed the door and went inside to relax in peace. My head was fucking pounding and all I wanted was some medicine and my bed. I went to the bathroom and got some pain meds. When I looked in the mirror, I cringed. I looked like hell. My eyes had deep bruises under them and my skin was pale, which was saying something since my parents were Brazilian. I removed the bandage from the right side of my head and examined the staples they had put in. The cut ran from my ear forward a few inches.

I went to bed and slept for a good portion of the day. When I woke again, it was to pounding, which just pissed me the fuck off. I told Knight where the fucking key was.

"Shut the fuck up," I shouted as I swung the door open. Lucy was standing on the other side, red cheeks and a startled look on her face.

"I'm sorry. I shouldn't have-" She turned and stepped away from the door, but I grabbed her arm and stopped her.

"Hey, I thought you were Knight. I was pissed because he said he was coming over and I told him where the key was. I didn't mean to snap at you."

"Oh, okay. I didn't mean to wake you, but Derek told me what happened and I wanted to make sure you were okay." She bit her lip as she looked at the side of my head. "Does it hurt?"

"That spot doesn't hurt so much, but I have a killer headache."

"Do you want me to give you a scalp massage? It helps me when I get headaches."

"I'll try anything at this point." I stepped aside and let her in, then went over to the couch to sit down. She sat down on the other end and patted her lap. "Why don't you lay down with your head on my leg?"

I did as she asked and closed my eyes as she started to massage around my temples and certain points around my eyes. The pain was slowly dulling and soon she was running her fingers through my short hair in a way that wasn't a massage, but still relaxing.

"I was scared when I heard what happened. Derek said you were very lucky."

I grunted, enjoying the feel of her fingers on my head.

"Do you remember anything that happened after you left my apartment?" I shook my head slightly and her fingers stopped moving. "Do you want me to leave? I don't want to bother you."

"Stay. I like the sound of your voice," I said, keeping my eyes shut. She was quiet for a moment and then what she said shocked me.

"When I was six, my mom died. It was winter and she got a bad cold, but she kept telling my dad she was fine. Then one day, she couldn't get out of bed. Dad insisted that she go to the hospital, but she just kept saying that she needed some rest. By the time Dad got her to go to the hospital, her organs had started shutting down. They couldn't do anything to save her. She had contracted pneumonia and it was slowly killing her.

"After that, it was just Dad, Claire, and me. Dad did pretty much everything to make sure that we were always happy. He never let Mom's death get him down. He used to have one of his friends take us into town to trick or treat on Halloween and he stayed home and made a haunted house for us. He would tape the light switches down so that we couldn't flip on the lights and he would have creepy music playing in the background. One time, we had to pass around organs that he made. I think there was a heart and lungs. It was disgusting. And then we had to walk through the whole house. He had taken wadded up toilet paper and put it all over the floor. It felt like we were stepping on mice. Then the vacuum cleaner started chasing us down the hallway. I still don't know how he did that one."

She was silent for a minute as she continued to run her fingers through my hair. It was soothing me to the point that I thought I might fall asleep, but I didn't want to waste this time I had with Lucy. I wanted to hear all her stories because chances were when she left, I wouldn't be seeing her again.

"I think my dad always worried that Claire and I didn't have a good enough life with him. Like he didn't make life interesting enough or something, but all the memories I have of growing up were great. There was one time that Claire and I were sure that there were ghosts in the house. We were walking down the hall to our room and there was a bookcase against the wall. I swear to God, there were pens and pencils flying off that bookcase and shooting into our room.

"And then there was the time that Claire and I stayed outside to watch the meteor shower. We were laying out on blankets in the dark and all the sudden Claire couldn't see. She started patting around on the ground and shouting, 'Lucy, I've lost my eye! My eye is gone!' We looked all over for it, but it wasn't anywhere on the ground. We ran inside to my dad and showed him that her eye was gone. He started laughing at us because her eyes were swollen shut. There had been cats outside and Claire was allergic. Dad never let her live that down."

I smiled as she continued to tell me stories from her childhood, but eventually, I drifted off to sleep. I hadn't been that much at peace in a long time.

I was grumpy after waking up on the couch alone. I had this insane idea that I would wake up in Lucy's arms and she would tell me she wanted another shot with me. Of course, that didn't happen, so I spent the rest of the day moping around my house. By the next day, I knew there was no way that I could spend another minute at home. I had to stay busy or I would end up going over to Lucy's and demand that she give me another chance. She would turn me down and I would be depressed all over again.

I went into work and into the conference room where everyone was sitting around the table, getting their assignments. They all looked up at me and Cap shook his head.

"Get your ass out of here. You heard the doc. No work for a week."

"I'm good. There's no way I'm sitting at home another day. I'll go crazy."

An evil look crossed Cap's face. "Alright. You can help Knight today."

I looked at Knight who was also grinning at me. "This is gonna be great."

Now I was nervous. "What's going on today?"

"Sean's sending over some possible recruits. We're going to put them through the course and see who has potential."

I started shaking my head immediately. "No. The last time we were looking at recruits, Knight got shot."

"Exactly," Cap grinned. "Good thing you're a medic. Just don't get shot. Kate's out of town at a conference. You'd have to tend to yourself."

"This sucks," I muttered.

"Hey, you want to be here? This is the job I have available for you."

"Fine." Anything was better than sitting at home.

After Cap finished handing out assignments, Knight and I made our way down to the training center. "I can't believe I'm doing this shit. They're not even recruits for here. This should be good."

"Relax. I do this all the time," Knight said, slapping me on the back. Sean Donnelly walked through the doors to the training center and came over to stand next to us. We watched as the recruits bantered with one another, each one thinking they were top dog.

"How do you deal with this shit?" I asked Knight.

"Kate taught me some breathing techniques. It's really been help-ing. Otherwise, I'd shoot half the people that walk through here."

"Half the people that walk through here are Reed Security Employees."

"Exactly," he deadpanned. "Alright. Here's what you do, take one deep breath in through your nose and hold it for five seconds. Then blow it out through your mouth. Repeat until you feel calm."

I nodded. "Yeah, I can do that. It actually works?"

"Not yet, but I haven't killed anyone, so it must be helping at least a little."

That didn't sound very promising. He walked forward and took in the recruits that were lined up. "Ladies, you are here today so that I can assess if you're good enough to join the police department. I'll be evaluating all of you along with my coworker, Pappy."

There were a few snickers and I saw Knight's body go rigid. "Something funny, asshole?"

"No, sir," the man said after clearing his throat.

I saw Knight taking in a deep breath and then blow it out. Shit, it actually looked like it was working.

"First thing you'll do today is run the course. If you can't pass it in under five minutes, you're automatically disqualified. Get your asses to the starting line now!"

The men hurried over to the starting line and Knight blew his whistle, starting the timer as the recruits took off. A few were very fast and obviously skilled. Another was fast, but a little uncoordinated. One was very slow, but obviously had heart. He pushed until he caught up with the guy that kept falling all over himself, then grabbed onto his arm and started pulling him through the course, picking him up when he fell and hauling him up the rope right along with him. I was impressed. Knight was too because when the timer went off and they still hadn't finished the course, he didn't cut them loose like he usually did. Instead, he waited for them to finish, obviously wanting to see how they did for the rest of the day.

The fastest of the group stepped forward, strutting like his shit didn't stink. "What the fuck? Call it. They didn't finish in time."

"I'll call it when I'm ready to, recruit," Knight yelled at him.

"This is bullshit. The one guy can't even climb the fucking rope without help."

"Recruit!" I shouted. "This is where we decide if you make it into the department or not. I would suggest you keep your mouth shut if you still want that opportunity."

The guy turned to another recruit and mumbled, "This guy's a washed up old man. That's why he's training instead of out on the job."

Knight stepped toward him, his eyes dark and lethal. I shook my head at the recruit's idiocy. "Old man? You want to step into the ring? See how old I am?"

The man snorted like that was the funniest thing he'd ever heard.

"I'll make a deal with you, you and me in the ring. If you beat me, I'll let you decide who stays and who goes. If I win, you walk out of here and you don't finish the training."

He looked around at the other guys, unsure if he should take that deal. He was bigger than Knight, but Knight was a trained assassin. He knew more ways to kill someone than most people in the military. And more than that, he liked it.

"And if I don't agree?"

"Then you walk out of here anyway," Knight grinned.

"I don't think this is a good idea," I said, shaking my head slowly. "Aren't you going to try to stop him from killing your recruit?" I asked Sean.

He shook his head. "Nah, I'm not worried about it. They're not on our payroll unless they pass the course. They're someone else's problem."

"I can take you," the recruit said with more confidence than he had.

Knight smirked at him and pointed to the ring. "Let's do this."

I shook my head, knowing this was going to end badly. I walked over to the medical room and grabbed my bag. There was no way that guy was leaving with anything less than a severe limp.

Knight pulled off his shirt, socks, and shoes, standing only in his jeans. Knight had stayed in shape and the scar that ran along his chest where he had been stabbed proved that he had seen action and lived to tell about it. He cracked his neck, jumping up and down a few times to loosen up. The other guy stretched a few times and then did a 'bring it' motion with his hands.

"Oh shit," I whispered as Knight's face grew dark and the assassin in him took over. He stepped forward and then waited. The other guy moved in, swinging left and right, but Knight always dodged his attempts at striking. Knight moved quickly, locking the guy's arms and striking repeatedly in his kidneys. He moved back, giving the man a chance to regain his breath. He grimaced as he panted through the pain.

The guy faked taking a knee and then shot forward, attempting to throw Knight off balance. Knight stepped aside and threw him into the ropes. He was toying with the guy. I shook my head and looked at the other recruits that could see the same thing happening. They were smart enough to keep their mouths shut.

Knight let him throw a few more punches, never landing any before I saw that look that I knew all too well. He was going in for the kill. The question was where would he strike and how much damage would he do? A kick to the chest threw the guy into the ropes, followed by a solid foot to the side of the knee, which had the guy screaming in pain. Knight finished him with a carefully placed throat punch. He wouldn't die, but he was definitely going to be having trouble breathing for a while.

Sighing, I stepped into the ring and went to tend to the fallen recruit. Sean smirked at me from the sidelines and Knight pulled his shirt back on, having not even broken a sweat.

"Jesus, Knight. You could have gone easy on him," I said as I examined his knee that was swelling rapidly.

"I did. He's not dead is he?"

"What the fuck, Knight?" Cap said as he entered the training center. "These guys are supposed to be training, not ending up in the ER."

"He accepted the challenge," Knight shrugged.

"Why the fuck didn't you stop this?" Cap asked Sean.

"He has a point. I don't know if I'd want him on the department if he can't back up what he shoots at the mouth. I kinda wanted to see what would happen."

Cap threw his head back in frustration. "You *knew* what would happen. It's Knight."

"Yeah, but it's been a while. He could have gotten sloppy in his old age," Sean shrugged.

"It's been like a year." Cap walked over to the recruit and looked down at him. "So what did you say to piss him off."

The guy groaned and held a hand over his throat, taking deep breaths. "I called him a washed up old man."

"You dumb fuck." He turned to Knight and shook his head. "We had a deal, Knight."

Knight pointed to the guy on the ground. "He's breathing. His kidneys will heal and he'll only be pissing blood for a week. His knee will be fine with physical therapy. I don't know what you're complaining about."

Sean ran a hand along his jaw and slapped Cap on the back. "Look on the bright side. At least we found out what a pussy he was before he joined the department. I'd say Knight did his job."

I pointed to one of the other recruits. "You get to take him to the hospital to be checked out." I stood, walking over to Knight. "I'd work on those breathing techniques a little more. I don't think they're working for you."

Chapter Nine

LUCY

Lucy: I'm here.
   Claire: In the bedroom

I got out of my car and headed for her front door. Ever since she and Derek got together, she'd become a girly girl and took extra time to get ready to go anywhere. It was kind of pissing me off. We had made plans a week ago to go shopping for some clothes for my weekend in Philadelphia for the teaching conference. I had plenty of clothes for teaching, but I hadn't had time to replace my day to day wardrobe.

I opened her door and walked inside. "Claire? You ready?" I sighed and walked back to her bedroom. The door was closed, so she had probably just gotten out of the shower. "Claire," I said, turning the door knob.

"Lucy! Don't come in-" she shouted as I opened the door and then screamed.

"Oh my, God! My eyes! I think they're burning!" I turned with my eyes covered and ran out of the room, straight into the hallway wall. I cried out in pain as my nose connected with the wall and I fell to the floor. Blood gushed from my nose, covering my shirt.

"Lucy? Are you okay?"

"I think I broke my nose," I whimpered.

"I'm so sorry. I didn't know it was you."

"I texted you."

"I'm sorry, I didn't see who it was. I thought it was Derek. I should have looked more closely."

"Yeah, you should have. Crap. Now I have to go to the doctor. You're going to have to drive me."

"Uh...I'm gonna need your help."

"Seriously? I just broke my nose trying to get away from that image and now you want me to go see it again?"

"Lucy, do you want me to take you to the doctor or not?"

"Fine," I grumbled, getting up and grabbing some paper towels to soak up the blood. I held my nose back, careful not to walk into any walls as I made my way back to her room. I walked over to her and had to laugh at her predicament. "What the hell is this stuff?"

"Would you stop looking and just get me out of it."

"I think I'm going to need an explanation to go along with this."

"After you get me out."

I sat on the edge of the bed and tilted my nose back. "Before."

She sighed and squeezed her eyes shut. "Derek and I like to experiment. One of my fantasies is being rescued by a superhero."

"Yeah, I've heard about that. You're kind of famous."

"Shut up," she shook her head. "Anyway. We've played out a lot of them, but this one is Spiderman."

"Oh, God," I groaned. "You two are so fucked up." I stood and tried to get the spider webs or whatever they were to come off, but they were stuck tight. "Hold on, I'll get some scissors." I went to the kitchen and returned a few minutes later with scissors and a knife. Her eyes widened and she shook her head. "Put the knife down."

"Sorry, Claire. I've got to get you out of there."

"Just be careful. I don't exactly trust you with a knife near me."

"Relax. I'm sure your superhero would save you."

"You can't breathe a word of this to anyone."

"You're no fun."

I worked on the bonds for well over fifteen minutes, but I couldn't get them off. My nose was still bleeding and my eyes were starting to swell shut.

"Claire, I have to call Derek. I can't do this and I need to get some relief for my face."

"Fine, but make sure he doesn't tell anyone."

"It'll be the first thing I say."

I pulled out my phone and couldn't see clearly anymore to find his number, so I used Siri.

"Hey, Lucy. What's going on?"

"I'm at your house and your wife needs you. She got herself in a bit of a predicament."

"Can you take care of it? I'm slammed at work."

"No, I can't because I need to go to the hospital. I'm pretty sure my nose is broken and I can hardly see anymore."

"Shit, can Claire drive you?"

"No, she's...indisposed at the moment."

"You tell him not to say a word!" Claire shouted.

"And you're not supposed to tell anyone," I relayed to Derek.

"I'll be there as fast as I can," he said with a sigh. I sat down on the edge of the bed.

"My face is killing me. I need some good pain relief."

"My wrists are killing me. This is not very comfortable."

"How did you get yourself like that anyway?"

"It's too embarrassing to tell."

"I'm pretty sure we're past embarrassing."

I tipped my head back after getting more paper towels and waited for Derek to get there and the bleeding to stop.

"Claire bear?"

"Oh thank God. My arms are killing me," she whined from the bed.

"I don't want to hear it. I'm pretty sure I won't be able to see for a week."

"What the fuck?" I looked up to see Hunter and Derek standing in the doorway, staring at the bed. Derek quickly shoved Hunter out of the room and closed the door. "What the hell is going on here?"

"I was trying to surprise you."

"Uh, a little help here. I'd like to get out of this very strange situation and get my face looked at before this shirt turns to solid blood."

"Right," Derek said, helping me up from the bed and out the door. "Hunter, take Lucy to the hospital. She thinks she broke her nose."

I held out my hand and he grasped onto it, pulling me into his side and wrapping his arm around me. "Come on. You can explain on the way."

He led me out to his truck and helped me inside, then took off for the hospital. "So, you want to explain what that was back there?"

"That was why I have this," I said, pointing to my face. "We were supposed to go shopping, but apparently she forgot and thought I was Derek. By the time I opened the door, it was too late. I ran from the room screaming with my eyes closed and ran straight into the wall."

"Ouch. Do I want to know what she was doing?"

"Apparently, she was wrapped in Spider-Man's webbing."

"Those two are so fucked up."

"Tell me about it. I think I'm going to have nightmares. I should never have seen her like that. I think I'm going to be scarred for life."

"Emotionally or physically?"

"Both," I sighed.

"We'll get you some pain meds and hopefully your nose isn't broken."

We pulled into the hospital and Hunter helped me inside. The nurses got me back right away since I was bleeding all over the place and the doctor came to check me out.

"How did this happen?"

"I walked into a wall."

The doctor looked skeptically at the nurse. "This is much worse than just walking into a wall."

"Well, I kind of ran at it full force with my eyes closed."

"Why would you do that?" the doctor asked. I didn't want to give my sister away. It was a weird enough story as it was.

"I saw something I wasn't supposed to."

"Right." The doctor nodded to the nurse, who immediately left the room. "It looks like you have a deviated septum. We could see how things look in a day or two, but it would be best to get you in for surgery and get that fixed. You could have breathing complications, frequent nosebleeds, and facial pain without it. The surgery is like any other. There are some minimal risks such as scarring, decreased sense of smell, deformed nose-"

"Deformed nose?" I screeched.

"It's very unlikely. Our surgeon is very good. Those are just minor risks."

"When would this happen?" Hunter asked.

"Today. We'll have to check the schedule to let you know the time, but it's better if we get this taken care of right away. It's an outpatient procedure and only takes about ninety minutes. We'll put you under general anesthesia, so you'll have to have someone drive you home and stay with you a day or two."

"I can do that." Hunter grabbed my hand and gave a small squeeze. I was grateful that he was there. Ideally, I would stay with my sister, but I was pretty sure that after what I saw, I would be avoiding her for at least a week.

The doctor asked Hunter to step outside for a minute, which could only be a bad thing. Was something more serious going on?

"I have a counselor on the way to see you. I want you to talk to her and only then will we proceed."

"Um...okay. What kind of counselor? Like emotional?"

A knock on the door had the doctor spinning around. "Here she is. This is Jane Carson. Please, listen to what she has to say."

The doctor left on that cryptic note and I watched as the counselor took a seat. "I want to ask you some questions and I need you to know that this is a safe place to talk. Nothing will go further than me."

"Okay."

"Did someone attack you?"

I scrunched my nose, causing pain to shoot through my face. "Excuse me?"

"This looks like a very vicious attack and that young man with you is easily twice your size. I just want to be sure that you're safe."

"I am. I promise you, that man would never hurt me."

She sighed. "A lot of women come through here and say the very same thing. Please, don't let him get away with this. There are people that can help."

I could see that I was going to have to explain if I didn't want her calling the police on Hunter. "Look, I was supposed to go shopping with my sister. I went to her house and she thought I was her fiancé. They have a little kink in the bedroom and she had created some webbing in which she was tied naked. I walked in and saw that and proceeded to go running from the room screaming and straight into a wall. No one hurt me but my sister for not locking her bedroom door."

The woman stared at me, trying to decide if she should believe me. "Would you like me to get her on the phone for you? Would that make you feel better?"

She nodded and I pulled out my phone, dialing Claire. "Oh, Lucy. Are you okay?"

"Claire, I have a very concerned counselor here that is going to have Hunter arrested if you don't tell her exactly what happened. I'm going to hand her the phone."

I handed the phone over and watched as the counselor went from disbelieving to staring at me in total shock. She nodded, not saying anything until Claire had finished. "Thank you, ma'am. I hope you're okay now."

She handed me the phone back and rubbed her forehead. "I never saw that coming," she murmured as she stood. "Feel better," she said as she left the room.

Hunter appeared a few minutes later with a confused look on his face. "What was that all about?"

"You just got out of a night in jail for domestic abuse."

"What?"

"I had to call Claire and have her clear it up. They were certain that you were beating me."

He stared at me for a moment and then started laughing. "Claire told her what happened?"

"Yep," I smiled. "I told her that they were going to arrest you if she didn't tell the counselor exactly what happened."

"I don't think they actually can do that. Don't you have to file a police report?"

"Maybe," I shrugged. "Call it payback for Claire making me see her like that."

"Is that the only reason?" he asked seriously.

I dropped my eyes to my hands and shook my head slightly. "I didn't want anyone thinking that you were capable of something like that. No matter what happened between us, I know that you could never do something like that."

His face softened at my answer and he looked away. "But I did hurt you."

"Hunter, what happened-"

He shook his head and cut me off. "I may not have hurt you like that, but I told you that you were mine and then I refused to let you in. It was over before it had a chance to go anywhere, and I'll always regret that."

"I may have pushed a little too hard," I said sheepishly. "I guess neither of us is very good at relationships. Maybe we're better off as friends?"

He nodded defeatedly, refusing to meet my eyes. "Sure. Friends."

I didn't know what was going on in his head. Part of me hoped that he wanted to give us another try, but I wasn't sure I was ready to face that kind of rejection again.

**

*H*unter held my hand as I waited most of the day to get into surgery. They had to be sure that I waited a certain amount of time between meals so that I didn't get sick. There was a whole list of instructions that I had to follow after my release and from what I understood, a very ugly nose piece. And Hunter was going to witness it. It bothered me more than it should have. After all, I was the one that told Hunter we would just be friends. So why did it bother me if he saw me at my worst?

I was so nervous for the procedure that the doctor ordered some medication to calm me. It took the edge off, but also made me a little giddy. I couldn't stop staring at Hunter and his amazing arms. They were so big and buff and it made my lady parts tingle. Was it wrong to want him so much when I was about to go have surgery on my nose?

"Has anyone ever told you that you look like The Rock?"

"I look like a rock?" he asked with a quirked eyebrow.

I laughed and rolled around the hospital bed. "You're so funny. Not a rock. *The* Rock. You know, Dwayne Johnson. You have those bulging muscles and the same beautiful skin tone. It was the reason I picked you up that first time in the bar."

"You didn't pick me up. I believe that was all me."

"No," I said, dragging out my words a little more than necessary. "I saw you with those big, hulking muscles and I knew that I had to feel your arms wrapped around me. Can you do the eyebrow thing?"

"What eyebrow thing?"

"You know, how he raises one eyebrow really high?" I tried to do it, but with my nose hurting like it did, I couldn't really move my facial muscles the way I needed to.

"Umm, let me try." He raised both of his eyebrows and I burst out laughing.

"You're just raising both of your eyebrows really high," I smiled at him and sighed, slapping my hand against his cheek. "You're so pretty."

"Men aren't pretty."

"You are. You have pretty eyes and long, beautiful eyelashes that are so thick, they make me jealous. And your lips," I sighed. "They're so plump, just like every woman dreams of having. It's really not fair that you got so lucky."

He chuckled and ran his thumb in small circles over my hand. "You're beautiful. You don't have anything to be jealous of."

"Tell me more," I whispered. I wanted to hear exactly what he thought of me.

"You have gorgeous, silky brown hair. It's one of the things I love most about you. And your eyes are really big, like doe eyes. They just draw me to you. They have from the first night I met you. And you have the most beautiful smile I've ever seen."

I didn't know if it was the drugs talking or if I was really falling for this man. My heart beat wildly in my chest as he continued to tell me what he loved about me.

"And I love that you know how to have a good time. I don't think I've ever had as much fun with a woman as I do with you. You're the only woman that I ever want to spend more time with."

"Do you still spend time with other women?" I held my breath as I waited for his answer, not sure if I would like what he had to say.

"There hasn't been anyone but you for a very long time. Even before I knew you were mine, I wasn't sleeping around because my body only craved you."

My breath stalled in my chest at his admission. Was I hearing things? Was this some crazy alternate reality? All I knew was that I wanted to tell him exactly what I loved about him. I wanted him to know that I still craved him just as much as the first time I met him. Damn these drugs for making my lips so loose.

Chapter Ten

HUNTER

" o you want to know what I like about you?" she said with a small grin.

I nodded. "Of course."

"You have such big muscles," she said to me from her bed. Her eyes were glazed over and she had a silly grin on her face. I was trying really fucking hard not to laugh at her right now, but she was hilarious on drugs.

"I work hard for them," I nodded.

She gestured for me to come closer until my ear was next to her mouth. "I love it when you're fucking me up against the wall. The way your arms flex makes me want to suck you into my mouth while I play with your balls. I have fantasies about you shoving your cock down my throat and fucking me hard until I can hardly breathe."

I pulled back sharply. She just took this from hilarious to downright painful. As in, my cock was straining against my zipper and it was fucking painful. She patted me on the cheek and sighed.

"You have the perfect face. A masculine face. Nice, sharp features that scream how manly you are. Your teeth are so nice and it gives you this perfect smile, and every time you show it to me, I fall in love with you a little more."

My whole body relaxed at her confession. She loved me. Even if she said it while she was on drugs, there had to be a part of her that really felt that way. That meant that I still had a fighting chance with her. I just had to go slow so that I wouldn't scare her off.

"Ah! There's my favorite sister," she shouted as Claire and Derek walked in the room. I adjusted myself quickly so they wouldn't see that I was hard as a rock while Claire's sister was in a hospital bed.

"I'm your only sister," Claire said.

"And my favorite brother," she grinned, then her face turned serious. "You two are very dirty. Like, way dirtier than I had ever imagined. I mean, I thought the things Hunter and I did were dirty, but he's never tied me to the bed naked. Although, that might be an interesting idea."

"Okay," Derek said, clapping his hands together once.

"Although, he has tied my hands behind my back and then fucked me from behind," she said with a grin. "That was fun. And then there was the time that we were at the bar and he fingered me under the table. I almost spit my drink all over everyone else there."

"I think that's enough stories," I interjected, not needing all the dirty things that I did to her told to her sister.

"Oh, come on, Hunter. Don't be shy now. After all, we did just see my sister tied to a bed in some kind of webbing. I think anything we've done is tame in comparison."

"How are you feeling?" Derek asked, saving us from any more of her tales.

"Not bad considering a wall hit me in the face."

"I'm really sorry, Lucy."

"Pssht." Lucy waved her off. "A little pain with sex can be a good thing. I just don't think it was supposed to be me that got the pain."

Claire turned bright red and bit her lip in embarrassment. "So, when's the surgery?"

"They're coming to get her in an hour. She was a little nervous, so they gave her some drugs to calm her down," I told Claire.

"If they were supposed to calm her down, why does she look high as a kite?"

I shrugged. "I guess everyone reacts differently."

They came and got Lucy shortly after to prep her for surgery. Derek and I were asked to go to the waiting area since we weren't family. I paced the large area, not able to sit still. I knew it was a pretty simple procedure, but it still made me nauseous to think of her back there about to be sliced open.

"Would you sit down? You're making me dizzy."

"You know, Lucy wouldn't be here if you and Claire weren't so fucked up. Spider webbing? Really?"

"Hey," he held up his hands. "She's the one that comes up with the ideas. I just let her live out her fantasies."

"Well, her fantasies just landed her sister in the hospital."

Derek laughed and slapped me on the back. "Shit, you are so far gone for that girl. Are you seriously blaming Claire for Lucy ending up in the hospital?"

"You know this is her fault."

He shook his head. "No, I know this was an unfortunate accident and you're feeling a little overprotective of Lucy right now. She'll be fine. She didn't seem like she was holding any grudges against Claire when we showed up, so chill the fuck out."

I knew he was right. I was practically foaming at the mouth over what was going on with Lucy. I had to pull my shit together. It was obvious to everyone that I had completely lost my fucking mind over this woman.

*W*hen she finally opened her eyes after the anesthesia wore off, I took my first normal breath. I knew that the doctor said the risks were minimal, but I couldn't help but be anxious over the whole thing. I was two seconds away from asking for some drugs of my own just so I didn't flip out. Lucy meant more to me than I could have ever imagined and the thought of her in pain was more than I could take. Derek had assured me that he would take care of Lucy when she was released, but I just couldn't deal with that. I needed to be with her and make sure with my own eyes that she was okay. The only way I was leaving her side was if she asked me to.

"How are you feeling?" I asked as she finally came around. She had packing inside her nose to hold everything in place and then she had a "mustache dressing" under her nose to catch blood that would leak out. She would have to keep it on for about twenty-four hours. I didn't care. I just wanted her to not be in pain, but based on the size of the swelling around her nose, I would guess that she was going to be in pain for a while.

"Hmm?" she looked around the room, blinking a few times and then focused in on me again. "Good. How'd it go?"

"It went great. The doctor said that your nose is a little deformed, but he could probably fix it with another surgery."

Her eyes went wide and she jerked up in bed, cringing from the pain. I stood up, regretting the joke instantly. "Shit, I'm sorry. I was just joking. There's nothing wrong with your nose."

"You big jerk," she muttered as she laid back down.

"The nurse is going to check on you and then we can get out of here now that you're awake."

"Awesome."

"Do you want me to take you to your sister's?"

"I thought that you were taking me home?"

"I can. I'd like to," I admitted. "I just wasn't sure if you would want me there."

"I don't think I can stand to be around Derek and Claire just yet." I wondered if she really felt that way. She had admitted to me earlier that she loved me, but I wasn't sure if it was just the drugs talking.

"I can stay with you. If you want, you can come back to my place. I have that nice, big bed."

Her eyes lit up and I smiled. "That sounds like heaven right now. I love your bed."

"Well, my bed is yours for as long as you want."

I took her back to her place after she was released and we got a bag packed for her to stay a few days. She insisted that she only had to stay one night, but I convinced her that my king size bed would be more comfortable for a few days. She didn't really put up that much of a fight.

"I just need to call the school and let them know that I'll be out for a few days. And then I need to call Graham. We were supposed to go to a conference this weekend, but that won't be happening now."

"You could probably still go."

"Are you kidding? I'm not going anywhere looking like I had my face bashed in."

I didn't argue because I didn't want her to go away for the weekend with Graham anyway. She got the week off work and then called Graham. It sickened me to hear him gushing over her. Yeah, I stuck close enough that I could hear him on the other end, offering to bring her soup and take care of her. She glanced at me as she told him that she was staying with a friend and I could swear that she blushed. I was going to get her back. I just knew it. I was going to take advantage of our time together, and I would win her back.

✯✯✯✯✯

"Just stay in bed, Lucy. I'll bring you breakfast."

"That's ridiculous. I'm perfectly capable of going downstairs for breakfast."

"You might be, but I just want to take care of you."

"Do I really look that bad?"

I cringed, not wanting to answer. Her nose was so swollen and I had changed her mustache dressing several times since we got back here yesterday. Her eyes weren't quite as swollen, but she had bruises under both eyes.

"Okay, don't answer that. I don't really want to know."

"You look beautiful."

"Sure, I believe that about as much as I believe you want a relationship," she laughed.

I forced a smile to hide the fact that that hurt a lot more than I wanted to admit. How could she not see how much I wanted her? What did I have to do to prove to her that I only wanted her? I stood and walked to the door.

"I'll be back in a few minutes with your breakfast," I said as happily as I could muster.

"Hunter, I'm sorry. I shouldn't have said that."

I smiled at her, not wanting her to feel bad for pointing out something that had been true up until a few months ago. "Don't worry about it. It's like I told you, I'll wear you down."

I went downstairs and shook my head as I placed my palms on the counter. Fuck, I didn't know what more I could do. How the hell was I supposed to show her that I was serious?

"Hunter."

I hadn't heard her come downstairs. She was standing in the doorway to the kitchen, looking at me in a way that I couldn't comprehend.

"Yeah," I said, clearing my throat. "I was just about to start breakfast. You should go back to bed."

I started busying myself around the kitchen, pulling out fruit to make a smoothie for her. She had a very limited diet for a few days.

"Hunter," she said softly. I didn't look at her. I couldn't. If I did, she would see how utterly devastated I was to know that she didn't really believe that I could give her what she needed. "Hunter," she said more urgently, placing a hand on my arm.

I finally looked up at her and realized that she was blurry. Fuck, I was crying. I was actually crying because the woman I loved didn't want me. Her eyes softened and she placed her hand on my cheek.

"I'm sorry. I know that you've been trying. I can tell and I shouldn't keep sniping at you. I guess I just was trying to keep my defenses up. I didn't want to get hurt again."

"I know," I said softly, and I couldn't blame her. She had every right to be wary around me. I couldn't just change the rules of our relationship out of nowhere and expect her to believe that I had changed.

"Can I ask you something?"

"Anything," I said, turning and swiping the moisture from my eyes before I embarrassed myself any further. I turned back to her with a smile.

"Do you really think you're ready to try? I just want you to be honest with me because I don't want to get my heart broken."

"Lucy, I can't guarantee that I won't fuck up again, but I am ready this time. I may need a little guidance from you, but I understand a little better now what you need and I'm ready to give that to you."

"I'm not asking that you be perfect, Hunter. I know I'm not, but I just want to know that you won't freak out on me."

"I'm not going anywhere. Even if you need more time, I'll still be here, waiting for you. I'd wait forever for you."

"I don't need forever. Maybe just until I'm not wearing a gauze mustache anymore," she grinned.

"I can do that. Alright, breakfast. I'm going to make you a smoothie and then we're going to binge watch *Poldark.*"

"You want to watch *Poldark?*"

I shrugged. "I don't know. Your sister told me about it. She said that you really wanted to see it and there are three seasons out right now." I waggled my eyebrows at her and she slapped me.

"We don't have to watch that. Don't you want to watch something like *Die Hard?*"

"Nah. When you work around violence all day, sometimes it's nice to just watch something a little lighter."

"You don't fool me. Derek told me how you guys all got together and watched sappy movies one day."

"Hey, that was strictly privileged information that he should not have told you."

"Yeah? What are you going to do about it?"

I wrapped my arms around her and pulled her into my chest. "I'm going to kidnap you and keep you here for the rest of your life so that you can't tell anyone else."

"I kind of like the sound of that."

★★★★★

I laid on the bed next to her, running my fingers over the smooth skin of her leg in the early morning light. She was everything I wanted and I needed her to know exactly that. There was no holding back with her anymore. Her eyes slowly opened and small smile tilted her lips.

"I love you, Lucy," I said in all seriousness. "I think I've always loved you, but I just didn't want to see it. I didn't know what the hell love was. But when I'm with you, my heart feels like it's going to pound out of my chest. My fingers tingle until I can touch your skin. The first thing my eyes look for are yours. I want to see that sparkle that lights up the room."

I shifted on top of her, cradling her body in mine. She had on a t-shirt and panties and I could feel her heat pressed against me. "Say you'll really give me another chance," I said, pressing a kiss to her stomach. "Say that this is really happening." I bit the bottom of her shirt and dragged it up with my teeth until her entire stomach was exposed. "I'll give you all of me. Anything you want is yours if you say that you're mine."

"Hunter," she whispered. "I want to, but I'm scared."

"I know. I know that you worry I'm going to run away." I pressed another wet kiss to her stomach and then looked back in her eyes, needing her to see how serious I was. "I promise that I'm ready for this. The only thing that scares me anymore is the thought of you walking out that door and never coming back. I'd be fucking lost without you. I'm not saying I'll never fuck up, but I promise that you're mine forever."

"I love you, too."

I ran my tongue along the top of her panties, watching as her eyes drifted closed. Her legs squirmed beneath me, trying to open for me. I took the lace into my mouth and pulled it down her thighs, over her delicate knees, and down to her ankles. When I pulled them off, I tossed them off the bed and pressed a kiss to the instep of her foot. I swirled my tongue along her ankle, circling the bone and then licking and kissing up her leg to her knee. I kissed every inch of her beautiful legs until she squirmed with need.

Her lips glistened before me as I sucked her into my mouth, tasting her salty flavor. I knew I would never find anything as great as this. Lucy was everything to me and now she would be mine for the rest of my life. I would make sure of it.

She wrapped her legs around my neck as I sucked her harder and harder, flicking my tongue against her clit as she squeezed me so hard I thought I would lose oxygen. When she came, I swore I blacked out momentarily from the pressure around my neck. When her legs finally loosened, I came up gasping for air. She was panting heavily and I started to worry that it had been too much. She was only a few days out of the hospital. I didn't want her to end up back there.

I started to move away, but she wrapped her legs around me again. "Where are you going?"

"I think that's enough for now. I don't want you to overdo it."

"I'll let you know if we get to that point."

"Lucy, I'm serious. That's all for today. We're not doing anything else."

"Says you."

She sat up and wrapped her hand around my cock, squeezing slightly. I groaned and shut my eyes tight. "Lucy," I said with a strangled cry. She spit in her hand and then rubbed my cock up and down from root to tip. Shit, this was the best hand job of my life. She started working me harder and harder. I should stop her. I should tell her that she needed to rest, but I had never felt anything so sweet. Well, besides her pussy.

"Hunter," she whispered. I looked into her eyes and saw lust shining bright. "When my nose is better, I'm going to suck you into my mouth and then let you fuck my mouth." I groaned as she flicked her tongue against my ear. "You're going to come in my mouth and I'm going to swallow every drop of your cum."

"Oh shit, Lucy." I could feel my balls pulling up and my whole body tensed.

"And then I'm going to lick your cock until it's clean," she whispered and then sucked my ear lobe into her mouth. I exploded in her hand, jerking so hard that I almost knocked her off the bed. I wrapped my arm around her to steady her and then pulled her in close. Her hand was still wrapped around my still hard cock. I couldn't help it. With her, it was like it was impossible to calm my body down.

"Fuck, Lucy. You're a she-Devil, you know that?"

"Well, I have to be creative for the next couple of weeks until I can make that a reality. Next time, I'll tell you what I want you to do to my ass."

And just like that, I was ready for another round.

Chapter Eleven

LUCY

*A*fter spending the week with Hunter, I was pretty sure that there was nothing he could do to ever push me away again. I had fully given my heart to him and there was no going back now. He asked me if I wanted to stay with him longer, but I wasn't ready for that yet. I think we both needed some space to make sure that we didn't rush things too much. As much as he told me that he wasn't scared anymore, I didn't want to jinx that.

I walked into the school Monday morning feeling like a new woman, despite the fact that my face was still swollen and bruised. It didn't bother me though. I didn't have anyone to impress.

"Lucy," Graham called to me as I walked toward my office. I smiled and waved at him.

"Good morning."

"I see you're feeling better," he grinned.

"Much better. It wasn't the most pleasant experience."

"You must have been running pretty hard to hit the wall like that."

I hadn't told him exactly what happened. My sister still needed her secrets. "I wasn't. It was just one of those klutzy moments that ends really badly."

"Well, I'm glad you're feeling better. How about I take you out to dinner tonight, as a sort of welcome back?"

I smiled slightly, but knew that I couldn't accept. Hunter wouldn't like me going out with Graham. He didn't like him to begin with and it would only piss him off considering what Graham had said to him at the barbecue.

"I'm really sorry, Graham, but I'm seeing someone and I can't go out with you to dinner."

His smile dimmed, but he took it well. "Lucy, I just meant as friends, but I understand. I wouldn't like it if my girlfriend was going out with someone else."

"Thank you for understanding."

I stood there for a moment, feeling slightly awkward. The last we had spoken, neither of us were dating anyone. Not that we really talked about it, but one minute I was going with him to the conference and the next, I had broken my nose and gained a boyfriend.

"How was the conference?"

"It was good. You missed some really good speakers."

"I won't miss it next time."

"Listen," he cleared his throat. "I have class. I'm glad you're feeling better."

"Thanks, Graham."

I walked into my office and set my bag down. That had bordered on painful. How was I going to continue to work with him if things remained awkward? Ever since that kiss, things just weren't the same between us. I got to work, trying to forget about Graham. I had a lot of work to catch up on. I got through most of the day relatively unscathed. The classes went quickly and luckily, the teachers that had filled in for me had followed my plans well. By the time I packed up for the day, I felt pretty good about getting back to work.

Walking out to my car, I stopped when I saw a figure hunched over by my car. I couldn't tell who it was, but whoever it was, was up to no good. I walked forward, hand on my mace and looked closer. It was Seth.

"Seth, what are you doing-"

My tires were slashed. My mouth gaped and I took a step back.

"Ms. Grant–"

"Don't!" I yelled, holding up the can of mace. "Don't move."

I pulled out my phone and called 9-1-1, all the while Seth was talking to me. I ignored him, choosing to let the police deal with him. A man approached that I recognized as the football coach.

"Seth, what's going on here?"

"He slashed my tires. I just called the police."

"Seth?" Coach Boots asked.

"I came out here and the tires were already slashed. The knife is there on the ground."

"Did you touch it?" the coach asked.

Seth looked down at the ground.

"Seth, we talked about this," the coach said cryptically.

The police arrived a few minutes later and given my statement and Seth's lack of explanation, they cuffed him and took him away. While they were dealing with him, I called Hunter and asked him to come pick me up.

"Seth really is a good kid. He just–" Coach Boots sighed and ran a hand over his head.

"Coach Boots, Seth has been following me around school, saying weird things to me since I started. I filed a complaint against him with the dean. I didn't want to, but it's bordering on harassment. My apartment was broken into, and now he's standing next to my car with my tires slashed and he touched the knife. I tried not to jump to conclusions, but this has to stop."

"I understand. I just never pictured Seth doing something like this."

I nodded, understanding what he was saying. No one wanted to believe that someone they liked was capable of doing such things, but it happened.

"What happened?" Graham asked as he walked up. "Holy crap. Who did that?"

"Seth. He was kneeling down next to my car when I got here."

"Shit. Do you need a ride?"

"No, Hunter's on his way."

He nodded and took a step back. "Well, I'll wait with you until he gets here. I'm sure this was a frightening thing to see."

"Thank you. I appreciate it."

Hunter pulled up a few minutes later and got out of his truck, walking over to my car to take a look. I could see the tension in his body as he examined the tires. The police had already taken the knife and had left. Campus security was still waiting close by. Hunter walked over to me, glaring at Graham.

"Graham was waiting with me until you got here," I said in explanation. Hunter didn't explode like I thought he would. Instead, he held out his hand and shook Graham's.

"Thank you. I appreciate you looking out for her. Lucy says that you've been walking her out to her car most nights."

Graham nodded. "Yeah, well, it's not safe for women to walk alone at night. There was a girl that disappeared from the campus last year, and after Seth started following her, I thought it was best if someone walked out with her."

"Like I said, I appreciate it."

I was totally shocked. Hunter was standing here and not only being civil to Graham, but also thanking him. He really was trying to turn things around for me and I felt myself melting more and more every minute I was around him.

Graham walked away and Hunter turned to me.

"I would really like for you to stay with me until this is all sorted out."

"I don't know that that's a good idea. We're just finding our footing and that might confuse things."

"Lucy, I'm not going to get scared if you stay with me. Besides, I'll just sit outside your apartment and worry about you if you aren't with me. I just need to know that you're safe."

"Well, shit. Who could say no to something like that?"

He grinned and gave me a kiss. "I'll call a tow truck and have your tires fixed by morning, but if you want, I can drive in with you and make sure you get in okay."

"I think I'll be fine driving on my own. Besides, the police took Seth into custody. I'm sure things will be fine now."

He didn't look like he believed that, but he didn't argue with me. "Come on. I'll take you back to your place to grab some stuff for a few days."

As we drove home, Hunter seemed a little irritable and I couldn't figure out what was bothering him. Was he having a change of heart already? I stared out my window, hoping that I hadn't laid it all on the line again, only to be disappointed. When we pulled up alongside my apartment, Hunter sat there for a minute staring out the windshield.

"Lucy, I need to tell you something and I need you to not freak out about it."

Shit, I knew this was going to happen. He was changing his mind. That took a whole half hour. He turned to me and I could see that he was really nervous.

"Just spit it out, Hunter. You've changed your mind." I shook my head and let out a deep breath. "I knew this would happen. I knew you would freak out."

"What? No, Lucy, that's not it at all." He took my hand and ran his thumb up and down the back of my hand. "I know that I told you I wouldn't do anything to manipulate you and I swear that's not what I was doing."

"What are you talking about?"

"Derek and I have had someone following you for the past few weeks. After everything that happened with the notes and your apart-ment, I didn't want you to be left alone when you were out."

I sat there silent for a moment. I couldn't say that I was necessarily angry with him, I was more just stunned. "Wait, if someone was following me, then they must have seen who slashed my tires."

"Chance was following you to work and then he was coming back around the time you normally leave. You left early today. He was just about to come to sit in the parking lot when you called me."

"Oh."

"I'm really sorry I didn't tell you before. I just wanted to make sure you stayed safe after your apartment was broken into."

"Is that why I haven't been getting any notes?"

"Probably. There's also something else you need to know." I looked at him warily. "I have a theory that whoever shot me was the same person leaving the notes. I think they're mad that you were spending time with me and they were trying to get rid of me."

My mouth dropped open in shock. That was insane. "But, I've seen you a lot since then. I've stayed with you. Why hasn't anything else happened?"

"We've been taking extra precautions. Since I was shot, I think he doesn't want to hurt you. I think he just doesn't want you with anyone else. I should have told you sooner though. Then, maybe we could have had someone staying on the campus with you. It would have been safer."

I had a choice to make. I could be mad at Hunter for keeping me in the dark about what he and Derek were doing, or I could see that he was trying to protect me and get over my expectations that everything always went my way.

"What do we do from here?" I finally said.

He looked at me, a little shocked that I hadn't started yelling at him. "Why don't we go inside and discuss our options?"

Progress. Both of us were learning to deal with each other in a calm, rational manner that was respectful of each other's feelings. We got out of his truck and walked up to my apartment. I didn't even bat an eyelash when he held out his hand for my keys. He unlocked the door and held my hand as we walked inside and he entered the security code. He checked out the small space and then came to sit at my corner table with me.

"Now that you know the situation, what would you like to do?"

"I think I should leave it up to you to decide."

"It's not really my decision. I'm not allowed to be on your protection detail, if that's what you decide. I'll call Derek over and he can go over options with us."

While Hunter called Derek, I got my bag out and started packing a few things to take to Hunter's. By the time I was done, Derek was out in the kitchen talking with Hunter.

"So, what did you decide?" I asked, walking into the kitchen.

"Well," Derek started. "Here are your options. We can take you to a safe house, which would be probably the safest option for now, but then you wouldn't be able to go to work. We wouldn't want to risk being followed back there and give up that location. Second, you could stay with Hunter and have a security detail on you, with at least one person that would stay with you at the school during the day to make sure that no one tries to get to you there. Third, we could continue with our current arrangement, but you'd have to tell us exactly what time you'd be leaving the school so that someone could always be there to walk in and out with you."

I turned to Hunter, wanting to defer to him for now. "What do you think, Hunter?"

"It's up to you," he shrugged. "I want you to be safe, but I'm not going to tell you what to do."

"Would I be safe with our current arrangement?"

He looked to Derek and Derek rolled his eyes. "Yes, you'd be safe."

"What do you think I should do, Hunter?"

"What would you like to do?" he asked.

"I want to do whatever you think is best."

"I just want you safe. I'll go along with whatever you think you can handle."

"Well, this is your area of expertise, so I think it should be your decision."

"I won't tell you what to do. We'll keep you safe no matter what you decide."

"Still, I would feel better knowing what you think is best."

"I understand that, but-"

"Good God," Derek broke in. "What the fuck is wrong with you two?"

"What are you talking about?" Hunter asked.

Derek's eyes bugged out and he slapped himself a few times in the face. "You two. Something is seriously fucked up here. Both of you went from being so goddamn stubborn that you fought each other tooth and nail on everything and now neither of you can make a decision for fear of hurting the other's feelings."

"I'm just trying to be respectful. I walked all over her before and I won't do that again."

"And I'm trying to defer to him. I understand that this is his area of expertise and he knows what would be best."

"And while that's true," Hunter cut in with a grin, "I never want to steamroll you again. I know how I fucked up before and I won't do that again."

"I kind of like that intense side of you."

"Yeah?" he quirked an eyebrow at me.

"Yeah, just in the right situation."

"And what's the right situation?" he asked.

"When you know what's best for me," I smirked.

"I can think of several occasions when I know what's best for you."

"Maybe later tonight you can give me an example."

"Please, make it stop," Derek groaned. "This is like a really bad porno flick." He sighed and sat down at the table with us. Hunter and I were still grinning at each other. "Hey," Derek snapped his fingers in front of us. "A little concentration here, please."

I pulled my lips between my teeth, trying my best to bite back my smile.

"Alright, here's what we'll do for now. You'll stay with Hunter and we'll post a team with you at Hunter's. They'll all take different watches, taking you to and from school. While you're in school, we'll keep watch on the building and your apartment, see if anyone tries to leave anymore notes for you. You aren't to go anywhere without letting one of us know. For now, we'll keep our distance so that you still have some privacy. Does that sound like a plan?"

"Sure," I grinned, still looking at Hunter. Honestly, I didn't care what the plan was. All I cared about right now was getting back to Hunter's house and seeing what he had in store for me. The glint in Hunter's eyes promised all sorts of delicious things.

"Are you two even listening to me?" Derek asked.

"Heard every word you said, man. What team are you putting with us?" But his eyes never left mine.

"I'll put Chance's team with you since he's already used to the routine. Go ahead and grab everything you'll need for the next week or so. We can always come back and get anything you forget. I'll have Gabe come over to help you with whatever has to be done." Derek started texting as he shook his head.

"Sure," I said, still smiling at Hunter.

"This is fucking ridiculous, Pappy. You were the last person I thought would ever get so fucked up over a woman."

"You have no room to talk," Hunter said. "You showed me the way."

"That sounds like a really bad country song," Derek said in disgust.

"Just telling it like it is. Sinner was right. When you know, you know. Might as well enjoy the ride."

"I think I'm going to go home and get away from...whatever this is you two are about to do."

"See you later, man." Hunter's eyes darkened as he continued to stare at me. I vaguely heard the door shut and then Hunter was out of his seat, pulling me to my feet. "God, I want that mouth so fucking bad."

"I can't yet."

"I know. We'll have to be a little more creative."

He lifted me up and set me on the counter, pulling my pants off me and spreading my legs apart. His fingers grazed my stomach as he lifted the hem of my shirt and tore it over my head. He flicked the strap of my bra, unhooking it with just one simple move.

"Gorgeous," he said as he took a step back. He pulled his own shirt over his head and then shucked his pants and boxers, leaving me drooling over his enormous cock. I never got tired of seeing it. He fisted his cock and started stroking it slowly. "Touch yourself. Now." I slid my fingers down to my pussy and ran my fingers through my juices. "Open your mouth." I did as he said. "Good. Now, flick your tongue over my cock." I quirked an eyebrow at him. I wasn't sure what that was supposed to mean. He was standing at least five feet from me. "Don't make me tell you again. I'm gonna fuck that pretty, little mouth hard."

That's when it hit me. He said we were going to have to be creative. I flicked my tongue out and watched as his eyes flared. His fist pumped up and down as his chest started heaving. "Open wide for me. I'm gonna shove my cock all the way to the back of your throat."

I opened my mouth wider and my fingers started working my clit, chasing the sensation that was building inside. "Fuck, yeah." His eyes zeroed in on my fingers and his nostrils flared. "Fuck it. I don't want your mouth anymore. Now I need your pussy."

He stormed over to me and spread my legs wider as he pulled me to the very edge of the counter. He pulled my fingers out of my pussy and shoved them in his mouth. His eyes slid closed as he slowly sucked every last drop off my fingers. "Damn, that's good."

I barely felt his cock at my entrance before he rammed himself inside me, hitting so deep that my body actually tried to flinch back. I screamed out as I threw my head back. His mouth found my nipples as he took me hard and fast. With every suck, my screams grew louder and louder, and when he thrust in one last time and buried his cock inside me, I felt like I would split in two.

The door swung open, hitting the fridge with a bang. I whipped my head to see what was happening. Gabe was standing at the door, chest heaving and a look of shock on his face. Hunter already had a gun trained on him and I had no idea where it had been hidden.

"Uh, shit. Sorry about that. The new noise alarm was going off like crazy. I thought..." He cleared his throat and swallowed hard. "I'm gonna have a talk with Cap about that noise alarm." He nodded repeatedly as he continued to stare at us.

"Gabe," Hunter said over his shoulder, lowering his weapon.

"Yeah?"

"You want to leave us the fuck alone and stop looking at my ass?"

"Right. Sorry about that. Not the looking at your ass part. I wasn't. Looking, I mean. Anyway, why don't you just call me when you're ready to go and I'll ignore all sounds coming from here."

"Sure," Hunter replied, not seeming fazed at all. Still, Gabe stood there awkwardly. "Gabe."

"Shit. Yeah." He turned on his heel and walked out of the apartment, leaving the door wide open. I heard his boots clomp down the stairs and then head back up. He reached in and grabbed the door handle. "I'll just shut this."

"Thanks, man," Hunter said. He turned back to me and we both started laughing.

"Noise alarm?"

"It was a new feature. If it gets too loud, it goes off. It's supposed to be an alert that there may be an issue."

"Ah, well, maybe Sebastian will rethink that now."

He nodded. "Yeah, I'm thinking he will. We have quite a few clients that I wouldn't want to see naked."

"I'm sure your clients would appreciate it also."

He pulled out of me and set me on the floor. "Go take a shower and we'll head back to my place."

"What did you have in mind for there?"

"I guess you'll find out," he said, smacking my ass as I headed off to the bathroom.

Chapter Twelve

HUNTER

"Seth Mackenrow got out on bail," Cap informed me as I walked into Reed Security. "Sean called me this morning when he couldn't get ahold of you."

"My phone died. Shit. How the hell did he get out?"

"They didn't really have much to hold him on. Even so, someone paid his bail."

"Fuck, this is fucking killing me. I don't know what the hell to do. I can't be with her twenty-four/seven."

"We have a plan in place. We're watching her everywhere she's going. Eventually, this guy will make a mistake and we'll catch him."

"Yeah, but how long is that going to take? She's trusting me to keep her safe."

"Look, I read this Seth Mackenrow's profile. I don't think it's him. From what I can tell, he's just concerned about other women disappearing like his sister. I honestly don't think he's the one you have to worry about. I don't think he was the one that slashed her tires. We need to be looking elsewhere. Who else has been around her?"

"There's the guy from the school that she teaches with. He's always around, but as much as I don't like him, I don't think it's him."

"Graham Kinsey?"

"Yeah, that's him."

Cap pulled out a folder and set it down in front of me. "He was a suspect in the disappearance of the Mackenrow girl. Apparently, they had a meeting right before she left the school."

"Yeah, but it says that police cleared him."

"Read the next page."

I flipped the page and scanned over what was written. I couldn't believe my eyes. "What the fuck? Why is he still teaching there?"

"Student/teacher relationships are only against the rules if he's actually her teacher. The "meeting" was about what they were going to do the next semester when she had to take his class. According to him, they agreed that they had to end things because he didn't want to lose his job. He disclosed all of that to the police and to the dean."

"How can they be sure that she didn't agree with him and he took matters into his own hands?"

"Cameras in the school showed him still in the building an hour after she left the building."

"Did they track him that whole time? Are they sure that he didn't leave?"

"Well, they can't be one hundred percent sure that he didn't leave, but they couldn't find any evidence to suggest that he had left or that he had gone anywhere. Her body was never found, which would suggest that she was taken off campus. There just wasn't time for him to take her off campus and get back for the cameras."

I ran a hand over my top lip. "Still, I don't like it. He's been hanging around her a lot. They're supposed to be friends and he hasn't mentioned this to her at all."

"Well, would you want someone to know that you had been investigated in a kidnapping and possible murder?"

"Alright, so if it wasn't Graham, then who posted bail for Seth? Let's look at that."

"Um..." Cap went over the report and then frowned. "It says that bail was posted by his coach. Guess he doesn't think he could do something like that."

"I saw him when I picked up Lucy. I didn't get to talk to him though."

"We'll keep looking into things, but it isn't necessarily anyone from the school even. She's had most of her notes delivered to her at her apartment. The vandalism was at her apartment. This is most likely someone from around here."

I shook my head. "I don't know—wait. She had a date with some guy a few weeks back. He got rough with her and I had to step in. He walked away, though."

"Do you have a name?"

"Noah. That's all I got. They met in the grocery store and went out to dinner later that night at that new restaurant in town. Maybe we can find out his last name from the restaurant. I'll look back at my calendar and try to remember when the date was."

"Good. Let me know. In the meantime, I have a job for you and Derek. Home installation. They want the works. Derek's already loading the truck with the equipment."

"On it, Cap."

I walked out of his office and took the elevator down to the supply floor. Derek was packing all the equipment we needed and I took it to the truck. "Where's the job?" I asked as we got in after we finished loading.

"Across town. I'm thinking it'll be an all day job based on the size of the house."

"Did they say why they wanted that much security installed?"

"Nope. They're not going to be there. They left a key for us outside and asked that the job be completed before they get back tomorrow."

"That's weird. Usually people want to be around for this kind of shit."

"Yeah, well, they live in an uppity neighborhood. Doesn't surprise me at all."

"Let's get this shit done. I want to be home by the time Lucy's home."

"She has protection with her."

"Yeah, well, Gabe walked in on us fucking last night and I didn't like the way he was looking at Lucy. He couldn't take his eyes off her."

"Are you sure it wasn't you he couldn't take his eyes off?"

"Dude, don't even go there. I didn't ask and I don't want to know."

"I'm just saying, you shouldn't assume."

I thought back to the way he was looking at us. Lucy had been mostly covered, but it was my ass that was hanging out. "Shit. You don't really think he's gay, do you?"

Derek shrugged. "Never asked."

"I've fucking showered when he was around. Now I'm never going to be able to look at him the same way. I'm always going to be wondering if he's looking at me."

Derek laughed and slugged me in the shoulder. "Good thing he wasn't in there when everyone was checking out your wax job." We pulled up to the house that was at least twice the size of my house. "Alright, let's go see what we have to work with."

We got out and walked to the front door, finding the key hidden where they had told us. I unlocked the door and stepped inside, stopping in my tracks when I saw what was in front of me. Fuck. Time stood still as I took in the device. There was a chair sitting directly in front of me with a box on top and a motion sensor on top of that. The box had cables running out of it, down to a battery on the floor.

I knew I had to move. I knew that the device would go off, but all I could see was Lucy and all the things we were going to miss out on. I heard Derek swear behind me and I felt him grab onto my arm and yank me out the door. I grabbed the door handle on the way out, slamming the door shut behind us. I dove left and Derek went right as the bomb exploded, sending us flying into the lawn. I felt something pierce my shoulder and my ears were ringing, but other than that, I was fine.

I stood and looked over at Derek. He was standing also, brushing debris off himself. He looked over and gave a chin lift, which I returned, signaling I was fine. Looking back at the house, the door was missing and the door frame was completely mangled. There were big holes where the interior walls once stood.

"Fuck me. Claire's gonna be pissed that I got this shirt all dirty."

"Stop thinking with your dick. This isn't the time for superhero scenarios," I said, pulling at my ears to try to get my hearing back.

"What's wrong with your dick? Did you get hit?"

The ringing in my ears was persistent and I could only pick up certain words he was saying. "Dude, I told you to stop fucking talking about Gabe. I don't need to know if he likes dick."

Derek walked over to me and pointed at my back. "You have a nail sticking out of your back."

I shoved his hand away and stepped back. "Dude, I'm not fucking gay. I'm not taking anything from behind."

"Hold still and this'll only hurt for a minute."

The ringing in my ears was starting to dim and I heard sirens in the distance. He turned me around and I felt him yank something out of my back. "Fuck! Why the hell didn't you say I had something sticking out of my back?"

"I just fucking told you that."

"When?"

"While you were talking about fucking Gabe."

"I didn't-" He grinned at me and I shook my head. "You were fucking with me."

"I couldn't help it. You're such an easy target."

We looked back at the door, both of us knowing that this job had been a complete setup. The question was, who was trying to kill us?

"Someone fucked up," Derek said. "That should have gone off as soon as we opened the door."

"Whoever it was forgot to take the plastic strip off the sensor. It delayed it."

"Had time to see that, huh?"

"I had a bit of a brain malfunction in there."

"Yeah, I noticed that when I had to drag you away from the bomb that was about to blow us to bits."

"We need to call Chance and check in on Lucy."

"Fuck, I was really hoping this didn't have anything to do with her."

"It might not, but I don't want to take any chances."

Derek got on the phone with Chance while I called Cap. I explained what happened and as much about the bomb as I could.

"Jesus Christ. What a clusterfuck."

"Cap, what's the name on the job?"

"David Emerson. Ring any bells?"

"None. I thought maybe this was related to Lucy, but I've never heard that name before."

"I'll do some more background on the guy, but you should know that you were requested for this job."

"By who?"

"David Emerson. I didn't think anything of it. He said that he met you a few weeks back and you gave him your card when you talked about security."

I thought back and shook my head. "No. I haven't given out a card in months, and I don't talk up the business because people always want favors."

"Alright. I'll get Becky on it. After you finish dealing with the police, head over to the campus and check on your girl."

"I was going to do that anyway."

"That's why I said it."

He hung up without another word and Derek and I went over what happened with the police. It took way too fucking long and I just wanted to get to Lucy, even though Derek had already talked to Chance and everything was fine. We were about halfway to the campus when Chance called back.

"Yeah?" Derek answered.

"We have a problem. Someone called in a bomb threat and the school is being evacuated. They won't let me inside to get Lucy."

"Why the fuck weren't you with her?" I barked.

"Because that's not what I was supposed to do. We've been hanging back to give her some space."

"Fuck," I swore as I hit the dashboard.

"They're emptying the school now. Gabe and I are at the exits watching for her. I'll let you know if we see her."

"We're about fifteen minutes out," Derek told him. "We'll see you soon."

He hung up and looked at me warily. "I guess we know why that bomb was there this morning."

"Yeah, take me out and get her alone."

"Except, she's not alone. She has Chance and Gabe with her, so what was his plan?"

"Get her alone in the school," I said, thinking out loud.

"Yeah, but they're clearing out the school."

I nodded, trying to figure out what the hell his play was. I pulled out my phone and called Cap.

"Cap, has Chance checked in with you?"

"Yeah, he filled me in."

"I need you to do me a favor and call whatever department responded to the bomb threat. We need to find out if any of their guys are missing or didn't respond to the call. Anything suspicious."

"Why? What are you thinking?"

"He set that explosion to take me out, to get Lucy alone. But Chance and Gabe are still with her, just not inside. So, to get her alone, he needs her inside."

"Right, but they're evacuating."

"Exactly, and who would go in to make sure that everyone was evacuated?"

"Gotcha. I'll find out who's running things and get a check on all personnel that are involved." He hung up and Derek shot me a questioning look.

"Are you thinking it's a cop?"

"I'm thinking if it's not a cop, it's someone impersonating a cop. Maybe someone that has a friend that's a cop with that department. He could have taken his place."

"And because they would be wearing face masks, nobody would know that he didn't belong."

"Exactly."

"It's a stretch."

"Yeah, but it's all we have to go on right now."

Derek nodded and turned down the road to the campus. We were about five minutes out. "Okay, one problem. He has her inside. How does he get out with her? If he's not wanting to harm her, which he could have done long before we got involved with protecting her, then what's his play? To keep her for himself?"

"I guess."

"So, he has to get her out of the building somehow."

"And he can't do that with the police surrounding the building. There's no way he could just walk out with her."

"Unless he has someone working with him," I surmised.

"Possibly, but that's still tricky with so many people around. He'd have to have one hell of a distraction to get her out without anyone noticing. Even if he drugged her and acted like she was unconscious, the paramedics would check her over. That's too many fucking people involved."

"This has all the markers of a stalker. Stalkers don't usually work with a crew. If I had to guess, I would say that he's working alone."

"Which brings us back to square one."

We pulled up to the building a few minutes later and found Chance standing by the exit, arguing with one of the cops.

"I'm fucking telling you that I need to get in there and find her. She's been under our protection because someone's been after her," he yelled at the officer.

"Sir, I already told you that we're doing a sweep of the building now, but it's going to take time."

"Excuse me," I interrupted, turning to the officer. "I'm Hunter Papacosta. I work for Reed Security. We think that our guy may be impersonating one of your officers. Do you have a list of officers that are in the building right now?"

"I don't know what information you're allowed to have. You're going to have to speak with my captain about this."

My blood boiled with every word he said. My body clenched and I couldn't hold it in. "Look, asshole. That's my woman in there and I'm fucking telling you that someone is trying to get her. If you don't help or at least let me in there to go find her, something's going to happen to her and then I'm going to have your badge and make sure you're picking up dog crap the rest of your life."

"I'll get my captain on the phone," he said, turning away from us.

Derek leaned in to whisper to me. "Picking up dog crap? Is that actually a job?"

I shrugged. "I don't know. I'll buy a dog and make sure he only shits in his lawn if I have to."

It took well over ten minutes to get the captain to get his ass on the phone with Sebastian, who was already on his way here.

"My captain is coming over to assess the situation," the officer said.

"Are you fucking kidding me? This is taking too long. He could have her already and we're just fucking sitting here."

"Calm down, man. Cap is almost here and he'll get shit sorted out." That didn't make me feel any better. "I've got Chance, Gabe, and Jackson questioning people and looking for Lucy."

"Wait. What about Graham? Has anyone seen him? He wouldn't have left without her."

"Are you sure?"

"Yeah, ever since that shit with Seth Mackenrow started, he's been making sure she gets to her car."

"Chance," Derek spoke into his microphone. "Look for Graham Kinsey. If he's out here, we need to speak with him. We also need to find Seth Mackenrow."

"He just got out on bail this morning. Chances are, he's not at the school."

"Still, we should find him."

Cap screeched up to the barrier in his pickup truck and got out, slamming the door behind him. Knight got out of the passenger side, decked out in all his gear, complete with shoulder and leg holsters. Never had I been so happy to have him on my side.

"Where's Captain Martin?" Cap growled.

"He's on his way, sir." The officer took a step back, obviously intimidated by Cap. Cap crossed his arms over his chest and glared at the man. "I'll just check on when he'll be here," he said, pulling out his phone.

"What do we have?" Cap asked.

"We're looking for Graham Kinsey right now. He's our best bet to finding out where Lucy is. We're also looking for Seth Mackenrow, but we don't think he'll be here."

"As soon as the captain gets here, I'll get Sean Donnelly on the phone to vouch for us. Hopefully, that will get us into the building to look for her. You'll go in two teams and search for her. Knight, you'll be with Derek and Pappy. Chance will take his team in. I'll stay out here to coordinate with the captain and make sure we have control of the situation. Get suited up."

Derek and I went to the back of the Reed Security SUV and pulled out our gear. Luckily, we were always prepared for anything. I strapped my knife to my ankle and attached my leg holster after putting on my vest and shoulder holster. Derek was doing the same. After checking my weapons, I walked back over to Cap, who was now arguing with the captain.

"You let my teams into the building now. They have more experience than any of the guys you've got in there and they know how to handle the situation. We've been vouched for by the department. Now, get your head out of your ass or I'll get the chief on the phone and make sure you're knocked down off your high horse to patrolman. Are we clear?"

The captain was fuming by the end of Cap's speech, but he lifted the tape and allowed us to enter. I pushed in my earpiece and pulled my weapon as we entered the building.

"Chance is taking his guys in the south entrance," Cap spoke into my earpiece. "The police are currently sweeping the first floor. Lucy's classroom is on the second floor. Room 225."

"Copy that. Have you found Graham?"

"Negative. Seth was also in class today, but he hasn't been seen either. His football coach is also MIA. His name is Kevin Boots. 5'11", 240 lbs, short, dark hair."

"We'll be on the lookout."

Derek took the lead going up the stairs, with Knight and I following. Her classroom would be about halfway down the hall. We were about halfway up the stairs when the lights went out.

Chapter Thirteen

LUCY

*T*he phone rang during my class and I was shocked when I picked up the phone and was told that we had a code black. I remembered reading through the employee handbook when I was hired and reading that if I ever got a call about a code black, I was to remain calm and let my class know that they needed to grab their bags and exit the school as quickly and quietly as possible.

I hung up the phone and smiled at the class. "Well, lucky you. We're running a drill, so you need to gather up your things and quietly head to the south exit."

The students all stared at me, obviously unsure if I was telling the truth or not.

"Well, let's not keep them waiting. Please go out to the south lawn and wait for further instructions."

The class picked up their things with a mixture of fear and curiosity and headed for the door. Once everyone had cleared out, I headed for my office, which was just a few doors down. I grabbed my purse and pulled out my phone, dialing Chance's number.

"Everything alright?"

"We've been instructed to leave the building. It's a code black. I'm going to the south exit."

"Alright. I'm coming to you."

He hung up before I could say anything else. I stood there for a moment, not sure if I should leave and hope to run into him or stay and wait for him. What if I left and then he was running all over the building looking for me? I tried calling him back, but the call wouldn't go through. That was weird. I didn't want to just wait around. I wasn't sure exactly what a code black was, but I knew that it meant we had a threat of some kind. I shoved my phone in my pocket and went to leave, but my office door wouldn't open. I jerked it, once, twice, but nothing happened. I checked the lock and saw that it was unlocked. I twisted the lock, trying to see if it was jammed somehow, but nothing happened.

Shit. I started banging on the door, but I could see that the hall was empty. No one was around to hear me. I pulled my phone out and tried calling Chance again, but I still got nothing. What the hell was going on? I started to panic. If there was a threat, I needed to get out of there fast. I ran over to my window and tried to pry it open, but it seemed to have been painted shut. I ran back to the door and balled up my fists, banging and screaming for someone to help me.

Finally, a face appeared in front of my door, but it wasn't a face that I was happy to see. Seth Mackenrow stood on the other side. I took a step back, not sure if I wanted him to help me or not. He tried the knob but nothing happened. His eyes met mine and a tingle went down my spine. This was the kid that had slashed my tires. His sister had disappeared. What if he had been the one responsible for her disappearance?

He stepped away from the door and I breathed a sigh of relief that he was gone, but then he was back moments later wielding a fire extinguisher. I stumbled back against my desk and shuffled around it to the back wall. He swung the fire extinguisher against the glass repeatedly until the glass broke.

"Ms. Grant, is the lock jammed?"

"Yes," I croaked out.

"Alright, stay back. I'm going to try and break down the door."

He didn't seem all that threatening right now. In fact, he looked like he was trying to help me. I was so confused and I just didn't know what to think about everything. He came running at the door full force, ramming his shoulder into the door. I flinched back as I heard it creak, but it didn't give. He went to the other side of the hall and rammed again. This time, the frame gave a little. The third time he rammed the door, it gave way fully and the door broke in. I stood stock still against the wall, not sure what to do now. My instincts were screaming at me to run.

"We should get out of here. They're evacuating the building."

"We aren't going anywhere," he said, taking a small step toward me. I swallowed hard and looked at the door, wondering if I could make it. There wasn't a chance.

"Why's that?" I asked, trying not to let my voice quiver.

"I've been trying to get you alone for weeks, but you always have someone around you. Now I finally have you alone and we're not leaving this room until I'm finished with you."

My whole body was shaking. I didn't know what I was supposed to do. There was no one in the hallway, no one that could help. My only hope was to draw him in, kick him in the balls, and run like hell.

"Seth, I really don't think now's the time to talk. If you want to schedule a time during office hours-"

"No! I won't wait anymore. It has to be now." He stalked toward me, his size easily twice that of mine. I looked around the room, hoping to see something that would help me defend myself, but all I saw was the chair and I didn't think I was fast enough to get to it before he figured out what I was up to.

He stepped right in front of me, gripping me by my biceps, squeezing a little too hard. I tried not to whimper, but I could already feel him leaving bruises.

"Seth, please..."

He looked confused for a moment and then shifted his weight. I glanced down and saw that he was right in line with my knee. I lifted and slammed my knee right into his crotch. I could feel my knee connect with his most sensitive parts. When he bent over, squeezing his eyes closed in agony, I raced around him, running out the door and down the hall. My heels and the tight pencil skirt I wore today were preventing me from running as fast as I could. My ankle gave out as I slipped on the tile and I fell against the wall. I tried to stand, but my ankle hurt too badly. I slipped off my shoe and tried to massage my foot, but everything hurt.

Hearing footsteps, I slipped off my other shoe and got up, hobbling down the hall. I glanced behind me as I braced myself against the wall. Seth was walking toward me at a fast pace. Panic roared through me and I hobbled faster, praying that I could make it out of there alive. Tears pricked at my eyes as I heard his footsteps just behind me. His large hands encircled my waist and lifted me off the ground. I screamed and kicked, trying to wiggle out of his arms, but he was too strong. He kicked open a door and slammed it shut behind us, setting me down on a desk. He bent down and examined my ankle, caressing my foot with his large hands.

"Seth, please, just let me go. I swear I won't say anything to anyone. I just want to get out of here."

He looked up at me in confusion. "Let you go?"

"Yes."

"Ms. Grant, I'm not trying to hurt you. I just wanted to talk with you. There are things you don't know and I'm afraid you're going to get hurt."

"Then let's talk outside," I said hurriedly. Not only was I terrified to be with this guy, but there was also the whole code black thing to be worried about.

"No," he said firmly. "I've been trying to get your attention for weeks and someone always gets in the way. This has to stop."

"What has to stop?"

"You, hanging around with Graham Kinsey. He's a murderer."

My eyes went wide and my mouth dropped open. I couldn't have heard him right. There's no way that Graham was a killer. "What are you talking about? Graham isn't a killer."

"Do you know about my sister's disappearance last year?"

"Yes, I've heard and I'm very sorry."

"Did you know that Graham was sleeping with her?"

"What? No, Graham would never..." I shook my head in disbelief. There was no way Graham would sleep with a student.

"He admitted it to the police. He was the last person that saw her alive that night. She met him in his office to discuss their relationship. See, he was going to have her in class the next semester and teacher/student relationships aren't allowed. Technically, at the time, he wasn't her teacher."

"No, you have to be wrong about that. How can you be sure?"

"Because I caught them," he roared. "Do you have any idea what it's like to walk in on your teacher nailing your sister?" I shook my head, not sure what else to say. "She was nineteen and he's almost thirty. He took advantage of her."

"I agree if that's true, but that doesn't mean that he's a murderer."

"I walked in on them that night. He was fucking her over the side of his desk, and then I listened as he told her that they couldn't be together anymore. She was devastated." He looked off in the distance, obviously caught in a painful memory. "She yelled at him, saying he never should have told her he loved her if he was going to break it off." He looked back at me, tears shining in his eyes. "She told him that she was pregnant. Do you know what he told her?"

I shook my head, not wanting to know what had been said.

"He told her that she had to get rid of it. That he couldn't afford the scandal. That he would lose his job!"

I covered my mouth with my hand, not wanting to hear anymore. This was all too much. I had spent time with Graham. I had considered him a friend and all this time, he was harboring a very dark secret. I wasn't sure if I believed Seth that Graham had killed his sister, but if the rest was true, he was not the kind of person I wanted to be associated with.

"He was the last one to see her. They have camera footage of him in the school later that night, but they can't account for the whole time."

"Did they arrest him?"

"They couldn't. They didn't have a body. They didn't have any evidence that she disappeared even. There wasn't a shoe left behind or her bag. She just vanished. She's still considered a missing person, but it's been a year. What are the chances that she's still alive?" he asked quietly.

All this time I had been afraid of Seth, but he was just trying to keep me safe. He must have noticed my friendship with Graham and worried for my safety. Suddenly, all his warnings made sense. All the times that he followed me to my car or watched from a distance. The night he followed Graham and I to the diner and then waited in the parking lot. He was concerned for my safety. He had even tried to tell me once, but he had been interrupted by Graham.

"Seth, I'm very sorry for what happened to your sister and I understand now why you wanted me to stay away from Graham. You just scared me. I didn't know what happened. I didn't know that he was a suspect."

He nodded and stood. "We should get out of here. I'll carry you outside. Just promise me that you'll stay away from him from now on."

"I will."

Seth lifted me up and started for the door, but stopped when he saw Graham blocking the entrance.

"Seth, put her down now."

I gripped onto Seth tighter, not sure that I wanted to be anywhere near Graham. I just couldn't wrap my head around all this right now.

"Seth, I'll only ask one more time. Put her down. Now." He raised a gun and my eyes widened in shock. Holy crap. He did do it. He's the one that murdered Seth's sister. I didn't know what to do, but I knew that I didn't want Seth shot, especially over me.

"Put me down, Seth," I whispered in his ear. "It'll be okay. We'll get out of this."

He looked at me and shook his head slightly, but I wiggled until he set me gingerly on my feet. I stood on my good foot, wincing as my other foot throbbed in pain.

"Come this way, Lucy."

I glanced at Seth and then slowly started making my way over to Graham. I noticed a coat rack in the corner behind him. It wasn't much of a weapon, but it was the best I could do under the circumstances. I walked until I was behind Graham. He didn't know that I knew about him yet. He probably assumed that I thought he was protecting me. When I was safely behind Graham, I inched my way over to the coat rack. Seth was saying something to Graham, but I wasn't listening. I was too focused on getting that coat rack. I wrapped my hand around the center of it, lifting off the ground. My body wobbled as I tried to balance on one foot.

"Seth, what happened with your sister and I was a mistake, but I would never hurt her."

"You're such a fucking liar. I heard you that night. I heard you tell her to get rid of the baby!"

Graham started to turn to me and I knew this was my only chance. I swung as hard as I could, hitting him in the side of the head with the base of the coat rack. His eyes rolled back in his head as his body dropped to the floor. The gun went skittering against the wall. I stared at Graham lying lifelessly on the ground. I hoped that I hadn't killed him. I just couldn't wrap my head around him being a murderer. He had always seemed so nice to me.

Seth walked toward me and looked down at Graham. "He would have shot me. I know it."

"Seth, I'm so sorry. I never would have thought...Graham always talked about hating guns. I just can't believe that he held one on you."

"It was all part of the deception."

"What did you do?" Seth and I looked up to see his coach standing in the doorway, a look of utter shock on his face. "I've let this go long enough, son, but this has to stop."

"What has to stop?" I asked.

"He attacked a student last year, insisting that he was responsible for his sister's disappearance. I talked the dean into letting him stay. He had already been through so much. I didn't think he should have to be kicked out of school."

I looked at Seth expecting a denial, but he just lowered his eyes in shame.

"Oh, God," I mumbled, stumbling back a step. I had just knocked out Graham based on what Seth had told me about him, but now I find out that Seth had accused someone else and attacked him also. I felt nauseous.

"Seth, I can't let this go on anymore. I have to turn you in."

"No!" Seth shouted. "I won't go to jail. I still have to find my sister."

Coach Boots raised a gun, the same gun that just moments before had been on the floor beside him. I was getting dizzy. This was all too much. I didn't know who to believe anymore. I didn't know what to think.

Coach Boots smirked and shook his head. "You won't find her. I made sure of that," he said, right before he fired a shot, hitting Seth in the chest. I screamed and ran from the room, pulling the door shut behind me. There was a chair outside the door and I jammed it up against the doorknob, making it impossible for the door to open, or at least, long enough to give me time to get away.

My ankle was killing me, but I hobbled as fast as I could, hearing the ramming of the door behind me. I made it to the end of the hall, but the elevator was out of service. The stairs were my only option, but it would take me forever to get down them. Hiking my skirt up as much as I could, I swung my leg over the banister and slid down, cringing when I hit the finial at the end. I worked my way over to the next one and slid down that until I reached the end. I was in a part of the building that I wasn't familiar with. I hadn't been down at this end of the building much. The south exit was halfway down the hall and I started for the doors, but then I heard running. Coach Boots was coming for me and I didn't think I could make it to the exit before he got to me. There was a dark hallway leading in the other direction and I went that way. Any sane person would make a break for the exit, so that's probably where he would think I went.

I found an unlocked door and shut myself inside, backing up until I hit the wall. It was extremely dark in the room, making it impossible to see where I was. I stood there in the eerie silence, counting each breath and praying that he would go the other way.

I could hear footsteps echoing down the hallway, knowing the minute they reached me I would be dead. I started panicking, each heartbeat thundering in my ears, making it impossible to concentrate on what was going on beyond those doors. And then I saw it. Coach Boots was in the hallway. He looked in through the window, cupping his hands around his eyes to peer in. I shrank back against the wall, praying that he couldn't see anything in the dark. I heard the door knob turn and then light peeked into the room. My heart hammered in my chest as the door started to open wider. I looked wildly around the room for a place to hide, but it was too dark and I couldn't see. As soon as he walked in the room and flipped on the light, he would find me.

The door was about half open when he suddenly turned and looked down the hallway. He raced down the hall, letting the door slam shut behind him. I let out a deep breath and tried to slow my racing heart. The shrill sound of my phone ringing had me letting out a yelp. I quickly dug into the pocket of my skirt and pulled out the phone that I had forgotten about, answering it before it rang again. I didn't say anything at first, just stood there waiting for Coach Boots to walk back into the room, but he didn't. I could hear someone yelling into the phone and I finally put it to my ear.

"Hello?" I whispered, afraid that someone would hear me talking.

"Lucy, it's Claire. Why are you whispering?"

"I'm hiding."

"From who?"

"Coach Boots. He shot a student in front of me and I ran."

"Are you serious? Where is he?"

"He just ran down the hallway. I think he heard something. I have to find a way to get out of the school, but I don't know what the hell to do. I don't know if I should stay here or try to find a way out. Plus, I hurt my ankle, so I can't really run."

"Okay," she said, taking a deep breath. "We are two very rational people. We can figure this out. Okay, what would someone in a book do?"

"Are you serious right now? You're referencing books to decide how I should get out of this situation?"

"Hey, when I'm reading, I always say, *don't go in there*, or *you should have gone the other way!* I'm telling you, you needn't look any farther than a good thriller."

"Fine, Madam Librarian. What should I do?"

"Okay, has he followed you yet?"

"He was just here. He tried coming in the room before he ran out of here."

"Okay, so he might already suspect that you're in the room. So, staying there probably isn't a smart idea. It's probably best if you leave."

"Great, but how do I know that he's not in the hall between me and the exit?"

"Well, you'll have to stay against the wall. Don't make any sudden movements."

"I couldn't if I wanted to," I grumbled.

"On the other hand, he could be trying to draw you out. Maybe he knew that you were in there and he's waiting for you."

"If he knew for sure that I was in here, he could have just walked in and turned on the light."

"That's true. Well, definitely don't go looking for him. That's when the girl always dies."

"That's very comforting, Claire."

"How far are you from the exit?"

My phone beeped in my ear, showing that my phone was on low battery. "Claire, you'd better come up with a solution fast. My battery is dying."

"Alright, first you need a weapon. Don't you dare leave that room without one."

"He has a gun," I said slowly, as if I was talking to a deaf person.

"Oh, right. Well, you should still have a weapon. You never know when it will come in handy. If I were you, I'd take my chances and head for the exit. You never know when he'll come back and then you're a sitting duck."

"Or, you could just call Derek and tell him where I am. I have a security detail outside the building."

"Why didn't you just say that?"

"Because you were over here telling me that I should figure out what someone in a book would have done," I said in exasperation.

"Well, yeah, but if I knew that Derek had a team there, I would have gone with that. You should have just said so."

I grunted in aggravation. "Claire, just get on the phone with Derek or Hunter. Tell them that I'm near the basement entrance in the southeast corner of the building. It's in the oldest section of the building....Claire?"

I pulled my phone away from my ear and saw that it was dead. Shit. Now I didn't know if she got any of that. What did I do now? Wait and hope for someone to come find me or take my chances out there with a killer? I crept toward the door and peered out through the window. When I didn't see anyone, I slowly pulled the door open and poked my head out just far enough to see down the hall. It was clear. I chewed on my lip, needing to make a decision and go with it. I couldn't just sit here and wait for someone to come. Now was my chance to make my move.

Just as I stepped into the hall, the lights went out, plunging me into darkness. Emergency lights came on sporadically down the hall, giving off just enough light to see that the coast was clear. I walked slowly along the wall, keeping my back as tight to it as possible. Each step hurt my ankle more and more, but I pushed on. This was my chance to escape.

I crept down the long, dark hall until I reached the opening where the stairs were located. Peeking around the corner, I didn't see anyone. I just had to make it halfway down the hallway and then I would reach freedom. But what about Graham and Seth? Seth had been shot. He could be bleeding out right this very minute, dying because he had come back to help me. To warn me. I couldn't leave him behind, but then I also knew that I wouldn't be able to make it up the stairs and even if I did, what good would I be? No, I needed to get out of here and tell someone where he was.

One step was all I took when a hand clamped down over my mouth and another snaked around my waist, pulling me back into the large figure behind me. I stifled a scream, breathing erratically through my nose.

"Calm down," a familiar voice whispered. "I'm going to get you out of here. Just do as I say."

The hand over my mouth loosened and I turned, seeing a figure dressed in tactical gear. I couldn't see his face, but that voice had sounded familiar.

"Can you walk?"

I looked down at my rapidly swelling foot and shrugged. "Sort of. I think I sprained my ankle."

"I'll carry you. We need to get you out of here, but I still need to be able to use my gun. I'm afraid this is going to be a little uncomfortable."

"That's fine. As long as I get away from that psycho."

He lifted me over his shoulder in a fireman's carry so he still had his right hand free. Then he turned around and went in the opposite direction.

"Where are we going?" I asked in confusion.

"He went that way, so we're going this way."

"But there's not an exit this way."

"There's an old route through the basement. We'll go that way."

It seemed a little odd to go that way, but then again, going back through the school in the same direction as the coach, who had just shot someone didn't seem like the wisest idea either. We made our way to the basement entrance and walked down into the darkness. He flipped on a light somewhere after the door shut and it illuminated the dark space.

"I'm going to set you down. I just have to find the door."

He leaned me against the wall and went in search of the door, returning a few minutes later, gathering me up over his shoulder like he had before. "Here it is," he said as we stood in front of an old door with a wheel handle. He set me down again and turned the old handle. It was obviously very old and hadn't been opened in a while.

"When we get to our exit, I'll call in and let them know we've made it out. They'll meet us at the exit."

"Why can't you radio them now?"

"Because this place is full of tunnels. I'm not sure which exit is still open. We'll have to go to each one and check to see if the door opens."

"Okay." That sounded logical enough, but I didn't really want to be carried over his shoulder anymore. It hurt my ribs. "Does anyone else know of these tunnels?"

"Not many people do. The coach wouldn't, if that's what you're worried about."

"Good, then I think I'll walk. At least for part of the way."

The man gave a firm nod and walked into the tunnel, motioning for me to enter. He handed me a flashlight from his belt and flicked on one of his own, pulling the door closed behind us.

"What was your name again? I didn't catch it."

"David. David Emerson."

"I'm Lucy Grant. It's nice to meet you."

Chapter Fourteen

HUNTER

*W*e made our way quickly up the stairs after the lights went out. All we had for light was the emergency lights in the hall. It wasn't much, but we'd gone in under worse conditions. It was slow going as we made our way down the hallway. We cleared every room as we went, not wanting to miss anyone that might be hiding in another room, even though I wanted to run down to her room and get her right away, there was a procedure to follow for a reason. When we finally got to her office, I saw the door broken in and my heart instantly jumped into my throat. Seeing something like this was never a good thing.

We moved on to her classroom and what we found there was even worse. Graham was kneeling over Seth Mackenrow, holding his hands over a wound on his chest. He glanced up at us with panic in his eyes.

"I didn't know what to do. I didn't want to leave him."

Seth's eyes were closed and I knelt down, feeling his pulse beating steadily under my fingers. The wound was in his shoulder and probably wasn't as bad as it looked.

"Cap, we have one down in room 225. Looks like a shoulder wound," Derek said into his mic.

"We're sending in paramedics now."

"Where's Lucy?" I asked Graham urgently.

"I don't know. Seth and Lucy were in this room and Seth was holding her. I thought...I thought he was trying to hurt her. I had a gun-"

"Wait," I interrupted. "*You* had a gun?"

"I bought it a few weeks ago. When Seth was following Lucy all the time, I got worried that this would end like with his sister."

"His sister that disappeared," I surmised.

He gave a slight nod. "Nobody knows what happened to her."

"Yeah, I hear that you're a suspect in that case," I said.

"I was cleared. I had a relationship with her and I was probably the last to see her alive, but I didn't do anything to her. The police know all that."

"Okay, so what happened here?" Derek asked.

"Lucy came toward me and stepped behind me. I was trying to calm Seth down. He looked like he was going to attack. I apologized for what happened between his sister and I and he started arguing with me."

"What were you apologizing for?"

Graham looked down in embarrassment. "That night, she told me that she was pregnant. I'm not proud of it, but I told her to get rid of the baby. I was worried about how it would look, that I would never get a teaching job ever again. When she left, that was the last anyone saw of her. Seth overheard us and we got in an argument and then he went after her, but she was already gone."

"How did Seth end up shot?" Knight asked.

"I don't know. I remember talking with Seth and then it was lights out. I woke up with a knot on the back of my head and Seth was lying on the floor in his own blood. Lucy was gone," he said quietly.

Seth mumbled something and I leaned in close to him. "What's that?"

"Coach Boots," he mumbled.

"Coach Boots? What about him? Is he the one that did this?"

Seth nodded slightly. "Killed...sister."

I looked up sharply at Knight. The paramedics and a few officers entered the room and started working on Seth.

"Graham, you're going to leave with the officers. We're going to finish checking this floor."

"Thanks. I'm sorry, you know, for what I said at your house."

"Oh, you mean the part about us being murdering assholes?"

"Yeah," he said sheepishly.

"Ironic how we're here saving your ass now, huh?"

He had the good grace to look ashamed as he followed the police out the door. Knight, Derek, and I stood, exiting the room and continuing down the hall. I paused when I saw a pair of women's shoes laying on the ground. Lucy must have taken them off to run. We continued down the hall, checking each room, but found nothing.

"Chance, are you finding anything?"

"Negative. We're almost clear on the first floor. We haven't found her yet."

"We're heading down the southeast staircase now. We'll coordinate with you at the south exit."

We finished making our way down the stairs and back outside. Chance, Jackson, and Gabe were already standing over by the police, looking at something on the map.

"We've got nothing. Are you sure she didn't slip out somewhere in the crowd?" an officer asked.

"We've checked everyone outside. No one remembers seeing her exit the building," Chance said. He turned to me and shook his head. "Cap called in more teams. He has Cazzo and Ice's teams checking the crowds again, but we've already checked. She's not out there. Besides, she would have tried to check in with one of us if she was out here."

"Where the fuck is she? We've already cleared the whole building."

Graham walked up and I almost snapped at him. I didn't need to deal with his shit right now. "Have you found her?"

"No, she's not anywhere to be found," I replied, slightly irritated that I had to discuss her with him.

"What about Coach Boots? Has anyone located him?" Knight asked.

"Police caught him on the first floor. He's already being taken back to the station," the officer informed us.

"What about the bomb threat?" Knight questioned. "Was anything found?"

"Not yet. The dogs and bomb squad are searching the second floor right now."

"We didn't see anything when we were up there, but that doesn't mean that we didn't miss it," I said.

"Pappy, you copy?" Cap's voice came through my earpiece.

"Yeah, what do you got, Cap?"

"Your girl talked to Claire. She was hiding from the coach. The phone cut out before Lucy could tell her where she was. That was a while ago, though. Claire couldn't get through to us. I'd say it was about twenty minutes ago. Also, Becky just called in. The name on the house this morning? His full name is David Noah Emerson."

"Noah. Fucking Noah. That was her date."

"I ran his name by the police chief. He's cousins with one of his police officers. He wasn't on duty today. The chief called over there and got no answer, so he sent some officers over to check it out. The officer was knocked out and tied to a chair. Looks like Noah's our guy."

"Fuck. But where the hell is he? We've had all the exits covered. We've cleared every room."

"What about the basement?" Graham asked.

"That was one of the first sections that was cleared," the officer said.

"So, he could have gone down there after it was cleared," Graham said.

"If he was posing as an officer? Yeah, he could have snuck down there. Nobody would have stopped him," Derek said.

"How would Lucy have gotten down there?" I asked.

"The basement is located in the oldest part of the building in the southeast corner," Graham said. "If she took the southeast stairs, it would have been easy to slip down that hallway into the old building. Nobody would have seen her and she might not have seen anyone."

"So, we need to do another sweep of the building, starting with the basement," I said.

"There are old tunnels down there. Not many people know about them. Before the school was built, there was an old shed that sat over where the basement is now. During Prohibition, the shed was used as a drop location for moonshine and the current basement was where the access to the tunnels was. I don't think anyone's gone down there since the school was built, but I have a map of the tunnels and where they let out."

"Where's the map?"

"In my classroom."

"Chance, take him up to his classroom to get the map. We'll meet down in the basement and start searching the tunnels."

Chance and Graham ran for the building. I placed my finger to my earpiece. "Cap, did you get all that?"

"Yeah, we'll be on standby. If you can give us a copy of the map, we'll start getting police over to the exits of those tunnels."

"10-4."

Chance was back within minutes with the map and we quickly got it over to Cap to be copied. I looked over the map with Graham, trying to find out the most likely routes he might take. Cap, Derek, Chance, Gabe, Jackson, and Knight all stood by, waiting for a starting point.

"There are a few that are under other buildings spread sporadically throughout this whole area," he pointed at a large area on the map. "Most of those are businesses or bars. I know a few of them have been closed off over the years."

He went down the list and quickly marked off locations that were no longer open.

"These five," he pointed at the map again, "lead out to fields and backyards. And then these access points have never been found. As far as I know, it's been at least ten years since anyone went down in the tunnels and probably longer since it was accessed from the school."

"Alright," Cap said. "We're going to break off into teams. I want the six of you to go into the tunnels and search out the access points that head off into fields. We'll have people waiting on the other end to head off anyone that comes out of the tunnels. We'll also inform all the businesses that police officers will be showing up in case those exits are utilized. We have no idea how communications in the tunnels will be, so no one goes off alone. Use your best judgement, but this guy is to be treated as a lethal threat. We try to bring him in unharmed, but Lucy's safety comes first. Understood?"

We all nodded and Cap started rattling off instructions over coms to Cazzo and Ice's teams. The six of us headed back into the school toward the basement. When we got down there, the lights were already on.

"How the fuck are the lights on in this part of the building?" I asked as we descended the stairs.

"Generator, over there in the corner. It must power the older part of the building," Gabe pointed out.

"You know, if Claire was here, she would point out that going in search of the killer in the creepy basement is what gets everyone killed," Derek muttered.

"Thanks for that," I snapped, not needing to hear his theories on murderers when my girlfriend was missing.

"Sorry, just pointing out the fact that this is exactly what would get most people killed in a book."

"But we're not in a book. We have fucking guns. Besides, what was the last book you read?" I asked Derek.

We scanned the room, looking for the exit Graham had told us about.

"I actually just finished a book with Claire. It was the romantic thriller *She Can Run*. It was definitely a chick book, but I'm telling you, it really gives you some insight into what chicks like to read about."

"I don't mind a good thriller, but I'm partial to books by Dan Brown," Jackson said. "I like the mystery."

Knight pointed to the far corner of the room where an old door with a hatch was located.

"I liked *The Red Sparrow Trilogy*," Chance said thoughtfully, "but I prefer to listen to audiobooks. Especially when I'm working out. I like to get lost in a good book because I can't stand how bored I get when I'm lifting weights."

"Really? I like a good jam when I'm working out," Gabe joined in. "I can't get into-"

"Ladies, please," Knight interrupted as we stood in front of the door. "Can we go catch the psycho and get the girl back or would you like to stand here and discuss your favorite books some more? I could order some tea and crumpets and we could have a little book club meeting."

I watched as the others stiffened up, puffing out their chests and standing a little taller. Rolling my eyes, I turned back to Knight and nodded for him to open the door. "That's gotta be it."

He turned the wheel handle and gave the signal. I stood on the other side of the door, holding my gun up, ready to enter when he swung the door open. It was pitch black inside and we all flipped on flashlights and made our way into the tunnel.

Chapter Fifteen

LUCY

I hobbled along behind David, starting to regret walking on my own. My ankle was throbbing more and more with every step. I had a feeling that he was irritated with me for holding him up and I almost asked to stop a few times, but he had a job to do and I didn't want to stop him from doing it.

"Are you ready for me to carry you yet?" he asked. I sighed and nodded, not wanting to hold him up further.

"Okay, I give up."

"Good. I don't like to see you in pain."

I wished that I could see his face, but he still had his police mask on and even if he didn't, one flashlight wouldn't illuminate the space enough. He hoisted me over his shoulder and I immediately wished I could just walk. It was so uncomfortable to be carried over his shoulder like this, but the trek through the tunnels was faster this way and my ankle was thanking me for the ease in pressure.

"How much further is it?" I asked.

"We're almost there. It should be just around that bend up ahead."

"How come we didn't take one of the other tunnels?"

"They're closed off. This used to be used for moving moonshine during prohibition. A lot of the businesses have sealed off the access to the tunnels. You don't exactly want employees wandering down here and getting lost."

"No, I suppose not. I wonder why they don't have tours down here. It would be pretty cool."

"The city won't allow it. They're not sure of the integrity of the tunnels."

"Should we really be down here then?" I asked, wondering if the tunnels were going to collapse on me at any moment.

"The alternative was to stay in the school with the guy that was after you. I thought this would be the safest route."

"When did you contact the police?" I asked.

"What do you mean?"

"You said that they would meet us at the end of the tunnel, but when did you let them know that you found me and that we were going out this way?"

"Earpiece," he said, tapping his ear. "They can hear everything I say."

"Oh." It was a logical enough explanation, but it still felt a little odd that we took this way out. If he had an earpiece, you would think that the police would have just sent in a few more guys to escort me out. Still, I didn't want to argue with him. He did get me away from Coach Boots after all.

"Here we are," he said, setting me down. "I'm going to open the hatch and then I'll give you a boost up."

"Okay." I leaned against the tunnel wall and held the flashlight for him as he used all his strength to open the hatch. I could see his muscles rippling through his shirt and the perspiration dripping from his face. He had gone above and beyond to make sure that I got out safely. I was going to have to make one hell of a thank you basket for this man.

Finally, the door gave and he pushed the hatch open. After catching his breath, he made a step with his hands and lifted me up through the opening. I had to pull at grass and earth to pull myself up because I couldn't use my foot to push myself. When I finally got out, the first thing I did was roll over and look up at the sun shining brightly in the sky. It was a relief after being in that dark tunnel for so long.

Wait. Where were the police? If they overheard him on the earpiece, they should have been out here already. They would have driven because they would know that I was injured, so where were they? I turned to see David hoisting himself up through the hatch and then he stood with his hands on his hips as he took a breath.

"Where is everyone?" I asked. I was getting more nervous by the minute. Something wasn't right here.

"They probably just got delayed."

"But we were down in that tunnel for at least a half hour. Shouldn't they be here already?"

"Relax, it looks like someone left a car for us." He pointed off in the opposite direction that I was facing and when I turned, I saw the car he was talking about. My brain was screaming at me that this wasn't right, especially when he pulled the car keys out of his pocket. They couldn't have left the car for him if he already had the keys. What the hell was going on?

"I think I want to call my sister and let her know that I'm okay. I had talked to her when I was in the building and I'm sure she's worried about me."

"I don't have a phone on me."

"Then, can I talk to whoever is on the other end of your earpiece? I'd just like to let them know to call my sister."

"They've heard you and I'm sure they are already in contact with your sister."

"Still, I'd like to talk to someone myself."

He sighed and pulled the mask off his head. No. This wasn't right. It was Noah. Noah, who I had gone out with on a date and Hunter had intervened when things got rough. I shook my head in disbelief.

"Noah, I don't understand. What's going on?"

"I just wanted some time with you. I've been watching you for a very long time. You know, some of the men you hang around with are all wrong for you."

"Noah, where are the police?"

"Back at the school, I would assume."

"They're not coming?" I asked.

He shook his head. "You don't need them. Even that guy that

you're obsessed with, the military one, he couldn't even protect you when the bomb threat was called in. I'm the one that went in to save you."

"Did you call in the bomb threat?" I had a bad feeling that this was all some twisted game on his part.

"How else was I going to get you away from your security detail? Those idiots should have been with you in the building. They couldn't even protect you from the psychopath in the school."

"Noah, I appreciate you coming to my rescue, but people are going to be worried about me. Maybe you could take me back and we can make plans to go out to dinner. I'd really like to thank you for all you've done for me."

He smiled and shook his head. "There's no need to thank me. When we get back to our house, I'm going to take care of you, like you should be. We'll get you all healed up and then we can make our plans for the future."

My heart beat wildly in my chest. I didn't know what to do. Did I fight him? Did I go along with his plan? Right now I was safe, but if I tried to get away, what would he do? Would he get violent? Then again, if I did nothing, would anyone ever find me again? What would Hunter want me to do?

I tried to think, but there were just too many outcomes. I wasn't sure what to do. Then I thought of Claire. She would tell me that the heroine should always fight back. That if the heroine got in the car, she would never be seen again. That sounded logical, but then I heard Hunter's voice in my head, telling me that he would always come for me. Chances were that if I left something behind, a clue or something, that he would find it.

"Would you mind bringing the car closer?" I asked, hoping I could get a minute to myself. "That way I don't have to walk and you don't have to carry me."

"I don't mind carrying you."

"I know, sweetie." I swallowed the bile at having to play along with this, but the fact was that without being able to make a quick getaway, I would have to play along and pray that Hunter could find me. "But you carried me through the tunnel and I don't want to wear you out. I'm sure I'll need more help later."

"Okay, pumpkin. I'll be right back." He leaned down and kissed me on the lips. I did my best not to cringe when his disgusting wet lips touched mine. He smiled and walked toward the car. I didn't know what to do. If I ripped my skirt or shirt, he might notice. But I still had my phone on me. Sure, it was dead, but it wouldn't be seen as easily out here. I slipped it out of my pocket and threw it down in the grass a few feet from me, hoping he wouldn't see it when he came back. Hopefully, Hunter would find it. It wouldn't lead him to me, but Hunter was good at what he did and I had to hope that he would at least find the phone and know where I had been. Maybe Reed Security could find me somehow. At least I wouldn't be vanishing without a trace.

Noah pulled the car up next to me and I stood on one foot as he came around. He opened the door for me and I slid into the front seat and buckled myself in. He pulled something out of his pocket. A syringe.

"Noah, what are you doing?"

"This is to help you sleep. I want you to rest on the way."

"No. Noah, that's not necessary. I'm already tired. I'm sure I'll sleep just fine without it."

"Now, Lucy, be a good girl and give me your arm. This won't hurt. I promise you, but you're going to have it one way or the other."

It went against every instinct I had to give him my arm, but I didn't know what else to do. I was already in the car and buckled in. It's not like I could fight back now. I wished more than anything that I had listened to Hunter more when I had the chance. I wished that I hadn't wasted so much time pushing him away. Especially now since I didn't know if I would ever see him again.

Noah took my arm and plunged the needle in. It didn't take long for the world to start to swirl around me. My last thoughts were that I hoped Hunter wouldn't be too upset with me.

Chapter Sixteen

HUNTER

"*L*ook at the ground," Derek said. "You can see where they were walking. This should make it easier for us."

We walked through the tunnels, being careful to watch for where the footprints led. There were no disturbances in the dust other than their prints and it led us to just one access point.

"The tracks stop here," Knight motioned. "They exited here."

"Cap, we're at access point four. That's where the tracks stop."

"Copy that. We've got Cazzo's team at that access point. There's nobody there."

"Shit. He's too far ahead of us," I said.

We opened the hatch and Cazzo pulled us all out. I shook my head as I sat in the grass, pissed that we were too late.

"There are tire tracks that run this way, but no signs of a struggle," Burg pointed out.

"So we have nothing to go on?" I asked.

"We'll find her," Knight said. "We just need to get back to Reed Security and regroup. We need information right now. Places he's been, favorite vacations spots, anything that will give us something to go on."

"Where's his cousin? Is he talking?" Derek asked.

"He's at the station," Cazzo replied. "I would suggest we go talk to him now. The police are already scouring his house for evidence of where he might go."

I started to follow the guys, but I turned back to the hatch one last time, hoping that Lucy wasn't out there right now completely terrified. I hoped that she was holding it together and knew that I would be looking for her. The light glinted off something and I walked over to see what it was. A cell phone. I picked it up and knew that it was Lucy's. She had left it behind for us. I tried to turn it on, but nothing happened. I wasn't sure if we would get any information from it, but it was something at least.

"I don't talk to Noah very often," his cousin, Randy, stated. "He's always been a little off, but I never thought he would do something like this."

"What happened today?" Cap asked. We were all at the police station, trying to figure out our next move.

"He had called me a few days back, wanted to know my schedule. He said that he needed to talk to me about some stuff. I told him today was my day off and he said he would be over by nine this morning. He came in and I asked him if he wanted some coffee. I turned my back and then I woke up when the chief sent over officers to check on me. I don't remember anything else."

"Where would he take her?" I asked impatiently. We were wasting time. We needed information now.

"I don't know. His parents live in Georgia now, but he wouldn't bring her there. They've never been too understanding of his eccentric side."

"And you have?" Knight asked. I could see the wheels turning in his head. He was thinking that Randy might be in on it.

"No. We just live in the same area. I'm his only family that's still around, but it's not because I want to be near him. He never moved away and I joined the force."

"Who would be understanding of his eccentric side?"

Randy shook his head slowly as he thought. "No one. I'm not even sure he keeps in touch with anyone anymore. But I don't know a single person in the family that wouldn't turn him in if he brought home a kidnapped woman. That's just beyond crazy."

"Okay, then what about someplace that your family owns that no one currently lives in?"

"None of us have any vacation homes or anything like that. We always-" he stopped and his eyes narrowed off into the distance. "There's this one place we always went on family retreats when we were younger. We haven't been there since we were teenagers, but this would be their off-season."

"Where's it located?" I asked urgently.

"Near Tuscarora State Park."

"That's gotta be, what? Five or six hours away?" I asked.

"About that. I can get you the information, but the place is huge. There's gotta be close to thirty cabins that you'd have to check."

"Shit." I ran a hand down my face. "He's got at least a good three hour head start on us."

"That's if she's out there," Knight said.

"I'm going. It's the only lead we have."

"I'm with you," Knight said. "I'm just pointing out that we shouldn't put everyone on this when we're not certain that's where she is."

Cap stepped forward and crossed his arms over his chest. "Knight's right. We can't afford to send everyone out there. If we're wrong, we'll waste valuable time getting to her."

"Let's load up. I'm leaving within a half hour." I turned and walked for the door, but Cap stopped me with a hand on my shoulder.

"Last I checked, I'm still in charge of things."

"I'm not waiting for everyone to figure out what we should do. I may be wrong about this, but I have to go now and see if I can find her. She's waiting for me."

"I know that, but you have us and we're backing you one hundred percent, but you're thinking with your heart, not your head. You'll get her killed if you go running off without a plan."

"I have a plan. It's simple. Grab my gun, find her, shoot him."

Cap smirked at me. "Not a bad plan, but how about you let us get just a few more details so we know what we're walking into." He turned to the rest of the guys, "We'll take three teams out there. Cazzo, Irish, and Chance, your teams will head out in the next hour. Get back to Reed Security, load up, and go. Knight, you'll make up the third on Irish's team. Ice, get ahold of the owners and get permission to get on the property and find our girl. I want your team to find out anything you can about the area and get schematics of the campground. Work with Becky and Rob. You'll guide them where they need to go. Alec, your team will coordinate with the police department and run down any other leads that come in. Let's move!"

⸻

*T*he ride out to the campground was fucking excruciating. Every minute, I was running scenarios in my mind of what was going on with Lucy. I didn't know if she was hurt. She was probably scared and had no one to rely on but herself. I at least had my team to support me.

"Have you heard from Lola recently?" Derek asked.

"No, have you?"

He shook his head.

"She told me she was headed to Hawaii for a few weeks," Knight said nonchalantly. I turned to him, completely puzzled.

"She fucking talked to you?"

"Yeah." He shrugged at my look of bewilderment. "What? I wasn't the one that screwed her over."

"We didn't screw her over," Derek said. "Well, I didn't. Technically, Pappy was screwing her over for a lot longer than any of us knew."

"You fucked Lola?" Knight asked.

"Jesus, are we back to this again? Who gives a shit?"

"Aren't there some rules about coworkers being involved with each other?" he asked.

"Not that I'm aware of," I muttered. "But it doesn't matter because we aren't fucking anymore."

"That's right," Derek said. "Now you're fucking Lucy."

"I'm not fucking her," I sniped. "She's more than that."

"Tell me how you really feel," Derek smiled.

"I don't have to tell you shit."

"Hey, all I'm saying is that I went and talked to Claire's father first. I told him exactly what my intentions were with her. Did you extend the same courtesy?"

"We haven't exactly had the smoothest relationship," I pointed out. "When exactly was I supposed to go talk to her father about what I intended with her? When I demanded that she stay with me and then I pushed her away? Or maybe when I followed her to the spa. That would have been the moment right there. *Hey, Harry. I want your daughter so much that I had my dick waxed for her.* Yeah, that would have been the real winner right there."

"I don't know, I think when you took a bullet to the head might have been a good starting point," Knight muttered. "It's not like he could shoot you for being an asshole to his daughter after you took a bullet."

Derek barked out a laugh. "Let's not overplay that incident. He didn't actually take a bullet to the head. More like it scraped his skull. If one of us gets grazed in the arm with a bullet, we don't bitch about it. We slap a bandaid on."

"Hey, asshole. I was in the hospital with a concussion."

"Yeah, and then Lucy went and made you all better," he smirked. "You can thank me for that any time you want, by the way."

"I'm just saying, there hasn't really been a good time to go tell him that I plan on keeping his daughter."

"Now you sound like a stalker," Knight said.

"You would know," Derek shot back. "How long were you watching Kate from across the street?"

"The difference was that she knew I was there."

"Not all the time," I snapped at him. "Let's not forget that you were watching her for a whole fucking year without any of us knowing about it. Well, almost none of us."

"Still sore about that, huh?"

"Well, when my old best friend gets stabbed and dies in a fire and I have to fucking bury his ass, yeah, I would say that kind of stuck with me."

"Wait, what do you mean *old best friend?* Who's your new best friend?"

"Derek. He's never faked his death and made me beat myself up for a whole fucking year about how I let him die," I sneered.

"I'm your best friend?" Derek grinned. "I'm touched, man. Truly touched."

"Dude, I had your fucking back in the desert. I can't believe you so easily replaced me."

"Hey, when you went on a killing rampage, I'm the one that broke you out of prison. I'd say I went way beyond the boundaries of best friend."

Knight quirked an eyebrow at me. "What? You mean like *lover?* I'm taken, Pappy, and even if I wasn't, I don't swing that way."

"That's not what I fucking meant."

"Are you sure? Because I heard that you gave Gabe quite the showing with Lucy. I heard you two had some kind of moment."

"We didn't have a moment. If anyone had a moment, it was him. And who's spreading that shit around anyway? You guys are worse than a women's book club."

"Been to a lot of those, have you?" Derek asked.

"Let's face it, Derek. The only person in the world that actually goes to a book club to talk about the books is Claire. The rest of them talk about men and sex."

"Aren't those two usually grouped together anyway?" Knight asked.

"Not necessarily," I told Knight. "Haven't you ever heard all the girlfriends and wives at our parties? If they aren't bitching about how often we want it, they're bitching about how we don't understand them."

"But, we don't understand them," Derek pointed out. "I mean, I understand Claire, but I don't get her half the time. Like this one time, I wanted to have sex and she was having some weird dream about Superman. I woke her the way every woman wants to be woken-"

"With coffee?" Knight smirked.

"No, with my mouth on her pussy, and she couldn't get into it. I mean, I was ready to get really dirty with her and all she could do was think about that dream."

"Sounds like you don't know what you're doing," I said.

"I know what the fuck I'm doing, but she's a woman. I'm telling you, they don't make any fucking sense."

"I don't know. I've never lost Kate's attention or couldn't get her to have sex with me."

"I can't say that I couldn't ever get Lucy to sleep with me, but I couldn't get her to do anything more than that with me."

"That's because you're a fucking idiot and you screwed it up with her. Did you tell Knight about that?"

"Tell me about what? Now you're holding out on me? You drop me from best friend status and now I don't even get to know what the fuck is going on with you?"

"Fuck, I didn't drop you from best friend status. You were out of my life for years. Sorry, I made new friends."

"Now I feel like the kid that no one wants to play with on the playground," Knight grumbled.

"You're not wrong about that," Derek muttered. "No one wants to play with you because someone always ends up in the hospital."

"Whatever. If you don't know how to properly fight, you don't step into the ring. So, how did you screw it up with her?"

"He wouldn't give her a drawer."

"A drawer? Like a kitchen drawer?" Knight asked.

"No, dresser drawer. He wouldn't share his dresser with her when he asked her to stay with him. He freaked out when she asked and it all went downhill from there."

"Look, I know I fucked up. Can we not rehash it? Besides, Lucy and I are in a good place right now. Well, we will be when I get her back."

"Are you going to give her a drawer this time?" Derek asked.

"No, I'm going to give her the whole fucking house."

★★★★

. . .

*W*e parked at the entrance of the campground by the office where the owners were waiting for us. Stepping out of the SUV, Derek and I walked toward them and shook their hands.

"We appreciate you letting us check out the property," Derek said.

"Well, if someone is trespassing and using our property, we'd like to know," the man said.

"Did you check out the names we gave you?"

The woman handed over some papers, fidgeting nervously with her fingers. "These are the locations they've stayed in the past, but I'm afraid it was always a different cabin. It's always based on availability, so really, he could be in any of the cabins. I also included a map of the campground. I hope that helps."

"Is there any power right now?" Derek asked.

"No." The man shook his head as he looked back behind him. "We shut everything down for the winter."

"Alright, it would probably be best if you left the property. We don't know the state of mind he's in and we don't need any other hostages around. When we're done here, we'll contact you and let you know what happened."

"What about damages?" the man asked.

"Any damage we cause will be covered by Reed Security," Derek assured them.

We walked back to the SUV as the couple scurried off to their vehicle and drove away. I pulled on my vest and strapped on my thigh holster and shoulder holster, then pushed my earpiece in.

"Ice, you copy?"

"Loud and clear. We're here with Becky and Rob."

"Any news from back home?" I asked.

"Police found quite a stash of pictures in Noah's apartment. He's been watching her for a while."

"How long is a while?"

"Looks like since earlier this summer." Ice said.

"That's well before the first note came."

"Yeah, it looks like you weren't the only one that purposely ran into her at the grocery store."

"Alright, let's not compare me to this asshole."

"Just saying..."

"Were you able to spot anything on satellite?" I asked, changing gears.

"Negative. Tree coverage is too heavy. I'm afraid you're on your own with that. We'll be here for anything else you need."

"Derek has the lead," I said, turning to the group of men surrounding me.

"Alright, we'll split off, each team taking a cluster of cabins. Chance, you'll take your team to cabins one through ten. Cazzo, your team has cabins eleven through twenty. My team will take the cabins at the back of the property. We think that's most likely where she's being held. If you see anything, check in immediately. We take this guy alive unless he's a threat to Lucy. Understood?"

We all nodded and broke off in our teams, heading out in the direction of our cabins. Our team had the furthest to walk, so the other teams would likely clear one or two cabins before we reached the back of the property. We hustled as quickly as we could, doing our best not to draw attention to ourselves. We had to cut through trees to get there quickly and the branches scraped at our faces as we ran through.

When we reached the first cabin, it was completely dark. My instincts told me that they weren't here. It was too dark, too still. But protocol made sure that we cleared each cabin or we might miss something. I just hoped that the time we wasted clearing each cabin wasn't the difference between life and death for Lucy.

Chapter Seventeen

LUCY

*W*here the hell was I? I tried to clear my vision as I looked around the unfamiliar room. My head was pounding and I felt nauseous from whatever Noah gave me. There was a fan above the bed that was spinning fast, blowing the sheer white curtains around the canopy bed. I couldn't look at it anymore or I would be sick. I sat up and pushed aside the curtain and let my feet fall to the floor, trying to get my bearings. When I felt steady, I stood and walked over to the window, my ankle still throbbing from earlier in the day, or whenever that was. There was a beautiful view of the mountain. Which mountain, I had no clue.

My skin cooled and I rubbed my arms, realizing that I was no longer in my own clothes. I looked down to see that I was wearing a long, silk nightgown with spaghetti straps. I had no bra on and unless I was mistaken, I wasn't wearing underwear either. I pushed aside the fact that I hadn't changed my clothes myself. I couldn't think about that now. I needed to figure out where I was and how to get out of here.

I walked around the room and started freaking out a little. The closet door was open and I could see women's clothing hanging in the closet along with several pairs of shoes on the floor. Lying on the foot of the bed was a silk robe and I hastily pulled it on to cover myself up. The door opened just as I was tying the knot in the front.

"My dear, I'm so glad to see you up and about. Did you have a good nap?"

A good nap? The man drugged me and took me away from my home. He was fucking delusional, but as long as he was treating me like something precious, he wasn't burying me in a hole in the ground. I did my best to smile back at him through my fear and anger.

"Yes, it was lovely. I was just a little chilly. I thought I might get dressed," I said, walking to the closet.

"Oh, no need for that. We'll be eating dinner and then going to bed." His eyes trailed over my body and I shivered at the slimy feel I was left with. He mistook my disgust for want because he walked forward and ran his finger down my cheek. "I have big plans for us tonight, but before we get to that, I've prepared dinner for us downstairs. I made it quite special."

I needed to play along. If I played into his fantasy, perhaps I could get the upper hand. *His fantasy.* Thank you, Claire! I knew exactly what I had to do. I smiled my biggest smile and took his hand. This was just like playing up a man's ego in a bar. I could do this.

"Thank you. Let's go eat. I'm starving."

He placed a kiss on my cheek and led me downstairs, holding onto my arm as we descended the stairs, making sure that I didn't fall. The whole place was lit with candles, which seemed like overkill. Why wouldn't he just turn the lights on? The cabin was quite beautiful and spacious, someplace I would stay if I ever went on vacation to someplace like this. That would never happen now. I would never ever want to come to a place like this. I couldn't without thinking of this incident. That's what this was, an incident. A small blip in my life and I would get out of here and never think of this man again.

There was a white table cloth covering the round table and food already set out. He had really gone all out preparing dinner. There was a baked chicken on the table with mashed potatoes, corn bread, asparagus, and a cake for dessert. How long had he been planning this? How long had we been here already? This was insane, but the food did smell good and I was starving. I just didn't know if the food was drugged in some way.

When he pulled out my chair for me, I took it and smiled up at him. He leaned down and gave me a quick kiss on the lips that felt more like kissing an eel and not because it was electric. He sat across from me and poured some white wine in the wine glasses, grinning as if this was the most special night of our lives. I quickly picked up my glass and guzzled half of it, needing some liquid courage. It went right to my head and made me feel dizzy. I wasn't a lightweight, but I had no idea how long it had been since my last meal. I needed some food in my stomach now.

"This all looks so delicious. How long did it take you to prepare it?"

"Oh, a few hours. The chicken has been in since we arrived, but the rest I did in just the last hour or so."

"Well, it smells wonderful."

"Let me dish out a plate for you."

"Thank you," I smiled. This was by far the weirdest moment of my life. I was pretending to be on some kind of date with a man who had kidnapped me, all so I could somehow gain the upper hand and get away from him.

He set my plate down in front of me and I waited as he dished out his own. It made me feel better when he took the first bite. I hesitantly took my own and sighed at how good it tasted. The man may be insane, but he was a hell of a cook. "Hmmm. This is delicious."

"I've been practicing since our date."

I looked up at him, a little nervous that I was the one being played. "You have?"

"Yes. When I sobered up and realized that the reason you were so upset was because I had fed you food you didn't like, I went home and started learning to cook. I wanted our next date to be perfect and so far it is."

Gag me now. This guy was saying all the right things and doing all the right things, but he was off his fucking rocker.

"And it's all the more special because you did that for me," I said sweetly.

"Darling, I'm learning that there's not a lot I wouldn't do for you. I would move heaven and earth to make you happy."

I tried my best to keep a smile on my face as I shoved more food into my mouth. I didn't know what to say to that and frankly, if I had to hear too much more of his bullshit, I might throw up my food.

"So, where are we?" I asked.

"In the mountains."

"Yes, I realized that when I woke up and saw the mountains outside. I was hoping you could give me some more insight. Maybe we could put it on our list of places to come back to someday."

His face lit up and he took a sip of wine. "I like the sound of that."

"Do we have any neighbors out here?"

"Not at this time of year. I thought it would be best to come out now when we wouldn't be disturbed."

An evil grin split my lips. "I like the way you think."

What I had in store for him, I didn't want anyone coming and ruining my fun. And I would have fun. I would take great pleasure in what I wanted to do to this man. The only thing I had to do was block Hunter from my mind because if I thought of him, it would feel like a betrayal.

"How long will we be staying out here?"

"That depends on you. If you'd like to stay for a few weeks, we can, but I know that you have a job to get back to."

"Yes, the students do depend on me."

At least I knew that he was planning to take me home, as long as he felt I was amenable to his plan. But I had no intention of sticking around and sleeping with him. I would be long gone before he had the opportunity to take things that far.

"Well, then we'll spend the weekend and head back home on Sunday."

"Perfect," I smiled as I took another sip of wine.

We finished our dinners in relative silence and then I let out a yawn, trying to signal that I was ready for bed. It was time to put my plan in place.

"Ready for bed, darling?"

"Definitely," I smiled. He took my hand as I stood from my chair and led me up the stairs. My heart pounded in my chest and I swallowed back the fear of what would happen if I couldn't convince him to do as I wanted. I had to go through with this. It was my only chance at escape. I would think about the rest later.

He led me into the bedroom and I pulled at his hand with a small smile. "I was thinking that maybe we could do something that I've been fantasizing about."

His lips turned up in an excited grin. "Why don't you tell me what you had in mind."

I put my lips near his ear, my hand brushing down the front of his chest as I let my breath huff out against his skin. "I want to tie you down and lick every inch of your body." I could feel him shudder against me, so I continued. "I want to know what it's like to ride you, knowing that you want to touch me but you can't."

I pulled back and looked into his eyes. I saw desire and need and I hoped that I hadn't just pushed too far. "I have just the thing," he said as he walked over to his suitcase. He dug through an outer pocket and pulled out a pair of handcuffs. "Will these do?"

"That's perfect," I said, walking over to him and slipping them out of his grasp. "Why don't you make yourself comfortable?"

I thought briefly of all the ways I could leave him handcuffed to the bed, but I decided that instead of humiliating him, I just wanted to get out of here. I didn't want to see him naked or let him think that I was actually going to go through with it. I just wanted to be back in Hunter's arms.

He sat back on the bed and I straddled his lap, letting my breasts hang in his face. The silky material did very little to cover me and I could see that he wanted more. I gently took his wrist and put one handcuff around it, locking it in place. I was almost there, almost free. I just had to get the other handcuff around him and the slat in the headboard. I swallowed hard as I threaded the handcuffs through the slat and then locked it around his other wrist. I was free. A smile split my face as I sat back and looked at his face. This would be the last time I would ever see him again.

"What are you going to do now?" he asked.

I stood from the bed and walked to the foot of the bed. "Now, I'm going to leave your ass here and I'm going home. Did you really think I would sleep with you after you drugged and kidnapped me?"

His face turned hard and red. He was furious, but I didn't care. He couldn't touch me now. His hands jerked in the cuffs and he growled at me. "Do you really think I'm going to just let you walk out of here?"

"You don't really have a choice," I smirked.

The look that crossed over his face told me that I was the one that was wrong. I didn't know how, but I knew that I was screwed. This wasn't going to go my way. I saw his fingers move to the center of the cuffs and then he flicked something and the handcuffs opened.

"Aww, you thought I would just hand over control to you. You really are stupid."

Two things crossed my mind at that moment. One, that if I was in a book and Claire were reading it, she would be yelling at me right now for having given away my plan instead of just taking my chance and running. The second thing I thought was that I was the typical cliche heroine that was going to be running from my stalker in a silk night-gown. In the cold.

I didn't waste a second waiting to see what he would do. I turned and ran from the room, ignoring the pain in my foot. I wasn't as fast as I hoped and he tackled me just as I reached the top of the stairs. I fell forward, smacking my head against the wall before we started tumbling down the stairs. I felt each stair dig into my hip as we rolled and bounced on the hard steps. When we hit the bottom, I was disoriented and couldn't get my bearings. I could feel Noah laying on top of me, but he wasn't moving. Shoving him off, I stumbled as I stood and felt him grab onto the bottom of my nightgown. I sent a kick back, hitting him in the face.

"You bitch!" he roared as he jumped to his feet and tackled me again. We flew back into a table, knocking the lamp to the ground. I heard it shatter against the floor and scrambled for something to grab onto. The shattered pieces weren't in reach. He grabbed my wrist, securing it in his, but I fought him off with the other, shifting my legs and trying to kick out at him. I was hindered by the length of the dress, but as long as I kept moving, I could keep him distracted.

His free hand grabbed onto my right strap, pulling at it until it ripped. I let out a scream, knowing he was just seconds from tearing the nightgown from my body and leaving me exposed. Out of the corner of my eye, I saw a candle on the edge of the table. I grasped at it with my free hand, feeling it slip further away as my fingers brushed against it. I heaved my body as hard as I could until the candle was in my hands. I threw the melted wax in his face, causing him to leap back and scream. I slammed my elbow into his face and scrambled to my knees, but he grabbed me from behind, flinging me over the back of the couch with him. I used our momentum to throw him into the glass coffee table. He held onto me, and together we crashed through the glass to the floor.

I felt glass slicing through my skin in several places, but it was his gasps that cut through the quiet. I glanced down at him, seeing red spreading across his side. I didn't know how badly he was injured, but this was my chance and I wasn't wasting it. I leapt to my feet and wracked my brain to figure out my next step. I was shaking so bad that I couldn't think straight. All I could think about was how close I had come to being assaulted by him.

With shaky hands, I knelt down next to him and felt in his pockets for his car keys or a phone. There was nothing. I glanced around the room quickly, hoping to find something, but I couldn't find a thing. I looked back and saw him lying still on the ground, covered in glass. He hadn't moved. I continued my search, opening drawers and digging through his luggage, checking him every few seconds when I heard him move. But every time I looked, he was in the same position. The roaring in my ears was making me crazy. I couldn't distinguish what was real and what I was imagining. I kept hearing glass shifting. I heard ragged breathing. I felt the air move behind me, but every time I looked, he was still lying as still as the time before.

I couldn't stay in here anymore. The longer I stayed, the more insane I felt with every second that passed. I ran out the front door, barely feeling the cold or the pain in my foot. My only goal was to get away before he woke up. I didn't know if he was dead or alive and I wasn't about to go back and find out. I ran through the trees, not wanting to take the road in case he woke up and went driving around looking for me. I stumbled through the woods until the adrenaline had left my body and I could barely walk anymore. I found a tree to lean against and slumped down on the ground, staring off into the night. I couldn't think anymore. I couldn't do anything. I was done.

Chapter Eighteen

HUNTER

*W*e had cleared three cabins with still no sign of her. "Chance, any sign of her?" I asked over through my mic as we headed to the fourth cabin.

"Nothing yet. Everything's quiet."

"Cazzo?"

"All clear. We have two more to check."

I sighed and followed Derek along the trail to the next cabin. I was getting anxious, needing to see her. If this didn't pan out and she wasn't here, we had nothing else to go on. No place else to look.

"Up ahead," Derek said ahead of me. My head whipped up and I saw the faint light in the cabin. It was dim, but it was definitely some kind of light coming from inside. We hustled to the cabin, peering in through the windows. There were candles lit all around the living room, but we couldn't see much else. Derek signaled for Knight to go around back and he and I took the front door.

"I'm in position," Knight's voice came over the mic.

"On my mark. Three, two, one, mark."

I kicked in the door, gun raised and ready to shoot. I went low and Derek went high, searching for any sign of her, but she wasn't here.

"What the fuck?" Derek whispered behind me. The living room

was torn up. The coffee table was shattered and there was blood all over the living room. Knight motioned upstairs and we headed silently for the stairs, guns trained on the doors that were open. All three rooms were clear, but one had women's clothing in it.

"She's not here," Knight said.

"Let's see if there's a blood trail," Derek said as we headed downstairs. "Chance and Cazzo, come in."

"Yeah," they said.

"We've found the cabin, but there's nobody here. We've got a hell of a mess. They obviously struggled and there's quite a bit of blood. We're looking for a trail now. Head on over to us. We're in cabin twenty-four. Keep your eyes open for anyone outside."

I followed the blood back over to the door and flipped on my flashlight so I could see where it went. The trail led out toward the woods. She was running. I prayed to God that she had made it far enough away from him and that it wasn't her blood. Derek, Knight, and I silently moved through the woods, tracking their movements. It wasn't hard. One or both of them had been moving quickly and without any care for the trail they were leaving behind.

We followed them for close to a mile before I finally caught sight of a feminine figure crouched down by a tree up ahead.

"Lucy," I called. Her head whipped around to mine and she stumbled to her feet, dressed only in a torn nightgown. It had once been white, but now it was covered in dirt and blood. "Are you okay?" I asked softly.

She took a step forward, gripping onto the tree. I started to run for her, but slammed to a stop when a figure stepped up from the shadows of my flashlight and grabbed her around the chest and thrusting a knife against her throat.

"Put the knife down," I shouted as I held a firm grip on my gun. I could see Knight and Derek positioning themselves further from me so that all of us could try to find a shot.

"She's mine. I'm not letting her go back to you. You're not good enough."

"That's fine." I said calmly. "Just move the knife away from her throat and we'll back off."

He was unsteady on his feet, barely able to hold himself up and I was worried he was going to slice her neck open if he stumbled. Lucy just stared ahead, no emotion on her face. It was like she wasn't there, but I couldn't worry about that right now. I had to focus on getting her away from this monster.

"Coming up on the other side," Chance spoke in my ear. "Getting into position."

"Alright. I'm setting down my gun," I said, holding my hands out in surrender. I bent down slowly, hoping that he would take it as a sign of good faith.

"Knight, do me a favor and take a step to the right so I don't put a bullet in your head," Chance said over the mic. I saw Knight shift and then I saw Noah glance around suspiciously. His hand tightened on the knife and I saw blood start to trickle down Lucy's neck.

"Chance, now would be a good fucking time," I said quietly and then heard the crack of the gun as Chance took out Noah from behind. His brain matter splattered out the front of his head, some of it flying at Lucy, but she still stood there completely still. I raced forward as Noah fell to the ground and pulled Lucy against me, holding her tight to me. She wasn't making a sound and that worried me more than anything. I pulled back and looked into her eyes, seeing a vacant expression. She was in shock.

Her skin was freezing and I quickly pulled off my vest and then my henley, pulling it down over her head. I didn't miss the broken strap of the nightgown or the blood splatter that covered her body. I didn't know how much was hers, but right now I just needed to warm her up. As I pulled the henley down, my fingers caught on something and I peered around her back. She had a piece of wood sticking out of her back. It wasn't large, but it was shoved in deep. How the hell was she still standing? How had she made it out here?

"Lucy? Can you hear me?"

Nothing. She didn't even blink. Her stare was blank.

"I'm going to get you out of here and someplace safe, okay?"

Again, nothing. I scooped her up in my arms and cradled her body in mine. I needed to get her back to the SUV where my medical kit was and then to the hospital. I didn't give a shit about Noah. He could be left to the wolves for all I cared. My only concern was Lucy and making sure she was okay.

I started jogging back to the SUV with Lucy in my arms, being as careful as possible not to jostle her too much. I could hear footsteps behind me, but I didn't bother to see who was with me. I was the only one here that could properly care for Lucy right now. It took ten minutes to get back to the SUV at the pace I set. Knight ran ahead of me and popped open the trunk. I set her inside as Knight pulled out the med kit for me. I quickly looked her over, seeing that most of the cuts on her were shallow and didn't need immediate attention. The wood in her back however, I didn't dare take that out. There was no reason that I couldn't take her to the hospital and they would be able to assess if she had any other injuries that we needed to be concerned about. They could also do a rape kit if needed.

I picked her up and placed her in the back seat, resting her head against my chest. Knight was in the driver's seat in seconds, with Derek in the passenger seat.

"Cazzo's covering clean up. He already called the police and asked them to coordinate with the department back home," Derek said.

He punched in coordinates for the nearest hospital and soon we were flying down the road to the hospital. It took a little over twenty minutes to reach the hospital and Knight pulled right up to the emergency room. I was out of the car and carrying her in before anyone else could even step out of the car. Everything happened so fast. Doctors rushed to us, a gurney was pushed up next to me, and I set her down, quickly giving the doctor a rundown on what had happened. She was wheeled away before I could even tell her I loved her.

As I watched the doors close, I collapsed to the ground, completely losing my shit. I was so fucking scared when I saw all that blood on her and the vacant expression on her face. Now she was back there and I couldn't be with her. I had no idea how she was or what had happened to her. I felt a hand on my shoulder, squeezing lightly and then the hand moved to my bicep and hauled me up off my knees. Knight dragged me over to the chairs in the waiting room and shoved me down into one.

I paced the waiting area when I couldn't stand to sit any longer and then I took to harassing the nursing staff about any information they had on her condition. Derek had to pull me back to the waiting area so that I didn't get kicked out of the hospital. We waited all night and little by little, Chance's team and then Cazzo's team showed up at the hospital to wait with me. Cap brought Claire out and got to the hospital about six in the morning and we still hadn't heard anything. It was past eight in the morning before the doctor finally came out to talk with us.

"Family of Lucy Grant?"

Claire stepped forward and pumped the doctor's hand. "I'm Claire Grant, her sister. She doesn't have a husband. I mean, she has a boyfriend. He's right here, but you can tell him anything you want. I mean, I think Lucy would be fine with that. Unless, it's not good news and maybe then I should hear it first."

Derek walked up behind Claire and placed his hand over her mouth. "Calm down, Claire bear. Let the man talk."

She nodded and Derek removed his hand. The doctor smiled kindly at her and I was ready to beat his ass for taking so fucking long to tell us how she was.

"Lucy is doing fine. She mostly has minor scrapes and bruises. She had one puncture from a piece of wood, but it wasn't as bad as we thought. It didn't do any internal damage and we cleaned it up and stitched it closed. We've given her a sedative because she was getting quite worked up while we were examining her. She's been through a lot, but medically speaking, she'll be fine. However, I would suggest a counselor to help her work through what's happened."

"What about a rape kit?" Claire asked. "Did you do one?"

"We did, but I'm sorry. That's not something I'm able to talk to you about. You'll need her consent for me to discuss that with you."

"But I'm her family," Claire said aghast.

"I understand that Ms. Grant, but all I can tell you is that medically she is fine."

That didn't answer any of my fucking questions. I needed to know if that slime bag had touched her. I saw the broken strap. I knew that he had gotten rough with her. I needed to know how serious this was.

"When can we see her?" I asked.

"Family can see her any time now. She'll be released shortly."

"Why the hell did it take you so long to come talk to us?" I barked at him.

"We had to be sure that she was okay and that takes time."

"I know. I was a fucking medic in the military, but you should have come and updated us."

"I'm really sorry it took so long, sir."

The doctor didn't say anything else as he stepped away, leaving me fuming. Jackson placed his hand on my shoulder. "Rape kits take a few hours to perform. They couldn't let anyone see her until they were done. It's just part of the procedure," he said quietly. I knew he was right, but I was fucking pissed. If a rape kit takes that long, did that mean that she had been raped or did they always take that long, no matter what?

Claire walked over to me and held my hand. "Give me just a few minutes with her. I know you need to see her and I promise I won't be long."

I nodded, knowing that I didn't have any fucking right to demand to go in there first. I wasn't her fiancé. Hell, I was barely her boyfriend. We had only just started over before she was taken. Claire disappeared behind the doors and I paced for another ten minutes before Claire came out.

"She's asking for you."

I breathed a sigh of relief. Thank God she was talking. "Is she okay?"

"She's...well, she's not quite Lucy, but she'll come around."

I nodded and followed the nurse back to Lucy's room. When I walked in, her eyes were closed and the blanket was pulled up to her chest, covering all of her. Just a few months ago, she had been in the hospital after being in a fire and I had been terrified then. This was a whole different level of scared. I was irrationally scared then because I didn't even know how I felt about her. I just knew that I couldn't lose her.

Now, I felt like if something had happened to her and she had been taken away from me, my life would be over. I wouldn't give a shit about work or any of my friends. I would just cease to exist. I knew now it was because I was so in love with her. The kind of love that Sinner, Cazzo, Cap, and Derek had all warned me about. The kind of love that brought a man to his knees and had him promising his woman the moon and stars if it meant that he was a lucky enough bastard to have her. That was Lucy for me. She was all I would ever need and I could see it crystal clear now.

I took a seat next to her bed and slipped my hand under her blanket to find her. She was still cold, but not nearly as cold as when I found her out in the woods. Now that it was daylight, I could see that she had scratches marring her already bruised face. Her nose hadn't healed fully from surgery yet. As far as the rest of her, I couldn't see her body to check her out and I didn't want to move the covers and make her cold.

Her eyes fluttered open a half hour later and she looked around the room in confusion. When her eyes found mine, I smiled hesitantly at her. I didn't know what she was thinking or feeling and I didn't want to make things worse for her.

"Do I look that bad?"

"You look beautiful."

"You're just saying that because you want to get laid." She laughed lightly and then closed her eyes again. When she opened them, she looked almost confused.

"What happened?"

"I was hoping you could tell me that."

"I remember running away from Noah, but then it's kind of a blur. I think I kind of blanked it out."

"We found you in the woods. He was out there with you, but he's dead now."

She nodded and blew out a breath. I hated to bring this up, but it was eating at me and I needed to know.

"Lucy, did he rape you?"

"No," she said firmly. "He would have tried. When I woke up there, he was being so sweet to me, so I figured it was best if I played along with his delusion. I pretended that I wanted to be there with him. He had been planning on taking me back home. I think he really thought we were in a relationship. After dinner, he took me upstairs and I convinced him that I wanted to be in charge and I cuffed him to the bed."

A grin lit my face. "That's my girl."

She laughed. "No, that's your stupid girl. Claire would have been so pissed at me. I thought I was being so slick. I told him that I was going home and that I was never planning on sleeping with him."

"How did he get out of the cuffs?"

"They were toy cuffs. They had that release button. I didn't even realize it until he popped them open. I could hear Claire in my head yelling at me for being the stupid heroine that didn't just run away."

"She probably would have been yelling at you the whole time she was reading the book," I laughed. "So, what happened then?"

"He chased me and we fell down the stairs. We pretty much destroyed the downstairs fighting each other. He tackled me over the sofa and I threw him into the coffee table. I wasn't sure if he was dead or alive and my mind kept playing tricks on me. That's when I ran, but everything's fuzzy after that. I think I was in shock."

"You were. When we found you, you were completely out of it."

"It's probably for the best. I don't really want to remember the rest."

I didn't want to either, but I could never forget the look on her face when I found her. I would never be able to get the gory image of her out of my mind.

"How are you feeling?"

"Sore. The doctor said that I had a piece of wood sticking out of me."

"Yeah, I didn't want to remove it because I didn't know if there was any internal damage. The doctor said that you're all good, though."

"Does that mean I can go home now?"

"Pretty soon. Where do you want to go?"

"Can I stay with you?"

"Of course," I smiled. All the pressure that had been building in my chest disappeared in an instant. "I didn't want to insist, but I was hoping you would say that you wanted to come home with me."

"Well, I'm still not over seeing Claire naked, so there's no way I'm staying with her and Derek."

"You can stay with me for as long as you want."

I leaned over her and kissed her lightly on the lips. I craved her so much, but after everything she had been through, I just wanted to feel her lips against mine and hold her tonight in my arms.

"*A*re you sure you're ready to go home? Because you can stay here as long as you need," I told Lucy. It had been a week and she was packing her bag to head home. I didn't want her to go, but I had to respect her decisions. The last time I had tried to force her to do things my way, she got so pissed at me that I almost lost her.

"I'm sure. I can't just stay here forever. I have to be able to live on my own again. If I always stay with you, I'll end up afraid of my own shadow."

"Lucy, there's nothing wrong with giving yourself some time to heal."

"I know that and I appreciate that you're looking out for me, but this is something I have to do."

"Okay," I said softly, kissing her on the lips. We hadn't had sex since she'd gotten out of the hospital. She was pushing for it, but I wasn't ready. I kept seeing her in that torn nightgown and it just didn't feel right. I felt like she needed more time to heal and I didn't want her freaking out if things went too fast between us.

"Alright, well, I'd better get home before it gets dark out."

"Do you want me to come with you? I could stay the night over there. You know, give you a chance to be used to being there again before you're alone."

"No, that's very sweet, but I'll be fine."

I pulled her gently against me and kissed her softly. "Be careful going home and make sure you lock your doors."

"I promise," she smiled. I walked her down to her car and as soon as she pulled away, I pulled out the keys to my truck and followed her discreetly to her apartment. There was no way that I was letting her stay there all alone. She had woken multiple times a night from nightmares and hadn't been able to fall back asleep. I couldn't let her go through that. I needed to be close to her, even if she didn't know it.

I waited for her to head up to her apartment and then I slipped in the building, turning my phone to silent as I sat down outside her apartment. It didn't take long before I heard her shutting off the lights and heading for her bedroom. I leaned back against the wall and waited for the inevitable. An hour later, she was screaming in her room and it took everything in me to sit out there and wait for it to stop. When I heard her shuffle out into the kitchen, I heard the sobs as she tried to calm herself down and I just couldn't deal with it.

I crept down the stairs and stood outside, dialing her number.

"Hello?"

"Hey, Lucy. I just needed to hear your voice and make sure that you were okay."

"Oh, I'm good." I heard her voice quivering as she tried to get herself under control. "I had a nightmare, but I'm okay now."

"Are you sure?"

"Yeah, you know it'll probably take time."

"Probably," I replied. "You know, I was thinking that Thanksgiving is coming up and I really don't have any family around to be with. Would you like to spend it with me?"

"Oh, um, Claire and Derek already invited me over to their place, but you could come with me."

"That's sounds like a plan."

"Okay, well, I should let you go. I'm sure you have to get to sleep for work tomorrow."

"Are you sure you're okay? I could come over if you want."

"No." I could hear the hesitation in her voice. She didn't want to ask me to come over because she didn't want to look weak. "I'm actually going to go back to sleep now."

"Okay. Call me if you need me. I can be over in no time."

"Thank you. Good night, Hunter."

"Good night, Lucy."

I hung up the phone and walked back inside, sitting back outside her door. I leaned up against the wall and prepared for a long night sleeping in the hallway. I had been through worse in the military and sleeping outside my girlfriend's apartment so that I knew she was safe was no great hardship for me.

When I woke up in the morning, I had a huge crick in my neck and my ass was pretty much asleep. It was already six-thirty and I had to be at work at eight. I walked downstairs after listening at her door for a few minutes and got in my truck, heading home to get ready for work. I was exhausted from bad sleep and I desperately needed coffee.

I walked into the break room at work and poured myself a mug of coffee, sitting down at the table and lowering my head to the surface. Just a little cat nap would do me wonders.

"Rough night?" Knight asked as he walked into the break room.

I let out a big yawn and shook my head to clear it. "I slept in Lucy's hallway last night."

"Why?"

"She insisted on going home, but she's been having nightmares every night. I didn't want to leave her alone."

"But if she didn't know you were there, what good did it do?"

"I knew she was safe." He rolled his eyes at me. "Hey, don't give me any shit about this. You followed Kate around daily and watched her from across the street at a coffee shop while she was at work in absolutely no danger."

"She was almost killed outside her office. I was doing the responsible thing."

"You were obsessed with her and you followed her everywhere. You watched her from your window at night."

"I never said you should be like me."

"I'm not being like you. I'm just trying to make sure that if she needs me, I'm close by."

Derek walked into the break room and gave me a chin lift. "Who do you have to be close to?"

"Lucy," I sighed.

"You look like shit. Didn't you get any sleep last night?"

"He slept outside in her hallway in case she needed him," Knight smirked.

"Now you're starting to sound like Knight."

Knight scowled and I huffed. "I'm nothing like him. I was keeping an eye on my girlfriend who was just terrorized."

Derek nodded. "Right, so did you ask her first if she wanted you to come over?"

"No, I asked her to stay with me and she told me she 'needed to do this'," I said, using quotes. "She doesn't need to do anything. Doesn't she realize that I want to be there for her?"

"So, she told you that she was going home alone. What did you do? Wait until she left and then follow her to her place?"

I took a swig of my coffee, not wanting to answer that question.

"So, you did do that," Derek laughed. "And then what? You sat outside her door all night?"

"Something like that."

"Did she call you?" Knight asked.

"No, I called her. I heard her screaming from a nightmare and I wanted to make sure she was okay."

"And was she?" Derek asked.

"No, but she didn't want me to know. I could hear it in her voice."

"So, you stayed the whole night, sitting outside her apartment door that's monitored by our security system because she might have a nightmare and need you," Derek surmised.

"Well, when you put it that way, it sounds a little creepy."

"Creepy is an underestimation. You sound like Knight and that's just downright terrifying."

"I don't sound anything like Knight."

"If you want," Knight interjected, "I could show you the easiest way to break into her apartment so that you can watch her sleep."

"That's crossing the fucking line," Derek said.

Knight shrugged. "I did it with Kate almost the whole year she thought I was dead. I didn't want to be away from her, so I broke in and watched her when I could."

"You know, you two are sick and seriously need some help." Derek turned to me and pointed a finger. "I'm thinking of breaking our best friend status. I can't be seen as a psychopath's best friend."

He walked out the door and I flopped my head back down on the table. I was seriously screwed.

"Come on. Let's go train. We've got shit to talk about."

I sighed and swallowed down my coffee, then followed him down to the training center. My ass was dragging big time and all I wanted was to go back to sleep. I got in my workout gear and met Knight in the ring. I didn't mind sparring with him. We used to do it all the time when we were in the military. I knew most of his moves, but he was also more calculating now than he was back then. But I was bigger and that gave me an advantage against him. Not that I won a lot. He was still the most trained fighter I had ever seen. He seemed to be able to read the minds of his opponents and always knew what the next move was.

We started out with just some light jabbing, but then the jabbing turned into full out brawling. I felt like I was in the middle of a bar fight, the way he was throwing punches. I took a step back and pulled out my mouth guard.

"What the fuck is your problem?"

"Where's Lola?" he asked.

"I don't know. She's not talking to me."

"So, what? You thought you would just leave her alone?"

"She went on vacation. What did you want me to do, follow her there?"

"Look, your woman comes first and I get that, but Lola's been fighting her demons for years and you just let her walk out of here."

"What the fuck do you know? I didn't let her just walk out. I was there every fucking minute for her."

"Until she decided she didn't need you anymore, right?"

"Well, yeah. When a woman says to fuck off, you leave her the fuck alone."

"Except you didn't do that with Lucy. You followed her around and did everything possible to get her back," he snapped.

"Yeah, well she's the fucking woman I'm going to marry."

"And Lola isn't, so you just left her alone."

"Look, I don't know what your problem is, but what goes on between Lola and me is none of your goddamned business."

"It is my goddamned business," he said, getting in my face. "She's fucking drowning and you just left her."

"I didn't leave her. She pushed me away."

"And you knew that shit wasn't right with her. You should have stepped in. You should have gotten her help."

"What the fuck? You've been working here for a fucking year and all the sudden you think you know us?"

"I'm telling you what you need to hear. You were fucking torn apart when you thought I was dead. How do you think you'll feel if something happens to Lola?"

"Don't even fucking say that. She would never do something to hurt herself."

"How do you know? How do you know what's going on in her head? You walked away from her. You're supposed to have her back."

"I didn't-" I couldn't argue with him anymore. He was right. I had been Lola's support system for years and then when she decided to break away, I had just assumed that she had it under control. I didn't talk to her about it or see if she needed anything. I had basically washed my hands of her problems and moved on. Maybe the reason she stopped using me was because it just wasn't fucking working anymore.

I sat down on the edge of the ring and flopped down on my back, staring up at the ceiling. Knight came and sat next to me.

"How the fuck do I fix it?"

"Well, first, you call her and bug her until she talks to you. Then, you need to convince her to come back here. She's not going to solve her problems by running away."

I huffed out a laugh. "I'd have better luck sending you after her."

"I've already talked to her. She sounds relaxed, but I can tell that this whole situation is eating away at her. She's not the kind of woman that can just walk away from her life here and be happy."

"Why are you telling me all this?"

"Call it paying it forward. You saved my life when you broke me out of jail. Then you helped me get a job here. Thanks to you, I'm not running anymore and I've got a woman that I would fucking die for. Right now, Lola needs a lifeline and you've always been that for her. The rest of us can help her, but you've always been the one that she trusted. Don't let her down."

He stood and walked out of the ring, leaving me alone and reeling. He was completely right. I had to make things right with Lola. She was one of my best friends and I couldn't let her down.

"*P*appy, before you leave, I have something for you." Knight walked over to me with a laptop. After his little talk with me earlier, I wasn't sure I wanted to hear this.

"What's that?"

"This, my friend, is a little insight into how I kept an eye on Kate."

He opened the laptop and handed it to me. There were several small screens filled with images of Lucy's apartment. It was the live feed from inside.

"Knight, we're not supposed to have access to the live feed. This is seriously fucked up."

"So is sitting outside her apartment every night. I figure this way you can watch from the comfort of your own home and know that she's okay."

"Thanks, man."

"Just don't tell Cap. He still doesn't know how I hacked the live feed from Kate's place and I'm not telling him how I did Lucy's either."

He walked away and I went home to get some shut eye. Except, when I got there, all I could do was stare at the live feed. I tore myself away from it for a whole ten minutes to take a shower and then I was back to staring at the feed. Lucy had just gotten home and she had already checked the locks at least five times. As the night went on, I could tell she was nervous about being there alone. I had called and talked to her, seeing if she wanted me to come over, but she insisted that she was fine.

As she got ready for bed, I couldn't help the uneasy feeling I got every time she got up and looked out her window or walked over to her front door to check the locks. I couldn't just watch from home. I had to be there. I took the laptop with me and headed over to her apartment. I wasn't sitting outside her door ten minutes when I heard the screaming. It broke my fucking heart to hear her so terrified and know that she wouldn't let me help her. I watched her on the monitor as she curled up in a ball on her bed and cried for ten minutes. Then, she got up and got some water. I wished that she would open the door. I wished that she would call me and ask for me. Anything so that I didn't feel so fucking helpless.

The door downstairs opened and Knight came walking in, shaking his head when he saw me sitting outside her door. "I figured you'd be here."

"Why are you here?"

"I can't let my old best friend sit outside his woman's apartment all night long and suffer alone."

"But why? She's not your woman?"

Knight sighed, "Look, you did a lot for me. I'm just trying to repay that."

He pulled out his own laptop and opened it up, showing video feed of his own house with Kate.

"That's seriously fucked up. You still watch her on the video feed?"

"Dude, you're fucking sitting outside Lucy's apartment and watching the feed of what's going on ten feet away. At least my woman is across town."

So, Knight and I sat there, night after night, watching our women on video as we sat outside Lucy's apartment to make sure that she was alright. She refused to spend the night with me and Knight refused to let me sit outside her apartment alone every night. It was a sick and twisted menage a trois that only Knight and I knew about.

Chapter Nineteen

LUCY

*A*nother night of no sleep and I was exhausted. My face looked a lot better from the surgery, but now I had bruises under my eyes from not sleeping. I wasn't sure exactly why I was refusing to let Hunter help me. A big part of me was worried that he would get tired of me and want me to go away. What if it ruined our relationship by spending that much time together? The smaller part of me just wanted to know that I was able to do this on my own. That I didn't need to rely on a man to save the day, even though I wanted nothing more than for Hunter to come running in and demanding that I stay with him.

I missed that side of him. He was always so demanding with me, but ever since we got back together, he had this other side to him, the side I always assumed I wanted, but now wasn't so sure about. Why had I pushed him away so much? I would give anything for him to burst into my apartment right now and demand that I go back to his house with him. He would tell me that he didn't give a shit what I wanted. That I was his woman and he was going to take me home and make sure that I was taken care of.

I sighed and drank down my coffee before getting in the shower. I had to go back to school today and I really didn't want to. I didn't know how I would feel about being in the school after everything I had gone through. Could I really be in the same room that I had seen a student shot? And what about Graham? Knowing that he wasn't the man I thought he was and he hadn't told me about his relationship with a student made me feel like a complete idiot. I didn't know how I was going to deal with him.

I flung the door open as I grabbed my purse and tripped over something outside my door, falling face first on the ground. Arms hauled me up by the armpits and I spun around to see Knight standing there grinning. I looked at the ground and saw Hunter shuffling something around and then he stood up.

"Hunter, what are you doing here?"

"Uh..." He glanced down at my messenger bag and then back up at me. "I wanted to wish you a happy first day back to work."

"Why were you on the ground?"

"I was tying my shoe. Sorry, I just noticed it as I got here and I wanted to tie it before I knocked on your door."

I cocked my head to the side, not sure why, but I didn't believe him. I turned to Knight. "And you came along to wish me luck?"

"Yep." He slapped his hands together and then turned for the stairs. "Well, now that that's done, have a good day. See you at work, Pappy."

He walked down the stairs and it didn't escape my notice that he didn't actually wish me luck. That was the weirdest encounter ever, but I didn't have time to dwell on it as Hunter pulled me into his arms and kissed me like we hadn't seen each other in years. I couldn't help but notice that he tasted like he had morning breath, which was odd because Hunter always brushed his teeth before he left the house. It was part of his routine and he never strayed.

"Well, thank you for stopping by, but I really do have to get going."

"I can't believe you're going back there after everything that happened."

We walked down the stairs and he held my hand the whole way. "I can't believe I am either, but I need a job and nobody hires in the middle of the year."

"You know, I hope you realize how fucked up that school is. They should have fired Graham for having a relationship with a student."

"They couldn't. He didn't technically break any rules, but I agree. He should have been fired."

"Have you heard how Seth is doing?"

I talked to the dean yesterday. He said that Seth is recovering, but he most likely won't play football again. Being out the rest of the year will really damage his chances of playing professionally."

"Well, at least he finally knows what happened to his sister. I can't imagine something like that happening and never knowing."

"I didn't hear what happened exactly. All I know was that Coach Boots killed her."

He nodded as he walked me to my car. "I guess he hit on her as she was stepping outside and she refused him. Things got a little out of hand and he freaked out. His plan had been to take her, but when she struggled, he accidentally killed her. He stuffed her in his trunk and dumped her in a lake. They found her body a few days after he confessed."

"That's so sad." I couldn't imagine having to tell her parents that their daughter had been found dead. At least as long as she was missing, they could still think that she was alive somewhere, but then again, not knowing had to be worse.

"Well, you know what would make me happy?"

"What?"

"If you looked for a different job. I just don't like you working there, knowing that all that happened and it's so far away."

"Believe me, I'm already ahead of you. I'm finishing out the year and then I'm done."

"Good. Now kiss me."

He pulled me in for a deep kiss and smacked my ass before helping me into my car. I stopped him from shutting the door. We had one last thing to discuss.

"Hunter, I know what you did for me with my apartment." A strange look came over his face. Something that resembled panic. "How you paid to have it fixed up? Claire spilled the beans. Our insurance payment will be coming through from the fire and I'll be paying you back every penny."

He shook his head and sighed. "I can't slip anything past you."

"No, you can't. But I appreciate all you did for me. I just don't want to owe you anything."

"Lucy, I just wanted to try to fix the mess that I was a part of."

"Thank you." I smiled at him and shut the door. I waved goodbye and watched in my rearview mirror as he stood staring at me.

I walked into the school with my head held high, but the more people that stared at me, the more my shoulders slumped. I wasn't used to being the talk of the campus. I just wanted to pretend like that whole thing had never happened. But the closer I got to my office, the more I started to wonder if I could actually go in there. The door had been fixed. You couldn't tell that Seth had broken down the door to get me out. I took a deep breath and walked inside. It felt strange being back here.

I put my stuff down and sat at my desk, trying to concentrate on getting myself organized for the day. Footsteps echoed in the hall and I found myself straining to hear where they stopped. They sounded close, but how close? Who was it? It was too early for students. I gripped onto my purse where I had my mace and dug around frantically in the bag for the canister. My head kept shifting between the door and my purse until finally I had a grip on the mace.

My nostrils flared with every breath I took. I was being irrational. There was nobody there. Nobody that would hurt me anyway. Why was I being so paranoid? Because I had been kidnapped? That was a terrible excuse to start seeing threats at every turn. At least, that's what I told myself. The school was secure and I would be fine.

I gripped the canister in my left hand as I started shuffling around the paperwork again. What I was really avoiding was going into my classroom. Logically, I knew there wouldn't be any blood left on the floor and there wouldn't be a body or a man standing there with a gun.

Logically, I knew that, but that didn't mean my head was catching on. I waited in my office as long as possible and then picked up my stuff to take to my classroom. I took a deep breath and blew it out in one long breath. I could do this.

I stepped into the hallway just as someone appeared in my peripheral vision. I screamed and raised my hand with the mace, not wasting a second in spraying it directly into the eyes of the person standing next to me. When the canister was gone, I finally lowered my hand and stopped screaming.

Graham was standing in front of me, groaning and scrubbing furiously at his eyes. I stared in horror at what I had done and then spun around when I heard feet stomping down the hallway. Chance was here, along with Gabe and Jackson running from the other direction. I sighed and leaned back against the wall, shaking hard as I struggled to get myself under control. I completely ignored Graham's whimpers of pain. I didn't have any sympathy left to give him. I was too busy trying not to lose it myself. Or, maybe I already had lost it.

"What happened? What did he do?" Chance yelled as he ran up to me. His eyes scanned my body, looking for injury and when he was satisfied, he turned to Graham and sneered at him. "What did you do?"

"I didn't do anything," he stuttered as he continued to rub his eyes. "I can't see. Can someone please help me? My eyes are on fire."

"Why were you outside her room? What were you doing?" Chance demanded.

"I was walking in the hallway. This is a school, after all."

"And you just happened to be outside her office when she was leaving?" Gabe asked skeptically.

"I was coming to see if she was alright. I knew that she was coming back today and I wanted to check on her! Now, can somebody please help me before I lose my eyesight?"

"You could have knocked like a normal person," Jackson sneered. "You knew she had been kidnapped. Why would you sneak up on her like that?"

"I wasn't sneaking up on her. I was trying to work up the courage to talk to her. I figured that she hated me at this point."

"I don't hate you," I muttered. "You helped them find me, but I am disgusted with you. Sleeping with a student? Asking her to abort her child so that you could keep your reputation? That's despicable."

He sighed and squeezed his eyes shut even tighter. I could see the tears streaming down his face and I tried to feel some sympathy for him, but I just didn't have it in me. "I know it is. I'm not suggesting that we just go back to being friends, but I hoped you could realize that I made a terrible mistake and you would be able to forgive me. I was young and stupid."

"Young? This happened a year ago, dude," Chance muttered. "I think that man bun is pulled a little too tight."

I could see now what the guys saw in Graham. He was a nice guy, but a little too naive to see the bigger picture. I couldn't imagine any of the men at Reed Security ever responding the way Graham had to Seth's sister. They just didn't have it in them to walk away from their responsibilities, no matter the cost.

"Graham, I appreciate all you did to help the guys find me, but I'm just not ready to pick up our friendship. I'm not even ready to be back here yet."

"Lucy, I made a mistake."

"I understand that, but we were friends and you didn't even think of telling me what had happened, even when Seth started following me. I would have understood the situation better. Maybe none of this would have happened."

Well, that wasn't entirely true. I still had a stalker after me, but perhaps the mess at the school could have been avoided.

"Gabe, take him and get his eyes cleaned out. Then someone's going to have to give him a ride home. He won't be able to do anything for a few days. Jackson, go talk to the dean and explain the situation."

Both men nodded and before I knew it, I was alone with Chance.

"I didn't realize you guys would be here today."

"Well, Hunter worries about you. He wanted us to wait outside the building and just see how your day went, but none of us felt right leaving you in here alone."

"Thank you," I said sincerely. "I'm not sure I'm even ready to be here."

"Where are you headed? I'll stay with you."

"That would be wonderful." I did my best to hold back my tears, not even realizing how badly I was shaken up after seeing Graham. I honestly didn't know if I could make it through the rest of the day, but I had to try. I walked into my classroom later than I would have liked and saw that I already had students waiting for me. I took a deep breath and tried to force myself to walk the rest of the way in, but I was stalled in the doorway.

My eyes drifted to the floor in front of me and red pools of blood oozed across the floor. Seth was lying there, bleeding out and Graham was lying next to him unconscious. My heart started hammering in my chest. This couldn't be happening again. Why were all these students just sitting there? Why weren't they trying to help Seth?

I had to get out of here. I couldn't do this again. I backed up quickly, right into a hard chest. Hands immediately gripped onto my arms to steady me and I felt a brush of air move past my ear.

"It's okay, Lucy. I've got you."

I knew that voice. It was familiar, but the image of Seth lying on the floor was still right in front of me and my whole body felt paralyzed. I began shaking my head wildly. I couldn't do this. No matter how much I wanted to, I couldn't be here and pretend that nothing had happened. I spun around and pushed my way out of the room and began running down the hall. I wasn't sure where I was going, but I knew I had to get out of there. I was just getting to the stairs when Chance wrapped his arms around me.

"Whoa. How about we calm down and not run down the stairs in high heels? Hunter would kill me if you broke your neck."

I couldn't catch my breath. I needed to get out of here. I just couldn't do this. The tightness in my chest was so painful that it brought tears to my eyes. Chance spun me around and cupped my face in his large hands. "Breathe, Lucy. It's alright. I've got you. I won't let anything happen to you."

I shook my head wildly as tears streamed down my face. "I can't do this. I can't be here." I squeezed my eyes shut as Chance pulled me against him and hugged my body to his. I gripped onto the back of his shirt and prayed that my heart would stop trying to jump out of my chest.

"Let's get out of here. You don't have to be here."

"What about my classes?"

"Fuck the classes. The dean will understand and if he doesn't, I really don't give a shit. After everything you've been through, he can't expect you to just walk back in here as if nothing happened."

He gripped onto my hand and led me over to the elevator, pressing the button. He wrapped an arm around my shoulder as we descended to the first floor and walked outside. I was freezing at this point and it had nothing to do with the cold weather and everything to do with what I saw when I walked in my classroom.

"Gabe will grab your things. I'll take you to Hunter."

I nodded numbly and got into his SUV. I sat in the front seat, disappointed in myself that I had let it all get to me. That I couldn't even come back and do my job. The drive to Reed Security went by in a blur and before I knew it, we were pulling into the garage and Hunter was yanking me out of the SUV and into his arms. His scent and the warmth of his body immediately calmed me and I found myself practically crawling up him to wrap myself completely in his arms.

"It's okay, Lucy. You're alright now," he murmured against my ear.

"I can't go back there," I whispered. "I just can't do it."

"You don't have to. You never have to go back there again."

"But what about my job?"

"I've already talked to the dean and explained the situation. He completely understood. He's going to find someone to cover your classes."

"How am I going to support myself? I don't have a job anymore."

"We'll get that all worked out, Lucy. I don't want you to worry about that right now. Just let me take care of everything, okay?"

I nodded and buried my head further into his chest. Everything was fine as long as I was with him.

I stayed at Reed Security with Maggie while Hunter finished up his work for the day. She came in halfway through the day with her daughter and just hung out with me. We didn't talk about anything in particular and mostly played with her daughter. When Hunter came to get me, I was calm and ready to head home for the night.

After saying goodbye to Maggie and Caitlin, Hunter brought me back to my apartment where my car was waiting for me.

"Did someone go get my car?"

"Jackson brought it back here."

"Oh, well, please thank him for me."

He came around to my side of the truck and helped me down, and then walked me upstairs. "How did you know that I would need someone with me today?"

"I didn't. I just didn't like the idea of you being at the school. I talked Cap into putting a detail on you for another week, just to be sure."

"Do you think I need one?" I asked nervously.

"Not at all, but it made me feel better and he knew that."

I opened the door and turned off the alarm while Hunter went and checked my apartment like he always did. "Are you sure you don't want to stay with me tonight?"

"I'm sure, Hunter. I need to do this."

He pulled me into his arms and kissed me. "I know you do, but I'm always here for you, no matter what you need."

"I know. I just need to know that I won't need someone by my side the rest of my life."

"It's okay to have someone by your side the rest of your life," he grumbled.

"That's not what I meant. What kind of life is it if I can't do things on my own?"

"I understand, but you have to give yourself time. It's been two weeks."

Hunter was my savior in every way. I wanted him more than I could ever have dreamed, but my insecurities that he would get tired of me gnawed at my brain. I just couldn't take the chance that I would lean on him too much and he would leave me. I just couldn't handle that right now.

"Come on. Let's eat some dinner and watch TV. Your choice."

I wanted more than a quiet night at home. I wanted him to take me and do unspeakable things to me, but he absolutely refused. Part of me wondered if it was because he saw me as damaged or if he worried I was too fragile. The other part of me worried that he didn't really want me anymore, but knew that I couldn't handle him walking away.

I started drifting off as we watched the movie and I felt Hunter pull me in closer. I glanced over at the clock on the wall and saw that it was already ten o'clock. I couldn't keep Hunter here anymore. He had to work in the morning and it was selfish of me to keep him up late at night.

"You should go home. I don't want to keep you up."

"I can stay the night, Lucy. You don't have to be alone."

"I'm okay. I promise."

He didn't look convinced, but he didn't argue. He stood and walked to the door, giving me a kiss before leaving. I made sure to lock the door and enter the code and then I went around and checked the window, even though they hadn't been opened the entire time I had lived here.

I plopped down in my bed and closed my eyes, refusing to acknowledge the noises I heard. I tossed and turned before finally falling asleep around midnight.

I ran through the halls of the school, trying not to make any noise as I hid from Coach Boots. He was going to kill me. I absolutely knew that. I had witnessed him murdering Seth and he wouldn't let me live. I ran down the hall of the older part of the school and locked myself in a dark room. I found the back wall and followed it until I reached the corner and slumped down to hide.

Every noise, every shadow had me jumping and caused my heart to skip a beat. How long would it be before he found me? Would he kill me quickly or would he torture me? Nausea bubbled up inside me until I was sure I would be sick. I couldn't take the not knowing. I almost wished that he would just find me and end my misery. I couldn't just sit here for hours on end and pretend that I was going to get out of this alive. Just come for me already!

Hours passed and my legs went numb from squatting for so long. I stood and slowly made my way along the wall. When I touched something soft, I gasped in surprise and took a step back. Cold fingers wrapped around my wrist, pulling me into a rough body. Nails scratched at me, clawing me until I could feel the blood dripping down my body. I tried to scream, but nothing came out. It was like I was paralyzed. No, this wasn't happening. I tried to yank myself back, but the hands gripped me tightly.

"Darling, don't you know that you can never escape me? You think I'm gone, but I'll always come back for you. You'll never get away."

I finally let out a piercing scream and yanked my arm back, running for the door. It swung open and I ran down the hall, but halted when I saw him. Noah. He was standing at the base of the stairs, blocking my way out. I turned and ran in the opposite direction, but the only door that was open was the one to the basement. I fumbled along the wall as I searched for the door to the hidden tunnels.

My breaths came out in ragged pants as my body shook in fear. I had to get out of here. I finally found the door and flung it open, running blindly in the dark. I stumbled and fell, then got back up and ran with my hand along the wall, hoping that I didn't run smack into another wall. When my hand left the wall and felt only air, I stopped and turned back. Feeling along the wall, I felt a tunnel break off in the other direction and I followed it until I saw a sliver of light peeking in. There was a door! I tried to turn the hatch, but nothing happened. I was trapped.

"Did you really think you could get away from me? I won't ever let you go, Lucy. You're mine."

He charged forward and I screamed as loud as I could hoping someone would hear me. I could hear ringing in the distance. Someone was coming. I just had to hold on a little longer. I screamed louder and louder, hoping that whoever was coming would get here soon.

I sat upright in bed with a jolt, sweat pouring down my face and in-between my breasts. My shirt was soaked through and I could feel my sheets drenched with my sweat. I took a few calming breaths and then realized what the ringing in my dream was. It was my phone. I scrambled out of bed as the ringing stopped, but picked it up as soon as it started again.

"Hello?" I tried to keep the fear and shaking out of my voice, but I failed miserably.

"Lucy? Are you okay? You sound upset," Hunter said, concern filling his voice.

"Bad dream."

"Do you want me to come over?"

"No. Of course not. It was just a bad dream. I'll be okay."

I heard him sigh into the phone. "Lucy, you can ask for help. It doesn't make you weak."

"I know, but there's no point in you coming over here. I'm just going to go back to sleep." There was silence on the other end, like he didn't really believe me. "What were you calling for?"

"I just wanted to make sure you were alright. I know that this has been tough for you and I just want to make sure you're doing okay."

"I'll be fine." That was my new catchphrase. If I had a quarter for every time I said that recently, I would be a millionaire. "Thank you for calling to check on me. I'll talk to you tomorrow."

"I love you, Lucy."

"I love you, too," I whispered.

I could hear in his voice how much he wanted to help, but I just couldn't allow it. Hunter was such a strong man. He didn't want a weak woman and the more he saw me as weak, the more he would realize that I wasn't right for him.

———

*T*he next day, I went over to Derek and Claire's house. Claire was still working at the library, but she worked in the afternoon, so I took advantage of her time off. I knocked on her door and heard her yell for me to come in. I opened the door hesitantly and then peeked inside. All clear.

"Claire?"

"I'm in my bedroom," she yelled.

"Yeah, I'm not going back there."

"Shut up! I'm just doing my makeup."

"Which damsel in distress are you becoming?"

She walked out of the bedroom with only half her face done up, sneering at me.

"Two face? Really? I wouldn't think that Derek would be into fantasies that involve another guy, but who am I to judge?"

"I'm not trying to look like two face. I'm trying out two different looks and I wanted to know which one looked better on me."

"Definitely the one on the right. The left side really does make you look like The Joker."

"Whatever. Give me a minute."

She walked back to her bedroom and returned a few minutes later with a freshly scrubbed face.

"So, how are things going?"

"Good. I had to leave my job, but other than that, everything's just peachy."

"Yeah, Derek told me about what happened. I was going to call you last night, but he insisted that Hunter was taking care of you and I should let him. Apparently he thinks that I can be too pushy."

"You? Too pushy? Nah."

"So, what are you going to do now? Are you going to find another job?"

"I'm not sure. I have to talk with the dean still. I'm sure the school won't continue to pay me if I'm not working there, so I'll have to find another job."

"Any idea what you want to do?"

"Well, I'd like to teach still, just not at the college, but nobody is hiring in the middle of the year. I could always substitute teach until I find something, but that's not steady income."

"You know that Derek and I will help you out with whatever you need."

"I know, but I don't want other people to pay my way."

"You're so stubborn. You have to give yourself time to heal."

"That's what Hunter says," I grumbled.

"So, how are you really doing?" she asked.

I tried to decide what to say. I didn't want her to think that I was going crazy, but I also needed to talk to someone about what was happening.

"Did you have nightmares about what happened with Derek in D.C.?"

"Are you kidding? All the time."

I blew out a breath and smiled. "I've been having nightmares every night and I was afraid I was going insane."

"Psh. You wouldn't believe some of the things I dreamt about. One night, I dreamt about the man that was chasing us. It was horrible." I nodded along, needing to hear what it was like for her. "He was in the restricted section of the library with us and he..." She shook her head and sighed. "He started yanking the books off the shelves and tearing them apart. He insisted that if I didn't hand over the book, he would tear apart the whole library."

I sat there stunned. "*That* was your nightmare?"

"Well, yeah. It was scary. I mean, at one point, I'm pretty sure that he ruined the oldest copy of the Bible. I also had a dream that I tried getting back into The Library of Congress, but they flagged me right away and I was hauled off to jail and then nobody would hire me as a librarian ever again. They said I had broken 'the code' and I no longer had the right to call myself a librarian."

"Claire..." I shook my head, unable to really fathom what she was telling me. "I meant scary dreams. I dream about people chasing me and being murdered. You're not talking about a nightmare. You're talking about your imagination running wild."

"Hey, it may not be scary to you, but it could actually happen to me and then what would I do?"

"I thought maybe you had dreams about the man who shot at you or something."

"Well, I didn't know that man. Maybe the reason you're having such bad nightmares is because you knew Seth, Graham, and the coach. And what happened with Noah, I mean, who wouldn't have nightmares? You can't compare what happened to me with what happened to you. I had Derek with me the whole time. You were on your own. I'm sure if I had been running from that man by myself, I would have ended up dead. You were running on your own and you survived. That's like, ten times more scary than anything I went through."

"I just feel like I'm going crazy when I have those nightmares."

"Lucy, I'm dreaming about books being destroyed. If anyone's going crazy, it's me."

She wasn't wrong about that.

Chapter Twenty

HUNTER

I called for the tenth time today. I needed to get ahold of Lola and find out if she was okay. I had been calling every day since Knight pointed out how wrong I had been to leave her alone. She wasn't answering my calls, but I wouldn't give up. I needed to know that she was okay.

"What the fuck do you want?" she asked. I almost forgot to speak because I really hadn't thought she would answer the phone.

"I'm surprised you answered."

"Yeah, well when you wouldn't stop calling, I figured I might as well find out what you needed to talk to me about."

"I just want to check in with you. See how things are going."

"I'm fine. I'm enjoying a wonderful vacation alone and not thinking about any of you."

I snorted because Lola couldn't stand to be away from the action. This had to be killing her. "Right. Why don't you just come home and work shit out? We all want you back. Derek and I have had the shittiest jobs without you here on the team."

"Really? Because Knight told me that he was filling in for me. Sounds like you don't really need me back."

"Knight filled in for you because Lucy went missing and I had to find her, which you would know if you were here with us like you're supposed to be."

"I can't, remember? I'm not allowed back in the field."

"Lola, all you have to do is follow Cap's instructions. You can still train with us. You're still a part of this team and it's not the same without you."

"Did you stop to think that maybe I don't want to be back on your team? Why would I want to be back with people that didn't have my back?"

"Lola, you know that I always have your back and sometimes that means doing what you won't do for yourself. I should have never let you push me away. I knew that you were still struggling and I told myself that you didn't want me anymore because you could handle it. But I fucking knew that everything wasn't okay. I'll never forgive myself for not being there for you."

"Hunter, I don't need you to feel bad for the rest of your life because I'm fucked up. I can handle my job. I had one freak out on the job in all these years. I don't think it was too much to ask that you mention *that* to Cap instead of agreeing that I needed counseling and couldn't perform my job."

"That's not what happened and you know it. Derek and I could see that we weren't helping you. All we want is for you to talk to someone. Is that really too much to ask?"

"Maybe it would have been fine if you had just talked to me about it as a team, but you cornered me in front of my boss. You made it seem like I couldn't handle myself. How will he ever think that I'm capable again?"

"You just have to show him that you are. We've all been pushed to our limits at some time or another. Look at Cazzo? Did you really think that he would come out of his situation the way he did? He came out stronger for it and I know you will too."

"Hunter, you're missing the point. You broke my trust and I'm just not ready to come back yet. I'm sorry. I can't do this right now."

She hung up without another word. That didn't go as I had

planned. In fact, it probably went worse. I was no closer to getting Lola to come back here than I was to getting Lucy to let me in.

$\mathcal{T}$wo weeks of sleeping outside Lucy's apartment was killing me. Knight joined me every night, but part of me wondered if it was to win back his best friend status. I called Lucy every night when I heard her screaming and she wouldn't wake up. She hadn't caught on yet that I seemed to always know when to call her. I'd also been able to play it off when I overslept outside her apartment and she fell over me.

But I didn't know how much longer I could keep this up. I was exhausted and I needed some sleep on a real bed. I knew Knight was getting a little tired of this also, but as much as I told him to go home to Kate, he insisted on staying with me. I was grateful. There was a very good chance I would go insane if he wasn't there to keep me company as I watched the video feed from outside her door all night. I wanted to be in there with her. I just didn't want to revert to my old ways and push my way into her life. She had to come to accept that I really wanted this and until that happened, I just had to go with the flow.

I groaned as I tried to stretch out my neck after leaning against the wall all night. I had been tempted a few times to lay down on the floor, but it was so dirty that I didn't dare put my face near it. I heard thumping up the stairs and then I saw Kate's pissed off face.

"I can't believe that you two are still doing this," she huffed. She walked past me and banged her fist several times against the door. I scrambled to my feet and tried to wipe the sleep from my eyes.

"Kate, you need to leave. Don't fuck this up for me."

"Fuck this up? Hunter, you're sleeping on a dirty floor in a hallway. I can't possibly fuck this up for you."

She turned and banged against the door again. The door opened seconds later and Lucy stood there with a questioning look on her face.

"Can I help you?"

"I don't know if you remember me, but I'm Kate, Knight's girlfriend."

"Fiancé," he said, stepping up behind her and pulling her against his body.

"Do you mind if we come in for a minute?" she asked.

Lucy waved us all in and looked at me strangely. *What's going on?* She mouthed to me. Before I could say anything, Kate spun around and started in.

"Look, I know we don't know each other, but I'm going to lay it out here for you. Hunter and Knight have been sleeping outside your apartment every night because Hunter is too chicken shit to tell you that he needs to stay here with you."

"I'm not chicken shit," I said defensively. Kate shot me a glare that told me to shut the fuck up.

"See, these men don't have boundaries. They don't know how to let a woman do things her own way, which is why they've both been sitting outside your apartment every night with video feed, watching both of us as we sleep. I don't know about you, but that's a little creepy to me. I've already been through this once with Knight and it's even weirder now that we're an actual couple and he's still doing it."

"It's not weird," Knight insisted. "I'm making sure you're safe."

"Right, from all those crazy people that are out to get me. I get it. You're a big, strong man and I will always need your protection." She turned back to Lucy. "Unfortunately, Hunter seems to have taken up Knight's stalking tendencies and is now going to continue to do the same thing to you until you let him stay with you every night so that he can assure himself that you really are okay. Which means that Knight will be sleeping out here with him every night, which is strange on a whole other level. So, I'm asking that tonight, you let Hunter stay with you so that they can both get some sleep and don't look like the walking dead anymore."

Lucy stood there stunned and then turned to me. "You've seriously been sleeping outside my apartment every night?"

"Yeah. I knew you weren't okay and I wanted to be close in case you called me."

"And you were watching me from fifteen feet away on video feed?"

"Ten feet," Knight clarified.

I slapped him upside the head, not really needing his help. "I'm sorry. I know it was over the top and I shouldn't have done something so stupid, but I love you and I don't like the thought of you alone and scared over here."

"But wouldn't it have made more sense to just tell me that so that I hadn't spent every night alone and scared? I didn't know you were outside my door, so it didn't make me feel any better."

"Well..." I didn't really have an answer for that. "I just didn't want to push."

She stepped into my arms and kissed me. "Thank you for doing that for me."

"So, we're good now?" Kate asked. "Hunter can sleep inside and Knight can come home to me?"

"Yes," Lucy smiled. "I'm really sorry, Kate. I never would have let Knight sit out here all night knowing that he was leaving you."

"Don't sweat it, Lucy. When these guys make up their minds about something, there's no stopping them. Sometimes, we just have to step in and take over."

Knight and Kate left, leaving me alone with Lucy. I wasn't sure if she was really okay with what I had done or if she just didn't want to explode in front of Kate and Knight. I cleared my throat and stepped back. "If you don't want me here, I can leave."

"Are you kidding? Then Knight would show up here again and it would creep me out to know that you're sitting outside my apartment. And watching video feed. That's just weird, Hunter."

"I know. I just wanted to keep an eye on you."

"So, I guess that's how you always knew when to call me."

"Yeah, we could hear you screaming and I wanted to try and wake you up. I kept hoping that you would ask me to come over. I don't like seeing you get so upset."

"I know, but it's still something I need to work through."

"Just promise me that you'll let me help you with that."

"Okay."

I kissed her hard and then pulled back before I mauled her. "I have to get to work, but tonight, I'm sleeping here with you. I need an actual night of sleep, so don't plan on staying up past six."

She laughed and slapped my arm. "Don't worry about it. I haven't been getting much sleep either, so I could use the early bedtime."

"So, everything's good now?" Knight asked as we walked into the conference room.

"Yeah. I'm staying over there tonight."

"Thank God. I need some fucking sleep."

"Hey, I never asked you to stay with me," I snapped.

"What's going on?" Sinner asked as he sat down. Cap, Burg, Cazzo, Derek, Gabe, Jackson, and Chance were already at the table.

"Hunter finally got an invite into Lucy's apartment, so now we don't have to sit out there every night anymore."

"You've been sitting outside every night?" Cap asked. "Why didn't you just tell her you wanted to stay with her?"

"Because, I didn't want to push it with her. We just got back together. I don't want to ruin things."

"What good did it do to sit outside her apartment if you couldn't go in?" Cazzo asked.

"Knight hooked me up with her video feed."

"You weren't supposed to say anything about that, jackass." Knight punched me in the arm and swore.

"What? Like Cap doesn't know what a creeper you already are?"

"He knew I was. He didn't need to know that I still do it."

"So, you two seriously sat outside her apartment all night and watched video feed of her inside her apartment?" Burg asked.

"I did. He sat next to me and watched video feed of Kate."

"You two have some serious issues," Cap said. "That's not what having a security system is about. We're supposed to make clients feel safe. Not like they're being watched."

"But these aren't clients. These are our women," Knight pointed out.

"It's still fucking creepy," Sinner said. He leaned his elbows on the table and whisper-hissed to Knight. "Can you show me how to get the live feed?"

Knight shook his head and shot me a nasty glare. "I told you not to fucking say anything."

"What I want to know is why Knight sat outside with you every night?" Derek asked.

"Because I'm his friend and he needed someone."

"I didn't need anyone," I said, not wanting to sound like a pussy.

"You're just trying to get back your best friend status," Derek grumbled.

"His best friend status?" Burg asked.

"Yeah. I'm his old best friend and Derek's his new best friend."

"Derek, don't be jealous, man," Sinner grinned. "I'll be your best friend."

"What the fuck?" Cazzo said. "I thought I was your best friend."

"Nah. That's me, you dickhead," Burg laughed.

"I would have sat in the hallway with you," Gabe said. "Why didn't you ask me?"

I glanced over at Derek, not wanting to say *because I think you're fucking gay and I didn't want you hitting on me.* Derek must have read my mind, because he burst out laughing and slapped his knee.

"What?" Gabe asked. "Why is that so funny? I'm a great friend."

"I'm sure you are," Derek laughed.

"Would you all shut the fuck up?" Cap shouted. "I'll get you all some BFF necklaces and we'll call it a day. Seriously, I can't believe I have to put up with this shit first thing in the morning."

He opened up some folders and started handing out assignments. Since we were still down one team member, Derek and I were stuck on security installations until Lola came back. I wasn't going to complain though. It ensured that I would be home with Lucy every night.

"Alright, Cazzo, I need you guys in New York City next week."

"Uh, Cap, I can't do that," Burg interrupted. "I need some personal time."

"Everything okay?" Cap asked.

Burg glanced around the table and sighed. "My dad's been battling non-Hodgkins Lymphoma. I just found out that he has more tests next week and he doesn't have anyone to take him."

Cap nodded. "No problem. We'll put Chance's team on this. If you need more time off, just say the word."

"Thanks, Cap."

I looked around the table, seeing that everyone looked as confused as I was. Why hadn't he said anything sooner? We would have all chipped in any way we could to help him out.

We finished up the meeting and Derek pulled me aside as we got our gear to head out. "Why didn't you tell me you were hanging out at Lucy's in the hall?"

"Because it sounds fucking creepy."

"Yeah, but I get it. I could have had Claire talk to Lucy. We could have worked something out if you were that worried about her."

"I know, but she wanted to do it on her own. She kept telling me that she had to do it herself."

"It's only been a few weeks."

"I know, but she's stubborn and I don't want to take over. That's how I pushed her away last time."

"Yeah, well if I recall, stalking didn't work for you either."

"She actually wasn't pissed at me for it this time. I'd rather have her at my place. I mean, I love her and I want to fucking marry her, but -"

"Whoa, back up. You want to marry her? Since when?"

"I don't know. I just know that that's where this is headed."

"Who would have thought my little Hunter would be all grown up someday?"

"Shut up."

"I'm happy for you. It's just that you've been telling anyone that will listen that it's a death sentence to get involved with someone and now you're talking about getting married."

"Yeah, just do me a favor and don't say anything to Claire. She'll tell Lucy and then I'll never see her again."

"Wouldn't you think that Lucy would be happy that you want that kind of commitment?"

"Nope. It's all too soon. She'll think that I'm doing it for all the wrong reasons."

"You know, you two really need to get your shit together. You're both a bunch of fucking idiots."

"That's not any way to talk to me if you want to hold onto your best friend status," I quipped.

I spent the next two weeks at Lucy's apartment every night. She still had nightmares, but I was always able to help her get back to sleep. She didn't look quite so exhausted and the nightmares weren't coming quite as often. But I was getting tired of going back and forth between my place and hers. I just wanted her to move in with me and end this madness.

Lucy rolled over next to me and her hand snaked down to my cock that was already painfully hard. I hadn't tried to have sex with Lucy since she had been taken. She told me she hadn't been raped, but I didn't know how aggressive that fucker had been with her and I didn't want to do anything to mess up her head.

I pulled her hand away from me and slid it back over to her side of the bed. She grunted at me and slid her hand back, gripping onto me so tightly that I almost cried out in pain.

"Hunter, you have to stop this. I want sex and you're leaving me very sexually frustrated."

"I just don't think we're ready."

"We're not or you're not?"

"I don't think you are," I said quietly, caressing my hand across her face.

"Hunter, I love you, but you're really pissing me off. I'm not fucked up in the head. He didn't touch me in any way, and if you don't start, I'm going to have to dump your ass and find someone else. There's only so much a girl can take."

"You're really okay?" I asked, not sure that I believed her.

"Yes!" she said in exasperation. "I don't know how many different ways I can tell you that, but you never believe me. I just want you to fuck me already."

"Oh, thank fuck!" I tore her nightgown off her and ripped her panties from her body. I needed her so badly and there was nothing that could stop me now. Her hands went around my back, pulling me in close, but I wasn't ready for close. I didn't want to fuck her and be done. I had waited too long for this moment.

I picked up her shredded nightgown and tied her wrists together and then tied the scraps to the nightstand leg. "There. Now you can't fucking move and I can have my way with you."

"It's about time," she gasped as my mouth latched onto her pussy. I had missed this with her so much. Not just the sex, but the intimacy of being with her. I craved it more than I ever thought possible. I ate her until she was screaming and writhing beneath me and then I shoved my boxers down and plunged deep inside her. I moaned at the instant relief I felt and thrust hard and deep inside her. My cock tingled with pleasure and it didn't take more than five minutes for me to shoot off like a rocket.

I panted hard as I came down from my high, but my body wasn't done yet. My cock hardened at the sight of her tied up in front of me and there was something I wanted more than anything, and I would have it. She had promised. I undid the ties and pulled her into an upright position on the bed. My cock bobbed in her face, and as her eyes flicked up to mine, a slow smile spread across her face.

I grabbed her by the hair as she opened her mouth. Her wet mouth licked and sucked my cock until I was hard as steel. I yanked back on her hair and shoved my cock deep into her throat. She gagged, but took me all the way in. Her hands wrapped around my ass, jerking me toward her every time I pulled out. She wasn't lying when she said she wanted this as much as I did. When she moaned around my dick, I felt the vibrations all the way in my balls. I exploded in her mouth moments later with my cock buried in the back of her throat. She swallowed all I gave her and then licked her lips in satisfaction, but I wasn't through yet. There was no way I was going to let her walk away with only one orgasm.

I threw her onto her back and latched onto her pussy one last time, sucking and biting at her clit. "You have to stop!" she shouted. "It's too much. I can't. Not again."

I didn't stop. My tongue flicked across her lips and up to her clit until she shoved her pussy up and started humping my face. I grinned as she rubbed herself against my lips until she came all over my mouth. When I came up for air, I felt her juices coating my lips and licked them clean. I loved the taste of her on me. And now that we were back, I would make sure that we didn't go a single night without getting what we both needed.

Chapter Twenty-One

LUCY

"So, how's everything going with Hunter?" Claire asked.

"Good. It's all going really good."

"Has he asked you to move in with him yet?"

"What? Why would you think he would ask me that?" I glanced over at Hunter, who was drinking a beer in the kitchen with Derek. It was Christmas Eve and we had all decided to stay home this year and celebrate together, even though Derek's family was doing a big get together. We just wanted to keep things low key.

"Oh come on," she rolled her eyes at me. "You spend every night together at your apartment. Why would you assume that he wouldn't ask you?"

"Because that's not Hunter. I mean, don't get me wrong, he's been great and I think he really is ready for more, but let's not push it."

"Lucy, you're blind. He wants to marry you. Anyone can see it."

I looked back at Hunter and frowned. "No, I don't think you're right. Besides, we haven't even officially been together that long. It's way too soon to even be thinking about something like that."

"You know, this is your problem. You think love works on some kind of time table. Now, I'm not saying that you have to run out tomorrow and get married, but I have a theory that you should only have to date someone for six months before you know."

"Know what exactly?"

"If you could marry that person. So could you?"

"I don't know. That's the most ridiculous thing I've ever heard. Nobody knows that fast."

"Derek did," she muttered under her breath. "Look, I'm not saying that you should know if you *will* marry that person, but if you can't see yourself married to the person you're dating after six months, then it's time to move on."

"How did you come up with that?"

"It's just logical. Think about it. If you've been with someone for six months and you're still thinking, *I don't know if I could stand the man for the rest of my life,* then what are the chances that you would ever get married? I'm just saying it's a logical way to look at things. If after six months, you think he has possibility, then you see where things go."

"You know, I would expect this of anyone else but you."

"I'm telling you, Lucy. You're still pushing him away."

"No, I'm not. He hasn't made any moves on me. He's gone all soft or something."

"So, now you want Hunter to go back to his domineering ways?"

"Well, it wouldn't be the worst thing in the world."

"You just have to show him that you want more," she whispered as she looked over at me. I watched as he talked to Derek and wondered if she was right. Could it be that he was waiting for me to give him some kind of sign? Claire was right. I did want to marry Hunter. I had been dreaming about it since he started sleeping over with me, but I hadn't wanted to get my hopes up. She was right though. I needed to find a way to show him I wanted more.

Derek and Hunter walked into the living room and Hunter bent down to give me a kiss. "You doing okay, baby?"

"Great," I smiled.

"Hey, I was wondering..." He glanced over at Derek and Claire and then cleared his throat. Hope bloomed in my chest because he looked really nervous. He would only be really nervous if it was something important. "I was thinking you could maybe stay over at my place tonight. You know, just for a change."

My face fell and I fought back the tears that were pushing to the surface. Why had Claire brought marriage up? I had been doing my best not to say anything about our relationship or get my hopes up and then she had to go open that bag of worms. I couldn't let him see me cry. I sat up quickly and ran off to the bathroom before I broke down in front of him. He didn't really want more with me. He was going back to his old ways. I slammed the bathroom door and slid down to the floor, holding my knees to my chest as I sobbed. Life just wasn't fair sometimes.

Chapter Twenty-Two

HUNTER

*W*hat the fuck had I done wrong this time? All I did was ask her to stay with me tonight and I had already pushed too far. Everything I did was wrong and I didn't know how to make it up to her. It seemed that everything I did in this relationship was wrong. Derek was right, I was a complete fuck up.

"What was that about?" Derek asked as he walked up to me.

"I don't know. I asked her to stay at my place tonight."

"And she ran out of the room crying?"

"Yeah. I don't know what the hell I did wrong. Do you think I pushed too hard?"

Derek shook his head and chuckled. "No, I think the problem is that you don't push hard enough."

"What did you do to my sister?" Claire asked as she stormed over to me. "We were having a perfectly nice night and then you had to go and make her cry."

"I didn't mean to," I said in disbelief. "I asked her to stay the night with me and she ran crying from the room."

"Men," she said, shaking her head as she walked off to the bathroom.

"What the hell does that mean?" I asked Derek.

"It means that you fucked up."

"No shit, Sherlock. But how did I fuck up? I don't know what to fix because I don't know what I did."

"It's what you didn't do. You should have asked her to move in with you."

"Are you kidding? She never would have gone for that. I can barely get her to stay over at my place. She's still convinced that I don't want a real relationship with her."

"Dude, I've told you this a million times already. You are so fucking stupid," he said slowly, emphasizing each word.

"Why don't you just tell me how to fix this instead of calling me names?"

"Here's how you fix it. You ask her to move in, you tell her you love her, you tell her you want to marry her!"

"But she doesn't want that with me."

"How do you know if you don't ask her?"

"Why the fuck would I ask her to marry me?"

"You don't want to marry me?" Lucy cried from the hallway.

I spun around and saw her crying in Claire's arms as Claire glared at me.

"What? Of course I want to marry you."

"But you just said *why the fuck would I ask her to marry me.*"

"That's only because you would say no anyway."

She sniffled and ran a hand under her nose. "Why would you assume I would say no?"

"Because you're so fucking stubborn," I roared. "Every time I try to get you to stay at my place, you get all wigged out and make excuses."

"That's because I didn't want to pressure you into anything, you stupid oaf," she yelled at me.

"Well, I wasn't trying to push you into a relationship with me. I thought you wouldn't think I was being genuine," I yelled back.

"How would I know if you want to be in a relationship long term with me when you don't ever talk about it?"

"Of course I want that from you. I spend every fucking waking minute with you. I love you and I want you to marry me. I've been carrying around the fucking ring in my pocket for the last month!"

"Then why haven't you asked me?"

"Because I thought you'd go crazy on me like you are now and walk away. I wanted to make sure you didn't have any doubts about me. Is it too much to fucking ask that you give a guy a hint? I'm not a fucking mind reader."

"Yes, I want to marry you. I just didn't want you to think that I was pressuring you into it."

"You're not. I've been wanting you in my house and my bed from the start. It just took my head a little time to catch up with the rest of me." I pulled her into me and kissed her like she would run away at any moment and this was our last kiss. Then I pulled back from her and dug into my pocket, pulling out the ring that had been burning me since I picked it out. I yanked her left hand up and pushed the ring on her finger. "There. Now you're my fucking fiancé and there's no take backs. You already told me you wanted to marry me."

"Fine. I guess we're getting married."

"Fine!" I shouted, pulling her into me and kissing her silly.

"Now they're back," I heard Derek mutter.

ALSO BY GIULIA LAGOMARSINO

Thank you for reading Hunter and Lucy's story. There's still more to come further down the line, so keep reading. The Reed Security gang will be back in Whiskey's story!

Join my newsletter to get the most up-to-date information, along with new content in the Reed Security series.

https://giulialagomarsinoauthor.com/connect/

Join my Facebook reader group to find out more about my obsession with Dwayne Johnson!

https://www.facebook.com/groups/GiuliaLagomarsinobooks

Reading Order:

https://giulialagomarsinoauthor.com/reading-order/

To find the individual series, follow the links below:

For The Love Of A Good Woman series

Reed Security series

The Cortell Brothers

A Good Run Of Bad Luck

Made in United States
Orlando, FL
30 October 2024